I0690106

A WING AND A PRAYER

THE DEVIL YOU KNOW: BOOK 3

CHRISTINE POPE

Dark Valentine Press

This is a work of fiction. Names, characters, places, and incidents are either the product of the author's imagination or are used fictitiously. Any resemblance to actual events, places, organizations, or persons, whether living or dead, is entirely coincidental.

A WING AND A PRAYER

ISBN: 978-1-946435-31-6

Copyright © 2020 by Christine Pope

Published by Dark Valentine Press

Cover design by Lou Harper

Book formatting by Indie Author Services

All rights reserved. No part of this book may be reproduced in any form or by any electronic or mechanical means, including information storage and retrieval systems—except in the case of brief quotations embodied in critical articles or reviews—without permission in writing from its publisher, Dark Valentine Press.

PROLOGUE

BEELZEBUB LOOKED OVER THAT DAY'S LIST OF new prisoners and found himself frowning. True, the numbers of damned souls admitted to Hell had been dropping over the past few weeks, but he'd attributed the reduction in volume to those ridiculous New Year's resolutions that humans seemed so fond of making. Everyone would have been on their best behavior during the month of January, but now that February had rolled around topside in the mortal world, he'd assumed that all the sinners and miscreants would have gone back to their usual lying, cheating, stealing, and so on.

Only...that didn't seem to be what was happening at all. This latest list had a paltry thousand souls on it. What in the world was he supposed to do with that? He glared at Belial, the demon who'd been working as his aide de camp ever since Asmodeus had, well, decamped.

"This is it?" Beelzebub demanded.

"Yes," Belial replied, looking remarkably unperturbed, blue eyes with their usual cheerful glint, a faint smile on a mouth framed by that ridiculous beard he'd grown over the past year or so. Then again, it seemed to take a good deal to upset Belial. Beelzebub had often wondered how someone with such a sunny personality had ended up in Hell, but he'd realized long ago that there were some mysteries which could never be fully explained. "I can double-check, if you like," the demon added, obviously trying to be helpful.

Not that there was any point. The list was the list; it always appeared at the beginning of the "day"—or what passed for day down here—on the desk of Lucifer's lieutenant, and was never altered or updated. Once upon a time, Beelzebub had been the Devil's assistant, but Lucifer had forsaken Hell in order to live a mortal life with the utterly unmemorable woman God had chosen for him, and so Beelzebub had taken over. He'd hoped that Asmodeus would occupy the position Belial currently held, but their fellow demon had turned out to be a traitor to their kind as well. At the rate they were going, soon there wouldn't be enough demons left to staff the place.

"No," Beelzebub said shortly. "That will be all."

Belial didn't bother to reply, only shot a grin of irritating good cheer in his superior's direction and strode out of the room. Scowling, Beelzebub stared down at the meager list he'd been given and wondered why he bothered.

"Ahem."

Beelzebub looked up from the enormous polished basalt desk where he sat—it had once belonged to Lucifer, but had come to Beelzebub along with all the other trappings of the office — and saw an elderly man in a shabby brown tweed coat standing a few paces away, gazing at him with mildly curious dark eyes.

Well, He looked like a regular old man. However, Beelzebub knew He was Someone far, far more important.

He was also the last person Beelzebub would have expected to find standing in his study.

"Yes?" he said, making no attempt to hide the irritation in his voice. Truth be told, Beelzebub lived in a state of constant annoyance, and of course, God knew that just as well as anyone else.

"Working hard, I see."

"Someone has to," Beelzebub growled. With Lucifer gone and Beelzebub's former partner-in-crime, Asmodeus, also settled down in apparent mortal bliss with a human woman in his bed, he was the only one left to keep Hell running. Well, the only one of any importance. Belial was supposedly a prince of Hell like the other upper-level demons, but he had never seemed like one, what with his foolish grins and "no problem" attitude. Still frowning, he added, "What do you want? I'm busy."

If anyone had been around to listen to this particular conversation, they might have been shocked to hear a demon address the Creator in such an impudent way. But since Beelzebub knew God most likely wouldn't retaliate, he felt it safe enough to give free rein to his feelings, which as usual, were sour as curdled milk.

As he'd thought, God only smiled. "Well, I thought I should come down here and give you the news myself."

"'News'?" Beelzebub repeated. He didn't much like the sound of that. News meant change, and he hated change. He wanted everything to continue as it had for the past few millennia. Or at least, continue in a way that didn't disturb his world too much. With both Lucifer and Asmodeus gone, Hell would never be precisely what it once was, but he had to hope it wouldn't suffer any more catastrophic alterations, either.

God inspected the sleeve of His brown tweed jacket. Possibly looking for lint, although Beelzebub couldn't detect anything amiss, nothing that would require such a level of close scrutiny. Looking up, the Creator went on, "I've decided to close Hell."

For a few seconds, the words didn't quite register. Beelzebub sat at his desk, the piece of parchment with that day's list of the damned still clutched in his fingers, as God's pronouncement slowly penetrated his thoughts. "What?"

"Oh, you heard me. I've decided to close Hell." God paused then, smiling slightly. Some people might have called that smile beatific, but its utter serenity only made Beelzebub want to grind his teeth in fury. "Lately, Hell has been serving as less and less of a deterrent to prevent people from acting badly. So, I've decided to shut the place down and move to a reincarnation model. Maybe putting some of the worst offenders through the spin cycle a thousand times or so will be enough to get them to see the light. So to speak."

Beelzebub could only stare at God, aghast. This couldn't be happening. How could there not be a Hell? Wasn't that the whole point, after all? To have the universe suspended between those two poles, to have utter light on one side and utter darkness on the other? How could God expect people to understand the perfection of Heaven if they didn't have the blackness of Hell to balance it out?

"You're closing Hell," he said, his tone flat.

"Yes, that's what I said." God paused there and sent Beelzebub a searching glance, concern clear in His brown eyes under the gray-frosted brows that framed them. "Are you quite all right, my boy? You look a little pale."

Voice a rasp, Beelzebub said, "I'm fine."

A pause as God appeared to consider that response. His eyebrows drew together, as though He knew the demon who sat before Him was lying.

Well, of course, He would know Beelzebub was lying. The Creator knew everything, after all.

That didn't mean Beelzebub intended to tell Him that he currently felt as if an entire legion of Roman chariots had just backed over him approximately ten thousand times. His head spun slightly, and he knew if he hadn't had the heavy stone desk to support his hands where they lay on its surface, they would have been shaking like aspen leaves in the first winds of autumn.

After a long, uncomfortable pause, He went on, "No need to worry, Beelzebub. I'm not going to leave you high and dry."

"How kind."

The Creator's mouth quirked a little at one corner, but He only said, "I won't offer you precisely the same deal I gave Lucifer and Asmodeus, mostly because I know you wouldn't accept it. You don't have much use for true love, do you, Beelzebub?"

That truth was so patently obvious, he didn't bother to reply, only stared back at God, hoping his face was as blank and unreadable as the stone surface beneath his fingertips.

"Still," He continued, "I can't have you staying here. The souls currently in Hell will be given their new assignments soon and sent back to Earth to relive their lives and see if they won't make such a hash of it the second time around. The other demons will be allowed their retirements, so to speak. In only a week or so, this place will be empty. And then…I will end it."

All this, gone? The great dark palace where Lucifer once dwelled and which Beelzebub now called his home? The vast pits where the souls of those damned here for eternity spent their painful, endless days? No more cold winds, no more scent of brimstone and smoke on the air?

In short, nothing that had made his existence here remotely bearable would be left.

No point in protesting; Beelzebub could tell that God's mind was made up. Neither did he question whether the Creator was capable of an act of such magnitude. After all, He had made Hell in the first place. He need only snap His fingers to unmake it. And any being capricious enough to wipe out all His Creation in a flood of, well, biblical proportions wasn't going to scruple at getting rid of a place like Hell if He'd decided it had served its purpose.

Somehow, Beelzebub managed to find his voice. "If I'm not to remain here, then where am I supposed to go?"

God's brown eyes twinkled, and a small finger of dread traced its way down Beelzebub's spine. When He looked that cheerful, it usually meant He had devised a plan that sounded wonderful to Him but would strike fear into any demon's heart.

"Well," He said, "I thought it would be easier if I had the three of you in the same place—that makes it easier for Me to keep an eye on you."

No, he wouldn't....

"Not there," Beelzebub said. Damn it, that comment had sounded just a bit too much like a whimper. He cleared his throat. "Anywhere else. Siberia. The Sahara Desert. The Australian outback. Antarctica."

God shook His head, eyes still twinkling. "Oh, you know I wouldn't put you anywhere so inhospitable. But don't worry—you'll have a nice house, something to your taste. And disposable income, because you've earned your retirement, Beelzebub." A pause, and He added, looking positively gleeful, "Or should I say, Benjamin Blake? That's the name you used when you were last on Earth, wasn't it?"

"Only as a matter of convenience," Beelzebub responded. The conversation was already slipping away from him, but he thought he needed to do what he could to maintain some semblance of control. "I'm not sure—"

"Benjamin Blake it is," God cut in. The words had such a tone of finality to them, Beelzebub knew there was no point in arguing, despite the nervous dread that currently gripped his stomach. "It suits you. And of course, I'll make sure you have all the necessary documentation—driver's license and Social Security card, birth certificate, vaccine records, medical history—"

"Please, stop," Beelzebub said, his voice strangled. Just the mere notion that he was about to be weighed down with all the trappings of a mortal life made him feel as though he was slowly asphyxiating.

God paused there, and sent the demon a look of concern. Not true worry, though; Beelzebub could tell He was enjoying this far too much. "I just wanted you to know that you will be taken care of. After all, I want you to have a smooth transition to your new life in—"

"Don't say it," Beelzebub interrupted. Anything to keep the Creator from uttering those fateful syllables.

"—Los Angeles," God went on inexorably.

"What better place for a former demon than the City of Angels?"

"Oh, God," Beelzebub moaned.

He might live for another eternity, but, as far as he was concerned, his life was over.

What the hell was he supposed to do in L.A.?

CHAPTER ONE

NAOMI KLEIN, MY NEXT-DOOR NEIGHBOR, sailed in through the back door of my kitchen and announced dramatically, "Have you *seen* our new neighbor?"

Since I was in the middle of making a fresh batch of the homemade miniature dog biscuits I whipped up on a regular basis for Frida, my two-year-old rescue chihuahua—and any other rescues who might be passing through at the time—I barely looked up from the bite-size bits of dough I was laying out on a cookie sheet. "Well, since I haven't gone outside in the past hour, I guess I'll have to say no."

"Eminently bangable," was Naomi's evaluation as she headed over to the fridge and got out the pitcher of sun tea I always kept in there...which, of course, was why she knew to get herself some. Brown eyes sparkling, she added, "*Super* cute. The universe has dropped a live one in your lap, Jillian."

"No one's in my lap," I said, somewhat wearily. I loved Naomi and was very glad to have her as a next-door neighbor, but I really wished she would stop trying to get me to date. Yes, almost a year had passed since my divorce was final, and yet I knew I just wasn't ready to get back out there. Honestly, I didn't know if I ever would be, and that was fine by me. Little Angels Chihuahua Rescue—my nonprofit organization that focused on fostering and finding homes for abandoned chihuahuas and chi mixes—took up pretty much all of my time. I recalled how demanding Tom, my ex, had been and guessed that most men probably wouldn't be too different, once they got comfortable enough to show me their true selves. "Anyway," I went on, since Naomi was eyeing me, clearly expecting me to say something else, "if he's so hot, you can have him."

"Can't," she said. "I'm only five days into my ninety-day man cleanse. What would I say to my viewers if I gave in to temptation less than a week into my detox?"

Naomi was a highly successful YouTube life-style guru and personality. She'd converted one of the rooms in the big Victorian house next to mine into a studio and interview space, and I was honestly kind of shocked at the celebrities she was able to lure in there for one-on-one talks. And honestly, although I still couldn't say I precisely understood how a YouTube celebrity could earn a salary in the low seven figures, obviously Naomi knew what she was doing.

So, while her comment about her "viewers" might have seemed self-centered, I knew it was only the truth. They looked up to her, absorbed her advice without question—or at least, not too much questioning—and if she was in the middle of a "man cleanse," then the last thing she should be doing was chasing after our new neighbor. I'd known someone would be moving in soon, just because the "for sale" sign on the house across the street had come down only a week earlier. However, since the two houses faced each other, I'd been able to catch glimpses of prospective buyers during the two months it had been for sale, and I knew I'd never seen anyone I would have referred to as "eminently bangable."

"Come on," she urged me. "He was out in the yard, inspecting the flowerbeds. In a suit, no less. And a bow tie. Who the hell wears a bow tie these days?"

"And yet he's still bangable?" I asked, my mouth curling into a grin despite myself.

"Yes, which should tell you something about

his looks. Let's go take a peek through the living room curtains—those dog biscuits can wait."

Since I'd forgotten to turn on the oven at the appropriate time and it was still preheating, I supposed that technically, Naomi was right. Still, it felt kind of silly to be peering past my living room drapes like a couple of gossips out of a 1950s sitcom or something. But since I could tell from my friend's expression that she was going to keep bugging me until I capitulated, I shrugged, went and ran my hands under the kitchen tap to get them clean, and then headed out to the living room.

Back when my house was constructed in the late 1890s, the living room had probably been called the parlor. Like all the other houses on Carroll Avenue—a famous street in L.A.'s fabled Angelino Heights—it had been built more than a hundred years earlier, a large Queen Anne–style Victorian with a five-color paint scheme, shades of blue accented with dark brick red and white. Not the kind of place that someone who managed a small, independent dog rescue operation should have been able to afford, but undisputed owner-ship of the house was the price my ex-husband had paid for this philandering. Cheating was no good, but when you were a high-priced lawyer having an affair with one of your clients, well, a million-dollar-plus house was a small price to pay to avoid getting disbarred.

I followed Naomi to the front window, which looked out on Carroll Avenue. Even in early February, the yards were all green, although most people's roses had been recently cut back and therefore weren't very showy. Even so, everything looked picture perfect, like something right out of a movie set—which made sense, since a lot of TV shows and movies had been filmed there. In fact, the house from the original *Charmed* television show was just down the road.

But there he was, standing in front of one of the flowerbeds in the house opposite mine, something of a similar vintage and style, only painted in shades of gray with dark green accents. My new neighbor had his hands shoved in his pants pockets and appeared to be scowling down at the close-pruned roses in the brick-encircled bed in front of him.

"A plaid suit?" I said, casting a skeptical glance at Naomi, who was hovering right behind me. "He's got to be gay."

"I don't think so," she replied, brown eyes wide with interest, full mouth under its coating of pinkish nude lip gloss quirking slightly. "My gaydar is usually infallible. I don't get that vibe from him at all."

About all I could do was raise an eyebrow. True, Naomi tended to have great instincts when it came to that sort of thing, but no one could bat a thousand all the time. And honestly, I couldn't imagine a straight guy wearing that suit—or the dark red bow tie that circled his neck.

However, I had to admit to myself that the new neighbor was damn good-looking. Tall, and with an athletic build that filled out the plaid suit he wore and kept it from appearing utterly ridiculous. Thick brown hair and regular features just this side of man-pretty. From that distance, I couldn't tell what color his eyes were. Not that it really mattered. I didn't have any plans to get close enough to find out for myself.

"Okay, he's cute," I allowed, and then stepped away from the window. "It's weird, though—I didn't see a moving truck."

She allowed herself one last glance at the new neighbor and turned toward me. "Oh, they came while you were out picking up that dog from Mount Washington."

"That dog" was Rufus, my latest rescue. I could already tell he was going to be a handful—he was feisty and wanted to act as though he ruled the roost, even though my own dog Frida had let him know, with a couple of not-so-uncertain growls, that this was her house and while she might tolerate visitors, no way was a new dog going to come in here and behave as though he was the one in charge. Anyway, Mount Washington was only about twenty minutes from my place, and the entire trip had taken me less than an hour, even factoring in coming and going and chatting for a bit with Myra Lopez, the gal who had found Rufus wandering her street and who'd called me to come get him.

"They unloaded an entire houseful of furniture in less than an hour?" I asked, knowing how skeptical I sounded.

"Yep," Naomi replied. "It was actually kind of amazing. A big commercial moving truck pulled up, followed by a van. There was a crew of six guys in the van, and they came out and met up with the two guys in the truck, and the whole gang of them moved everything from the truck to the house in record time. Nice stuff, too—expensive antiques, from what I could tell."

Which was exactly the kind of furniture you'd want for a home like one of ours. Inwardly, I found myself already approving of this new neighbor, simply because I thought if you were going to live in a vintage house, then you should have vintage furniture to go along with it. Not that I had anything against more modern styles, but there were plenty of modern homes in L.A. I didn't see the point in filling a Victorian house with mid-century furniture, any more than I'd want someone decorating a brand-new glass and steel house with antiques.

Obviously, if he could afford a house on this street and the kind of furniture Naomi was describing—not to mention a team of eight people to unload everything and put it away—then our new neighbor must have been doing okay for himself. I didn't recognize him, so I didn't think he was an actor, although I supposed he could have been; I didn't have enough time to watch most of the shows currently on the air and wasn't all that familiar with who was starring in what. Or maybe he was a designer of some kind… the suit was the sort of eccentricity that might be forgiven in design circles.

Not that it really mattered. The guy had moved in across the street from me, and so I guessed we'd wave and say hi from time to time, but I doubted our interactions would extend much beyond those surface pleasantries.

"And he only looks like he's a year or two older than you," Naomi went on. "Early thirties at the most. So, I think it's just about perfect."

"I have no plans to date anyone, least of all our new neighbor," I told her. "Just think how messy it would be if we did end up going out and then broke up later. Awkward."

"You need to stop jumping to the worst conclusions, Jillian," she said. Now she sounded brisk, as though she was talking to her YouTube audience and not someone in the room with her. "Maybe it would all turn out great."

"I kind of doubt it."

That exchange was all we had time for, because some yaps and growls coming from the family room told me that Rufus had woken up from his nap and decided to encroach on Frida's territory once again. Murmuring an apology to Naomi, I hurried over to the source of the commotion and picked up Rufus. He squirmed in my arms but obviously knew better than to try to nip at me. Down on the floor, Frida shot me a narrow glance, as if to tell me that while she understood that I had to take in these lost souls from time to time, she wished I'd do better at keeping them away when it was time for her all-important afternoon beauty sleep.

It was too early to take the dogs for a walk—I tried to head out around four every day unless I had an appointment or the weather was too hot—but the backyard had been thoroughly chihuahua-proofed, and so I knew it would be safe to send Rufus out there to cool his heels until it was time for that afternoon's constitutional. I took him over to the back door and let him out, and although he shot me a reproachful glance, he trotted down the steps cheerfully enough and off toward one of the lilies of the Nile that bordered the lawn so he could lift his leg and pee.

Although I could tell from the look on Naomi's face that she wanted to continue our conversation about the new neighbor, she must have glimpsed something in my expression that told her to back off, because she said breezily, "Well, I need to get back. I've got Elizabeth Gilbert dropping in tomorrow and need to get the studio squared away."

"Oh, that's all?" I responded. "I'm surprised you don't have Ryan Gosling or Emma Stone lined up."

"Next week," she twinkled, and let herself out. There was actually a gate that connected our two properties, and so she tended to come and go through the kitchen and the backyard, rather than walking in formally from the front of the house.

I reflected it was a good thing that we'd turned out to be close friends, or the gate could have been problematic. Once upon a time, when our respective houses were built, they'd been owned by a wealthy man and his adult son, and so I supposed the parties involved had wanted to have an easy way to get back and forth between the adjoining properties. When Tom and I were shopping for houses, the real estate agent had been almost apologetic about the gate, saying that we could probably replace that part of the fence if we wanted to, although she hoped we wouldn't, since doing so would alter something original to the house. Naomi had already been living there and seemed nice enough, and so we'd left the gate alone. At the time, I'd had no idea she'd become my best and closest friend—and someone I turned to for support and guidance when the truth about Tom's philandering came out.

Sometimes I wondered whether I really would have given up and headed home to Redding, the town in northern California where I'd grown up, if she hadn't been around.

But I'd weathered that storm, and life had settled down into a comfortable groove. My father —the honorable representative from California's 1st District, Congressman Henry Cunningham— had growled that I should have taken Tom for every last dime he had. I didn't want revenge, though. I just wanted to get on with my life. Now, I had to admit that it was wonderful to live in such an amazing house and not have to worry about its upkeep, since Tom paid for that as well. Donations to Little Angels Chi Rescue paid for the dogs' food and vet bills, and gave me a little left over to live on, and that, in addition to a small amount of spousal support, was all I needed. I'd never been one to worry about being "fancy," something Tom had initially said he loved about me but which began to annoy him as time wore on, since it practically required a crowbar to get me out of my jeans and into anything suitable for a cocktail party or the other sorts of upscale events he'd wanted me to attend as the wife of his law firm's newest partner.

No, I was better off without him, for a variety of reasons. And the sad thing was, I still didn't know for sure whether he had ever really loved me or had just thought I'd be useful to his legal career because I was a congressman's daughter.

After assuring myself that Rufus was fine, and appeared to be occupying himself by sniffing around the entire perimeter of the backyard, I went back into the kitchen and popped the trays of dog biscuits into the oven, since it was finally up to temperature. Next, I needed to wipe down the counters and check the calendar on my laptop for the next day's schedule. I had a meeting with a possible foster for Rufus at ten out in Rancho Cucamonga. The opposite direction that most traffic would be heading, thank God, and so I figured I'd be safe if I left a little after nine. Then I had a lunch meeting in Pasadena with some possible donors, but that was it for the day. I thought I should have the rest of the afternoon free —assuming, of course, that I didn't get any frantic calls that required me to drive out to someone's house or a shelter to rescue a dog that was in danger of being euthanized.

Well, all the chasing around was part of the reason why I drove a Prius. I needed something with good mileage. And since I was rescuing chihuahuas—the little dogs that had claimed my heart back in grade school and held on ever since—and not, say, German shepherds, it didn't matter that my car was small.

I looked out the kitchen window again, expecting to see Rufus wandering around the lawn, or maybe back to sniffing the lilies of the Nile or the patch of Icelandic poppies off to one side. But as my gaze passed over the yard, I realized I didn't see his furry little black and white body anywhere.

Panic rose in me, but I pushed it back. After all, he was a very small dog, even smaller than Frida. I didn't know for sure what was mixed with the chihuahua in him, although I assumed it must be another very small breed, maybe a rat terrier. Anyway, any of the border plants could have hidden him, or even the stately sycamore tree in the far corner of the yard.

Still, I figured I'd better find out for sure. It was just about time to bring him in and take him and Frida for a walk anyway. I pushed my glasses up on my nose—the damn things were always sliding down—and hurried out the back door.

"Rufus!" I called.

No response, but that didn't bother me too much, since I'd already discovered that Rufus only answered to his name about half the time…if you were lucky. I went and checked behind the tree, and along the hedges, calling his name the whole time, but there was no sign of the dog.

Damn it.

I came to the gate in the side yard—not the one that joined Naomi's and my properties—and that was when my blood really did run cold. Oh, sure, the gate was closed and latched securely. However, although I'd taken the extra precaution of fastening wire screen to the bottom of the gate so my little chi wards couldn't get out, I saw that it had been bent back at one corner. Not very much, but definitely enough so a wriggly little five-pound body could have squeezed past it.

Double damn it.

Allowing myself a single curse under my breath—anything else would have been wasted energy—I opened the gate and let myself out, my gaze immediately scanning the street for any signs of the wandering dog. Nothing—but no cars, either, thank God. My street was a fairly quiet one, even though it was well known and we got tourists wandering up there on a regular basis to take photos of all the picturesque houses. Otherwise, there wasn't much point in being there unless you were going to someone's home, since Carroll Avenue wasn't a throughway, just a couple of blocks situated between two north-south streets.

Then I heard it—Rufus's bark. I hadn't been around him for very long, but I already knew that was his excited, happy bark, the one you might hear when you got out his leash to take him on a walk. Or maybe when you played ball with him; that was what Myra had told me, since he'd been with her for a couple of days before she called to have me pick him up, although the dog and I hadn't yet had the time for any real play time.

I stared in the direction of the sound and realized it was coming from the new neighbor's yard. And yes, there was Rufus, dancing around the legs of Mr. Eminently Bangable himself, who stared down at the dog as if he'd never seen one before in his life.

Oh, boy.

Sheer instinct made me reach up to smooth my hair as best I could, even as I tried to tell myself that it didn't matter what the hell I looked like. I'd put on some tinted lip balm after lunch, but I had no idea whether any still remained on my mouth. Not that it mattered. What mattered was getting Rufus away from the new neighbor before he completely wore out his welcome.

Trying to look unconcerned, I marched across the street and up the walkway in front of the neighbor's house. About all I could do was hope that Naomi really was occupied with her studio, and not looking out her own front window. Otherwise, she'd probably think I'd cooked up this meeting on purpose, despite my protestations that I didn't care when—or if—I bumped into our new neighbor.

"Hey," I said, once I was close enough to the man to catch his attention. He turned at once, eyes fixing on me.

Oh, yes, definitely cute, in a boyishly handsome way. There was nothing boyish about his expression, which looked disapproving in the extreme, or in the way his hazel eyes narrowed as they took in my untucked chambray shirt—sporting a few stains from my dog biscuit–making activities earlier that afternoon—and jeans with the holes in the knees. No, he looked like the headmaster of some uptight boarding school who was about to give one of his unruly students a well-deserved reprimand.

Ten points from Gryffindor! I thought, and forced myself to hold back the unwelcome giggle that rose in the back of my throat.

"Is this your animal?" he asked, transferring

his glare to Rufus, who was dancing around his legs as if he'd just met the owner he hadn't seen for the past two years. Seriously, I'd seen dogs less excited when their soldier masters came back from Iraq.

"Sorry," I said, doing my best to look apologetic. With skills honed during years of herding chihuahuas, I bent down and scooped up the wriggly little mutt. He squirmed in my arms but didn't try to get down, probably because it was a long drop to the brick walkway on which we stood, and if nothing else, Rufus had keen skills of self-preservation. "He somehow managed to squeeze out under my fence."

"Then you should probably get a better fence."

The dripping disdain in his voice would have been worthy of Professor Snape himself, although the man who stood before me now bore absolutely no resemblance to that particular black-haired, long-nosed fictional character. Irritation flared, but I did my best to push it aside. Whatever else happened, this guy was my new neighbor, and we would potentially have to deal with each other for years. The last thing I wanted was to get off on completely the wrong foot.

"I'm really sorry," I said, tightening my grip on the dog, who wouldn't stop wriggling. "There's actually wire attached to the bottom of the gate to keep this sort of thing from happening, but Rufus here managed to push right past it." I paused, then added, "I'm Jillian Torres, by the way. I live across the street."

And I stuck out my free hand.

For a long moment, my new neighbor stared at my hand as if it was some particularly nasty specimen he'd just spied through the lens of a microscope. Then he let out a breath that sounded a little too much like a sigh, and took my hand and gave it a single pump before releasing it again.

"I'm Benjamin Blake," he said. "I just moved in to this neighborhood."

From the tone of his voice, he seemed to be regretting that particular decision.

"Nice to meet you, Benjamin," I said. No way in the world was I going to make any attempt at familiarity by calling him "Ben." If that was his preferred nickname, he could let me know. However, I got the distinct impression that he would like to have as little contact with me as possible.

So much for the "banging" Naomi had envisioned. Honestly, I couldn't even picture the disapproving individual in front of me engaging in such a messy activity.

Since he didn't seem inclined to respond in any sort of friendly way to my pleasantry, I figured I'd better cut our conversation short before I said or did something to embarrass myself.

"Well, I need to get this little guy back inside," I went on, after an awkward pause. "But if you ever need anything, both my next-door neighbor Naomi and I work from home, so we're usually around in case of an emergency."

Benjamin Blake's cool hazel eyes narrowed slightly. I had a feeling he couldn't imagine the sort of contingency that would require him to reach out to either of us for help. To my relief, though, he only gave a very small shrug and said, "Thank you."

His tone was dismissive enough, however, even if he hadn't said something overtly rude. I hefted Rufus in my hand, said, "Have a good one," and made myself walk back across the street. As much as I would have liked to glance over my shoulder to see if Benjamin's expression had altered at all, I knew that wasn't a very good idea.

No, I went through the side gate and shut it behind me—the front door was locked, and so I had to go in the way I'd come, through the back door off the kitchen—and then deposited Rufus on the tile floor there. He shook himself and then hurried over to the water bowl and begin slurping away at it. Apparently, his exertions had worked up quite a thirst.

"Troublemaker," I muttered. Although I loved pretty much all dogs and had fostered a few that were even bigger handfuls than Rufus, I found myself hoping that the interview with his prospective foster parent the next day would go well. The last thing I wanted was to have to keep chasing him out of Benjamin Blake's yard. I had a feeling he'd be less than thrilled by repeated interruptions.

But at least now the awkward introductions were over, and from then on, we could be indifferent neighbors if we chose. The couple who lived to the left of me were like that—Janine and Alton Widawsky. I maybe saw them twice a year, if even that much. Well, unless they were complaining about the dogs. I tried my best not to have more than three or four under my roof at any given time, and it wasn't as though I set them loose in my yard to bark their heads off and annoy the neighbors. But one time I had a whole litter of five barely weaned puppies dumped in my lap, and the resulting commotion had been a bit much, even by my standards. Still, I didn't think it had merited a call to animal control.

Let's just say my relationship with the Widawskys was a bit frosty after that.

Since Mr. Blake was across the street, I doubted noise would be an issue. No, it was more that I could tell he didn't have much use for anyone, let alone his crazy dog lady neighbor.

And that was fine by me. In a way, I was glad that he was so prickly. If he'd been at all friendly, I would have had a more difficult time coming up with reasons to avoid him.

Because I was doing just fine in my life…and the last thing I wanted was the kind of complications a handsome neighbor might cause.

CHAPTER TWO

My phone *binged*. I looked down at the screen and allowed myself a small eye roll.

One word. *So???*

Obviously, Naomi hadn't been so busy working in her studio that she didn't have the chance to peek out her front window and see me standing in the new neighbor's front yard, having some sort of conversation.

Nothing to tell, I responded. *Rufus got out and went over to the new guy's yard. His name is Benjamin Blake.*

You were talking for a couple of minutes, she sent back. *How'd it go?*

It didn't go anywhere. Actually, he's kind of a jerk. Not friendly at all.

Bummer. A pause, and then a second message

bubble appeared beneath that one. *Maybe he was just tired from the move. You should try again.*

The move where he didn't lift a finger and had eight guys helping out? I thought, but I didn't bother to send that particular question to my friend. I could tell she wanted to entertain visions of something working out between me and Benjamin Blake, and that definitely wasn't going to happen. Not every man was possible relationship material, and I was okay with that. I didn't want a relationship anyway. Therein lay madness.

Hoping to deflect her, I typed, *Want to come over for takeout tonight? We can order Thai.*

No can do, babe, she wrote back. *I have a gallery opening downtown to go to. I was going to ask you if you wanted to come, but then Eloy invited himself along as my date.*

Eloy Esparza was Naomi's stylist and manager. Theirs was a weird relationship—he was flamboyantly gay, or at least acted as if he was—and yet he was far too protective and controlling of her for someone who appeared as though he had no interest in her romantically. Or maybe "controlling" wasn't exactly the right word. It wasn't as though he interfered in her love life, but rather that he always seemed to find a hundred and one reasons why someone wasn't the right person for her, and always seemed pleased when her latest relationship fell apart. For someone who styled herself as a lifestyle guru, Naomi didn't exactly have her personal life together.

But her legions of fans didn't know anything about that, of course. They only saw that she always appeared flawless and in control of her world, and the only reason I knew anything about Eloy was because Naomi was my neighbor, and so of course I'd met him early on. Luckily, he seemed to tolerate me, probably because he figured it helped her to have a close female friend, especially one as harmless as I was. We moved in different worlds, and I certainly wasn't the kind of person who could draw focus from her. Not the woman with the revolving door of chihuahuas and the tears in her jeans, who usually managed to remember to comb her hair...but not always.

Actually, on more than one occasion, I'd contemplated cutting it all off, but I could never quite muster the courage. I'd been growing my hair since eighth grade, and it reached all the way down to my waist. Pale blonde and thick, it was probably the most noteworthy thing about my appearance, and although I didn't think I was particularly vain, something always stopped me when I thought I'd gotten to the psychological moment when I was ready to let it go.

So, the hair stayed. Most days, I pulled it back in a ponytail or braided it to keep it out of the way, but I had a feeling I was still far too attached to it.

Since I knew I needed to reply to her last message, I wrote, *No problem. Just thought I'd ask. Have a good time!*

I'll try to. And I'll bring you along to the next one. Promise.

Sounds good.

I knew it wasn't an empty promise, either. If Naomi Klein told you she'd do something, she did. End of story. Even if it meant telling Eloy to back off. Then again, it was easy for him to back off when I was involved. I wasn't a threat.

But since I really didn't want my thoughts to run down that particular path, I added, *Let me know if you have any celebrity sightings!*

At this party? Doubt it. But I'll dish if there's anything to dish. Later!

And that was the end of the convo. I set my phone back down on the kitchen counter and went over to the fridge, figuring I might as well forage rather than waste a takeout evening when I was going to be in the house by myself. Not that there was much to scrounge; I desperately needed to go to the grocery store, and about all I had to choose from was a carton of yogurt old enough I wasn't sure whether I should risk consuming it, a couple of Lean Cuisines, and some frozen chicken tikka masala from Trader Joe's.

Looked like it was going to be a tikka masala night.

With a sigh, I shut the freezer door and went to measure out Frida and Rufus's dinners. I always fed the dogs as close to six o'clock as I could manage, although I tended to eat at least an hour later. And I could be glad that, although Rufus was definitely a handful, he didn't try to steal any of my own dog's dinner. There'd been times when I'd had to place the bowls of dog food at opposite ends of the house, or lock up any visiting dogs in the kitchen while they ate so they wouldn't go marauding in Frida's bowl, but I didn't have that problem with Rufus.

As soon as the kibble began to hit their stain-less-steel dishes, both dogs came running, their toenails clicking on the tile floor. Despite that not-so-pleasant encounter with Benjamin Blake earlier in the afternoon, I couldn't help but smile as I watched the two little creatures attack their food with the appetite of much larger dogs. They were so sweet and funny that they always managed to brighten my day.

As I watched them, I wondered whether maybe I should adopt Rufus. After a little initial tension, it looked as though he and Frida were getting along well, and I didn't think her nose would be too out of joint about the situation, since she was used to strange dogs coming and going all the time anyway. However, I also knew that I had a propensity toward falling in love with whatever dog entered my care, and this definitely wasn't my first "crush." No, better to have Rufus go and stay with a foster family until he found his forever home. That way, I'd be able to have room for the next orphan who needed a temporary way station before they moved on to fostering or a more permanent situation.

Once they were full, both dogs eyed me with some curiosity, clearly expecting me to make my own dinner. I had to admit that I wasn't very disciplined about not giving animals table scraps; I'd always done it with Frida, and it seemed as soon as we had a new dog under our roof, they picked up the habit as well, no matter what might have been standard practice in their previous home.

"Not yet, kids," I said. Something stubborn inside kept me from eating dinner any earlier than seven o'clock. Maybe that still wasn't fashionably late enough for the party crowd, but it also wasn't getting the early-bird special at Denny's, either. A girl had to have some standards.

Even though he was newly arrived and thus hadn't had time to become accustomed to my routine, Rufus didn't seem too disappointed when I grabbed my glass of water and took it with me to the family room. Some nights, I'd have a glass of wine to wind down, but I had that early-ish meeting in Rancho Cucamonga the next day and figured I'd better take it easy that evening. And Frida was already used to me taking my time about dinner, and so she followed me without looking too annoyed… although I was also aware of her watchful eyes as I sat down on the love seat and lifted the remote for the TV.

The local news had barely flashed on the screen when someone knocked at the door. Surprised, I put down the clicker and got up from where I sat. Had Naomi changed her mind about having me come with her to the gallery opening? But no, that didn't make any sense—she would have texted me to tell me to put on some makeup and a decent outfit. I did own a few good items of clothing, although most people who saw me day to day probably wouldn't have believed such a thing.

People didn't often go door to door in my neighborhood, although such a thing wasn't out of the question, either. Was it Girl Scout cookie season already? Stocking up on Thin Mints and Tagalongs was definitely a good reason to answer the door.

However, when I peered out through the one bit of clear glass in the stained-glass panel on the front door, I didn't see any Girl Scouts standing out there. No, it was Benjamin Blake, of all people, looking just a little annoyed.

Actually, looking *extremely* annoyed.

For just the briefest moment, I contemplated not answering his knock. After all, he appeared aggravated enough that I doubted his attitude had materially improved from the time we'd met a few hours earlier. On the other hand, I knew for a fact that Rufus was safely inside, because he and Frida had followed me to the foyer and stood on either side of me, their ears up and their tails wagging. Whatever had set Mr. Blake off this time, it definitely wasn't a marauding chihuahua.

A deep breath, and then I opened the door. "Hi, Benjamin. What's up?"

This casual greeting seemed to only annoy him further, because his brows drew together in a scowl, and his lips—full in a pouty, pretty-boy sort of way—compressed for a few seconds. "I'm sorry to bother you," he said. "But you did tell me you were always home."

Which seemed to be his way of intimating I didn't have a life. Then again, I supposed I shouldn't allow him to bother me, since I really had told him I was usually around. And sadly, I didn't have much of a life, or at least what most people would think of as a life. Just me and the dogs, not much socializing or party-going or even stuff as simple as going to the movies. All right,

Naomi and I went out from time to time. But a social butterfly I was not.

"Mostly," I admitted. "What's the problem?"

"I don't know for sure," he said. "I went to turn on the heat, and nothing happened."

That sounded like an issue for an HVAC person to look at. However, it was past six-thirty, and the chances of getting anyone to come out and look at the thing at that hour were pretty low. Some people might have shrugged off such a problem—we were in Southern California, after all, not North Dakota or something—but the weather had been fairly chilly for the past week, and those old houses weren't insulated like new-construction homes.

And there was something else I thought I spied in Benjamin Blake's expression. Yes, the annoyance I'd noted earlier, but beneath that, something that looked almost like anger at himself for not being able to handle such a simple problem.

That seemed to decide things for me. More than once, I'd been accused of being too soft-hearted—Naomi thought I should've gotten a lot more out of Tom than the house and a very modest grand a month in spousal support—but I'd never seen the point in being a jerk just to be a jerk.

"I can take a look at it," I said. "Is it a new system?"

"I don't know," he confessed. "This is the first time I've lived in a house like this."

"You've always lived in newer places?"

"Older, actually."

I looked at him in some surprise, thinking he had to be from the East Coast or someplace else where it was no big deal to have houses that were centuries old. Here in California, a hundred years —or a little more than that—was about as old as you got unless you were talking about the Spanish mission buildings or something along those lines. But then I shrugged off my inner questions; I had a feeling my neighbor wouldn't appreciate me asking personal questions about his past.

"Well," I said, "let's see what's going on. Just let me grab my house keys."

As I hurried off toward the kitchen, where I'd left my purse sitting on the counter, I realized Rufus had scampered into the entry and was once more bounding around Benjamin Blake's legs. Why the dog had taken such a shine to someone who seemed like an inveterate grouch, I had no idea.

To my surprise, when I came back to the foyer, Benjamin had actually bent down and was scratching Rufus behind the ears, the little dog nearly flattened to the floor as his tail wagged ferociously.

"He likes you," I said, and my neighbor shrugged.

"It would seem so."

I went to the door and was about to close it so I could lock it behind me when Rufus started to whine. "I'm just going across the street for a couple of minutes," I told him. "I'll be back soon."

He whined again and then gave a little bark, standing on his hind legs and dancing about as his tail kept going a mile a minute.

"Does he often act like this?" Benjamin asked, looking vaguely alarmed.

Since I'd only had Rufus with me for the better part of a day, I couldn't profess to know all the ins and outs of his behavior. In this case, though, I had a pretty good idea what was going on.

"He wants to come with us."

Benjamin Blake's eyebrows shot up. "Why on earth would he want to do that?"

"Because he likes you," I replied, while silently adding, *Although I have no idea why....* "He's a very good dog," I went on. "I don't think it could hurt to have him come with us. But of course, I'll have him stay here if you want."

"Well...." He paused so long, I thought for

sure he was going to tell me to keep Rufus safely locked up in my house. But then he said, "If you don't think it will be a problem."

"No problem at all," I said briskly. "Here."

And I bent and scooped up the little chi mix, and handed him to Benjamin.

He looked so terrified, one would have thought I'd handed him a newborn baby instead of one very small dog. Luckily, though, Rufus settled down right away, pushing his nose against the lapel of Benjamin's jacket.

"Told you he liked you." I locked the front door and pushed my keys into my pocket. "Now, let's see what's going on with your furnace."

Still with Rufus cradled in his arms, Benjamin took me across the street and up the front walk to his house. I'd be lying if I said I wasn't curious about what I would see inside, especially after Naomi's comment about all the expensive antiques.

When he opened the door, my breath caught. If it hadn't been for the electric light fixtures, I could have almost imagined myself back in a Los Angeles from more than a hundred years earlier. Everything seemed absolutely perfect in every detail, from the reproduction William Morris wallpaper to the Eastlake-style antique curio cabinet against one wall, right down to the Persian carpet in rich shades of green and burgundy and deep slate blue on the polished honey-oak floor. Tom and I hadn't been quite that fussy with the little bits, since we'd decided against wallpaper and instead opted for jewel-toned paint on the walls, but I had to admire the dedication to the Victorian aesthetic I saw here.

"It's amazing," I said, and Benjamin cocked an eyebrow at me.

"What's amazing?"

"The house, of course," I replied.

He still looked a little puzzled. "Isn't your own house from the same era?"

"Well, yes, but I haven't done as much with mine. Was the wallpaper here when you bought it? I was hoping they'd have an open house so I could see what this place looked like on the inside in person, but there was so much interest in the place, I guess the realtor didn't see the need for one."

"I don't know about the wallpaper," Benjamin said. "My...agent bought the place for me."

I stared back at him, trying to figure out if I'd heard him correctly. "You mean you had someone else buy the house for you sight unseen?"

"Basically." He shrugged, then bent down and deposited Rufus on the Persian carpet. He sniffed at the thick wool pile but seemed as though he knew he needed to be on his best behavior, because he curled up in the center of the rug and lay there, panting slightly, ears perked so he wouldn't miss a thing. "That is, he knew my taste, so he knew what to get."

That still seemed like an enormous level of trust, especially considering that this place must have sold for close to two million. I didn't see how it could be any less, since it had six bedrooms to my own home's four—I knew this because of course I'd perused the listing on Zillow, even if I'd never actually gone inside the house before Benjamin invited me in—and the interior was clearly in better shape than ours had been when we purchased it. Tom hadn't been much of the fixer-upper type, so I'd put most of the sweat equity into the place. Maybe that was part of the reason why I'd been so fiercely determined to hold on to the house when our marriage fell apart; my ex had only seen the big Victorian as an investment, whereas I knew it also contained a little piece of my soul.

"Well, it's very nice," I said, realizing what a limp compliment that was. But Benjamin hadn't brought me over here to praise the house, just to take a look at the thermostat. At least, I hoped that was the issue. If he had a problem with the furnace, then probably his best bet would be to load some wood into the fireplaces and heat the house the old-fashioned way, at least for that night. "The thermostat?" I added. Might as well get on with it before I made a complete idiot of myself.

"Down this hall," he said. His expression was slightly relieved, as if he was glad that I wouldn't be forcing him to stand there and waste any more time with idle chitchat.

Sure enough, there was a very new-looking digital Nest thermostat installed in the hallway. Luckily, I had almost the same models in my own house, so I thought I should be able to help him out. "It's really simple, actually," I said. "You just push it up or down to adjust the temperature. What temperature would you like the house to be?"

Benjamin shrugged. "I don't know. What's considered comfortable?"

He sounded as though he'd never adjusted a thermostat in his life. "Um…usually somewhere between sixty-eight and seventy-two degrees, depending on personal preference and how much energy you're trying to save. But let's go with seventy for now," I added quickly, as I noticed a flicker of impatience in his eyes. Indoors, they seemed warmer-toned than they had looked outside, almost amber.

I knew I shouldn't be paying any attention to his eye color—or anything else about him. He was standing about a foot away from me, but even that felt a little too close. Maybe it was only that he seemed much taller in close proximity; I realized he had to be several inches past six feet, dwarfing my own five foot five.

All too aware of his gaze fixed on me, I made the necessary adjustments to the thermostat, then heard the telltale click of the device sending a signal to the furnace to wake up and get to work. Almost at once, a faint hiss of air emerged from the nearest vent.

"There you go," I said, inwardly grateful that it had been a simple fix. Even if it hadn't been, it wouldn't have been my fault, but I found myself wanting to avoid aggravating Mr. Blake any more than he already was. "They're smart thermostats, so they'll learn as time goes on and start adjusting themselves to make the house more comfortable for you without you having to fiddle with them."

"Ah," he said, his gaze flicking upward briefly, probably toward the second floor, where I assumed another of the devices must be installed. For an uncomfortable moment, I wondered if he was going to ask me to go upstairs and reset that one as well, something I really would have preferred to avoid. Being down there on the ground floor was one thing, but going upstairs to where the bedrooms were located would have felt downright weird.

To my relief, though, Benjamin only gave a brief lift of his shoulders, then went over to the register and held up his hand, presumably to feel the warm air flowing through the vent. "Yes, it does seem to be working."

"Piece of cake," I said. "You can get the app and use your cell phone to control it as well, which is helpful if you're away and want to reset the temperature before you come home."

"I don't have a cell phone."

"Excuse me?" Maybe I just hadn't heard him correctly. How in the world could someone exist in this day and age without a smart phone? All right, I could understand not having one if it was an expensive luxury and a person had more important things to spend their money on, but anyone who could afford a house like this one definitely had the cash to get the newest and shiniest iPhone or Android in existence. "How do you function?" I blurted, then realized that hadn't been the most politic thing to say.

"Just fine, Mrs. Torres." Now he looked almost amused, as if watching me insert my foot in my mouth had actually done something to improve his mood. "This home has a regular phone in case of emergencies. As for the rest—I don't see the need to walk around all day with my face buried in an electronic device."

Ah, a Luddite. No wonder he wanted to live in an old house. His avoidance of technology and anything too modern might also have explained the suit and the bow tie.

I knew better than to ask. "It's Jillian," I said. "Mrs. Torres is my former mother-in-law." As soon as I made that remark, I wondered if I should have kept my mouth shut. It was true enough—I'd never used "Mrs." in front of my name, and mostly hadn't reverted to my maiden name of Cunningham because the thought of all that paperwork, including changing the title on the house, seemed like an enormous time suck. But the last thing I wanted was for Benjamin Blake to think I'd made a point about my name because I needed him to know that I was single, and available.

Well, available in fact if not in intention, anyway.

"Jillian," he repeated. "If you insist. And thank you—the house seems to be warming up nicely. I think it's a little odd that the former owner would put such modern devices in a place like this, but...."

"I don't think they had any kind of thermostats when this house was built," I pointed out. "In which case, pretty much anything you put in would be an anachronism. I suppose the previous owners thought they might as well use something easy to work with and up to date."

He nodded, but in the briefest possible way, as

though allowing my argument without exactly agreeing to it. That seemed a little rude to me, but pretty much par for the course as far as Benjamin Blake was concerned.

"Well, enjoy your evening," I said, since it seemed obvious enough that he didn't want me hanging around now that I'd performed my one useful service for him. "And if you need to figure something else out about the thermostat, you can try Googling it."

I halfway expected him to say he didn't have a computer, either, but he only replied, "Yes, once I get my internet hooked up. They're coming tomorrow."

Right. I supposed I should have thought of that. After all, despite how completely "done" the house looked, he'd only just moved in. One would have thought he'd make sure a detail like that was handled before he ever got here, but, as my own squabbles with Time-Warner had taught me, sometimes all the planning and forethought in the world didn't mean squat when it came to fighting with the cable company.

"That's not too long to wait," I said, trying to sound cheerful about the situation. "Since the weather isn't going to change much from today to tomorrow, I think you'll be okay."

As I was talking, I headed back toward the foyer. Along the way, I paused to scoop up Rufus from where he was lying on the rug in front of the fireplace in the front parlor. It was currently cold and dark, but maybe the dog remembered fires in hearths from wherever he'd lived before. I honestly didn't know much about the little guy, except Myra had found him wandering the streets of hilly Mount Washington, and that no one had claimed him even though she'd put up numerous posters in her neighborhood and also added his picture to several local "lost pet" websites and bulletin boards and Facebook groups.

He went into my arms easily enough, but I noticed how he kept staring at Benjamin, something about the expression in his round dark eyes imploring. I could tell the dog wanted to stay here. Why he'd fixated on my neighbor, I had no idea, but no way would I even make the request. He was going to a wonderful foster home very soon…I hoped. I still had to check out the house and make sure it would be okay for him.

"Thank you," Benjamin said. Something about the stiffness in those two small words told me he wasn't the sort of person who was in the habit of thanking other people. Once again, I wondered where he'd come from, what his history was. He seemed so utterly different from anyone else I'd ever met.

"No problem," I replied. That much was true, at least. It wasn't as if I had any other claims on my time that evening. "Good luck with the cable company tomorrow."

I figured that was as good a way as any to end our encounter. Breezy, friendly, but also disinterested enough to make it clear that it would be just hunky-dory if we didn't have much contact after this. Yes, he was good-looking, but after dealing with my ex-husband, I figured I'd had enough good-looking jerks to last me a lifetime.

Not that Benjamin Blake had shown even the slightest interest in me. No, I wasn't sure whether he'd actually noticed I was female. That made the situation even easier to manage. I definitely wouldn't have to fend off any advances from him, that was for sure.

I walked across the street, Rufus still in my arms, and didn't look back.

INTERLUDE

He wasn't quite sure what to make of the woman who lived across the street. On the surface, she seemed friendly...but not too friendly, not in a way that might have spelled trouble in the future. Unlike his fellow demons, Beelzebub had absolutely no interest in forming a relationship with a human being. Just the mere thought of the sort of intimacies he might be expected to share if involved in such an association made him shudder slightly.

But, he reflected as he went back toward the kitchen to make himself a cup of tea, it seemed that Jillian Torres had no more interest in such a thing than he did himself. Although he'd been exiled to Earth for less than twenty-four hours, he'd been here long enough to learn that human females found this form he wore attractive enough

—at any rate, he assumed that was why the teller at the bank where he'd withdrawn some cash for his daily needs had smiled at him in such a way and told him to stop by again in the near future.

Perhaps he would, if his cash ran out quickly enough, but he would do his best to find a different teller to help him—a male one, if at all possible. The last thing he wanted was some ridiculous human female batting her false eyelashes at him and trying to flirt.

Beelzebub did not flirt.

Jillian hadn't been like that at all. No false eyelashes, for one thing; he wasn't sure whether she'd been wearing any makeup at all. In a way, he appreciated that, if only because it meant she wasn't trying to present a false image of herself to the world. Some people might have found her attractive anyway, since he supposed her features were pleasant enough, but human standards of beauty had always mystified him.

Her hair, though…it was quite striking. Thick and pale blonde, it fell to her waist and made him want to look at her twice. She didn't do anything to call attention to it, but she didn't need to. Those long locks drew the eye without any effort at all from her.

And then Beelzebub wanted to shake his head at himself, because he knew it was foolish of him to be thinking about her hair in the first place. He reassured himself that she'd been businesslike and nothing else. She hadn't even looked back at him before she crossed the street, that ridiculous dog of hers in her arms.

But no, it wasn't her dog, was it? She'd said something about it being a foster. Not that it mattered—like everything else about Jillian Torres, it was none of his concern.

Despite this inner admonition, he couldn't quite stop himself from considering the dog as he set the kettle on the stovetop and snapped his fingers to turn on the gas burner beneath. If he'd known how the thermostat worked, he could have done the same thing with it...and would do so in the future if necessary.

Once upon a time, he could have caused the water in the kettle to heat instantaneously just by the mere force of his mind, but God had seen fit to make sure that many of Beelzebub's demonic powers were no longer his to control. Trifles were left to him, ones that probably would have still seemed miraculous to a regular human being, but not so long ago, he'd been able to command far greater powers. Yes, he was blessed with abundant health and long life and an inexhaustible bank account, but even though he wasn't completely powerless, he was still annoyed that he also wasn't quite what he used to be.

Also, he couldn't possess people anymore,

which quite possibly annoyed him more than all of the other losses combined. Possession was such a handy way to gather information about people, and he knew he would miss it greatly before he was done.

That dog, though…it was far too friendly. In the past, dogs had always been able to sense his presence, which was why possessing someone who owned a dog could be problematic. Now, though, it almost seemed as though Rufus—ridiculous name—could also tell who and what he was…and didn't care. Beelzebub wasn't quite sure what to make of that. Perhaps the dog somehow could perceive that many of his powers had been taken from him, and therefore he no longer constituted a threat.

Possibly. That still didn't explain why the creature was so damnably friendly.

The water in the kettle began to boil, and he lifted it from the burner and poured some into the teapot he had waiting nearby. No bags of tea for him; he preferred to do this the old-fashioned way, with a tea ball of pierced tin and some oolong leaves he'd purchased down the hill in Chinatown earlier that day. As human as it was, the ritual soothed him, and he breathed in the fragrant steam as he returned the lid to the teapot.

As he waited for the tea to steep, he found himself frowning. It was too quiet here—a few sounds drifted up the hill from the busier streets below, but that wasn't the same as having the cries of the eternally damned continually echoing in one's ears. He supposed it could have been worse. At least God hadn't given him a house out in the middle of an uninhabited forest somewhere.

Still scowling, Beelzebub went out to the living room and turned on the sound system there. Immediately, classical music began to play —a piano piece by Bach. That was better. Although he would never have admitted such a thing to anyone, he found Bach soothing. So precise, so mathematical. No overwrought violins or weepy cellos, just pure, perfect progressions of chords.

He returned to the kitchen and poured himself some tea. For just the barest moment, he found himself wondering what Jillian Torres was doing. Immediately, though, he clamped down on that thought. There was no need to think about her, because she meant nothing, was no one.

And that went for her ridiculous dog as well.

Thus assured of his self-sufficiency, Beelzebub sat down on the living room couch with a cup of tea, and prepared to face the first night of his newly human life.

CHAPTER THREE

"Well, I'll let you know," I said cheerfully to Anita Olsen, the woman who wanted to foster Rufus. My cheer was all manufactured, but I didn't want to tell her to her face that there was no way in the world I'd leave my latest rescue with her. No, I'd handle that unpleasant necessity via the safe distance provided by email. "I just have to check on a few things, but you should hear from me by tomorrow at the latest."

"Great," she said, all smiles as she walked me over to the spot where my Prius was parked in front of her house. "I can't wait!"

Somehow, I managed to return her smile, but then I got in the car and pulled away as quickly as I could without being rude. What a waste of time. Anita had assured me her place would be just perfect for Rufus, but that obviously had been wishful thinking on her part. She already had two dogs, which wouldn't have been a disqualifier—except they were big and aggressive and would have eaten Rufus for lunch…figuratively if not literally. Even worse than that, her supposedly secure yard was enclosed with only chain-link and not the sturdy cinderblock wall she'd all but promised me over the phone. If Rufus could get out of my locked-down backyard, then he'd escape from Anita's before you had a chance to say "Scooby Doo."

Which put me back to square one. I had a long list of fosters I generally relied on, but all of them were already full up, and Janine Hartgrove, my backup, was traveling in South America and wouldn't be back until March. Yes, I could always keep Rufus at my place a bit longer, and yet I really would have preferred not to, since I could already tell he was getting on Frida's nerves. She was a patient dog, but she put up with the revolving door of rescue dogs because she knew they never tended to stay longer than a night or two before they went on to someplace more permanent.

I got back on the 10 Freeway heading toward Los Angeles and tapped my fingers on the Prius's steering wheel, trying to decide what to do next. There were several Facebook rescue groups I belonged to, and I could put out the call there, although I'd have to vet anyone who offered to help. People who fostered dogs tended to have very big hearts, but chihuahuas offered their own special set of challenges, and someone who wasn't used to working with them could run into trouble fairly quickly.

Too bad I couldn't get Naomi to help me out. With her living right next door, she would have been the perfect solution, but she had a big seal-point Siamese named Cleopatra who absolutely ruled the roost, and I knew she—the cat, not Naomi—would throw a hissy fit if my friend tried to bring a dog into her sanctum. Besides, Naomi really wasn't a dog person. She put up with my chihuahua fascination because I didn't make a big deal about it, but it wouldn't be fair to put her on the spot by asking her to take on Rufus when I knew she absolutely had no interest in dogs, chihuahuas or otherwise.

Then a thought sprang up in my mind, one from so out of left field, I actually laughed out loud and shook my head at myself. Good thing I was sailing along the freeway at seventy miles an hour and there was no one in my immediate vicinity to see me acting like a crazy woman.

Still....

What if I asked Benjamin Blake to foster

Rufus until I could find a permanent home for him?

The dog had already formed a strange kind of attachment to my new neighbor. Benjamin lived right across the street, so he could ask me for advice or help whenever he ran into any trouble. His yard had an actual brick wall, not just a wood fence, and therefore was even more secure than mine. All in all, it seemed like the perfect solution.

Well, except for the part where Mr. Blake didn't seem to be at all interested in any contact with his neighbors, let alone taking on the responsibility of watching a foster dog. I could only imagine the expression on his face if I tried to make such a request.

On the other hand, I didn't have a lot of options. Worst-case scenario, he'd laugh in my face and walk away, and I'd be left with the same pitifully few alternatives I already had. I figured I could handle Benjamin's scorn; after surviving the embarrassment of my husband's affair, I knew it would take a lot to discombobulate me.

And I just knew it would make Rufus happy if some sort of miracle occurred and my neighbor actually said yes.

That seemed to settle things. I stayed on the 10 until it merged with the 101 and headed north until I got off at Echo Park Avenue. From there, it was only a five-minute drive to get to my house.

All seemed quiet enough when I came in. I hadn't brought Rufus with me to Anita's house, simply because I didn't want to be put in the position of having him there and then having to decline the foster—which was exactly what had happened, even though I hadn't given Anita the bad news yet. Instead, I'd done my best to segregate the dogs, leaving Frida upstairs sleeping in her basket at the foot of my bed and with a child gate blocking the bottom of the stairs, and allowing Rufus free run of the downstairs. As I'd driven away, I'd prayed that he wouldn't cause too much trouble; he'd seemed well-behaved enough when it came to the furniture and the rugs on the floor, but dogs could get destructive when left alone if they were worried they'd been abandoned.

However, all seemed well as he greeted me at the back door, tail wagging and lopsided ears perking at the sight of me going to the pantry. I got out a couple of treats and walked through the rest of the downstairs, reassuring myself with the quick inspection that he hadn't chewed on the couch or peed on the living room rug.

"Good boy," I said, and bent down so I could give him a treat.

He took it at once and headed over to the dining room so he could settle on the rug there and happily chew on the homemade dog biscuit I'd just handed him. With him taken care of for the moment, I took down the child gate and went upstairs. Frida met me at the door to the master bedroom, and I fed her the second treat I was holding and scratched her back.

"Thanks for being patient, sweetie," I told her. "I hope you don't mind hanging out up here for a little while longer. I need to go across the street and talk to my new neighbor."

Frida's head cocked slightly as I spoke, but she seemed far more interested in the treat I'd given her than what I was actually saying. To tell the truth, I talked to my dog all the time, not because I thought she understood me one hundred percent—although she did have a pretty big vocabulary, and I had to watch what I said around her—but because speaking to her like she was another person made me feel a little less alone. Kind of pathetic, I supposed, but there we were.

Because I didn't want to provide Benjamin Blake with any ammunition for the sort of condescending glances he'd given me the day before, I paused in front of the mirror in the master bedroom and picked up the comb I'd left lying on the counter, then passed it through my hair a couple of times. A bit of tinted lip balm to freshen things up, and I figured that was about as good as it was going to get. At least I'd put on a newer pair of jeans and cute flats and a sweater, since I hadn't wanted to go over to Anita Olsen's house looking like a complete slob.

Then I wondered if the irritable Mr. Blake would wonder whether I'd gotten dressed up just to impress him, at which point I did my best to shove the whole conundrum out of my mind. It didn't matter what he thought. The only thing that mattered was whether I could get him to agree to foster Rufus for the next few days—or week, or however long it took to find the dog a suitable permanent home. He could sneer at me all he liked, as long as I knew Rufus would be okay.

I bent and scratched Frida behind the ears, and so of course, she immediately rolled over onto her back, exposing her tummy so I could scratch that, too. Used to this ritual, I obligingly rubbed her belly for a moment or so, but then I stood up. "That's all for now," I said. "I'll be back in a bit, and then I can take down the gate and you can go out in the yard."

Frida sat up and cocked her head, then gave an absentminded scratch behind one ear before returning to her basket. She assumed her usual perch, with her forepaws dangling over the opening in the front and her chin resting on her paws.

"You are the cutest dog in the whole world," I

said—another ritual—and went back downstairs, replacing the child gate as I went. Rufus ran up to the front door as soon as I approached, but I shook my head. "It's way too early for a walk," I told him. "But I'll let you outside when I come back."

Or maybe not, I realized as I closed the door behind me. If Benjamin Blake said yes, then Rufus would get a short walk as I brought him over to his new—if temporary—home, but that was a little different from being let out into the backyard to have free run of the place.

The day wasn't quite as gloomy as the one that had preceded it; a bit of sun peeked out from behind the gray clouds that had shrouded the sky for the first part of the week. No rain, which was too bad, since we definitely could use some. All the same, my spirits lifted a bit at the sight of the sun, and I hoped its appearance then was a good omen.

Benjamin Blake's house looked a little friendlier with the sun shining on it, the cool-toned paint scheme of gray and green soothing rather than cold. I pulled in a breath as I mounted the front steps and told myself that I was here for Rufus, and so I shouldn't worry about how my neighbor might react to my presence.

A simple *ding-dong* sounded when I pressed the doorbell—the old-fashioned kind, not a fancy "smart" bell to match the thermostats installed inside. I waited as the seconds ticked by…and waited…and waited.

Could he have gone out? I supposed that was a possibility, but I remembered how he'd said someone from the cable company was coming that day to get everything installed. You'd think he'd want to be home for that, although I supposed the Time-Warner van could have come and gone in the time I'd spent driving out to Rancho Cucamonga and back.

At last, though, the front door opened, and Benjamin Blake stared down at me. He looked a little different that day, mostly because he'd exchanged the blue plaid suit and bow tie for a white button-down shirt and gray windowpane plaid trousers. Still way too dressed up for someone who supposedly was hanging out at home and waiting for the cable guy to show up, but I had to admit he did look a bit more approachable.

A very small bit.

His eyes narrowed. "What is it?"

Mr. Congeniality, he was not. "Sorry to bug you," I said. "But I was wondering if I could ask a favor."

"Quid pro quo for fixing my thermostat?"

I blinked at him. "Um, no," I replied, wondering if he had to go out of his way to be a

jerk, or whether it was something that came naturally to him. However, my marriage to Tom had
given me coping skills with jerks, if nothing else,
and so I went on smoothly, "More of a neighborly
thing, I guess. Do you mind if I come in?"

His left eyebrow lifted ever so slightly, and for
one awful moment, I thought he was going to say
no. But then he shrugged and said, "If you must."

As welcomes went, it wasn't much of one. But
he hadn't declined, or thrown me bodily off his
property, so I figured that was a win. I smiled and
murmured a thank-you, and went inside.

Like the exterior of the house, the interior
seemed a little more approachable in the light of
day. I got a better look at the exquisite floral tile
that surrounded the hearth in the front room, and
was able to see that he had a fabulous view of
downtown Los Angeles through the large picture
window, bordered in amber glass, that faced out
onto the street. However, I reminded myself that I
was there on an important errand, and not to
gawk at the architectural details of the house.

Because Benjamin Blake was still staring at me
through slightly narrowed eyes, I realized I'd
better get to the task at hand before I annoyed
him any more than I already had.

"It's about Rufus, actually," I said, and he
crossed his arms.

"Your dog that crawled under your gate?"

I nodded, but then added, "Well, that's the thing. He's not actually my dog. He's a rescue. That's what I do—rescue chihuahuas. I have an organization called Little Angels Chi Rescue."

This noble occupation didn't seem to move Benjamin at all. Or at least, I couldn't detect even the slightest shift in the stony expression he'd been displaying for the past couple of minutes. His lack of reaction didn't seem to bode well for my errand, but since I'd already embarked on this mission, about all I could do was see it through to the end.

"Anyway," I went on, hoping I didn't sound as desperate as I guessed I probably did, "Rufus really seems to like you."

"No accounting for taste, I suppose," Benjamin Blake interposed, his tone so flat, I wasn't sure whether he was making a self-deprecating joke or not.

I decided it was probably better to ignore his remark and keep going. "Usually, when I take in a rescue, I have the dog fostered with someone I can trust until I can find them a permanent home. In fact, I just went to check on a possible foster for Rufus earlier today. But it didn't work out—and all my regular foster homes are unavailable—and so…." I made myself breathe, and forced out the words. "And so…I was wondering if you could take him. Just for a few days," I added quickly in an attempt to make the request not sound quite so awful, even though I knew I might be making a promise I couldn't keep. Sometimes it took a very long while to find the perfect forever home for a dog.

Benjamin Blake only stared at me. I swallowed, cursing myself for being such an idiot. Even if he'd been a regular, friendly sort of new neighbor, I was asking for an awful lot. But to approach someone like him, a man who clearly had definite boundaries drawn around himself, boundaries he obviously didn't want anyone to cross…well, I realized that I should have stuck to calling myself crazy and tried something else.

"I know it's a huge request," I continued when the silence grew too terrible. "And I would never have asked it, except that Rufus really seemed to take to you. But if it's too much—"

He cut me off there. Strangely, though, his tone was almost gentle, despite the way he'd just interrupted me. "You really don't have anyone else to ask?"

"No," I replied. "Naomi has a cat who hates dogs, and, like I said, all the usual people I'd approach have their hands full with the dogs they're already fostering. And I know," I went on, before he could point out one glaringly obvious fact to me, "I have room at my place, but Frida doesn't do well when I have other dogs around for extended periods. Otherwise, of course I'd keep Rufus for as long as necessary. But—"

"I'll take him," Benjamin said, and I found myself blinking again.

"You will?"

"As long as it's temporary."

"Oh, it will be," I assured him, relief flooding through me. "I'm going to post his info in all the usual places. He's such a sweet dog, I know he'll find a good family in no time."

For a few seconds, Benjamin didn't reply. One hand pushed at the turned-up cuff of his opposite sleeve. A nervous gesture? I couldn't guess, since I didn't know him well. Or at all, really.

Then he said, "Would you like to look at the backyard?"

"Um...sure. He's a little dog, though—he really doesn't need much room."

A very small smile touched the corner of my neighbor's mouth. It came and went so quickly, I hardly had time to recognize it for what it was, but even in that short second or two, the shift in expression altered his face considerably. Instead of looking like the sort of petulant pretty boy I could easily dismiss, he appeared handsome and approachable, the kind of man who definitely merited a second look.

Danger, Will Robinson! I thought, and did my best to push that image of him away. I did not want Benjamin Blake to be someone I might be interested in. The only way I could get this to work was if we were both casual and relaxed and indifferent to one another.

"Actually," he went on, "what I meant was that perhaps you should take a look to make sure it's secure, considering how easily Rufus escaped your own backyard yesterday."

"Right," I said. *I knew that.* "Definitely. Let's see what we're working with."

Once again, his lips twitched, but his expression was more mocking now, something I could easily ignore. "This way."

He led me out of the living room and down a hallway that appeared to bisect the lower half of the house. I spied a large dining room with a fabulous hand-painted glass chandelier hanging over an enormous mahogany table, and another, smaller room with dark wood bookcases that appeared to be a study. Then we emerged into the kitchen, far more up-to-date than the rest of the house, its counters pale, polished marble, with white subway tile on the backsplashes and the cupboards black-washed wood.

From there, we went through a service porch equipped with a brand-new state-of-the-art LG washing machine and dryer, and down a set of steps into the backyard. It was a little larger than mine, with eucalyptus trees bordering the lawn and neat, brick-edged planters, but what surprised me the most was the bar setup that had been built onto the back of the house, complete with tiled counters and barstools and a long shelf clearly intended to hold bottles of liquor. The whole thing was perfect if you were into backyard parties, but Benjamin Blake had to be the last person I would think of as a party animal.

Something in my expression must have shifted, because he said, "That was there already, obviously. I'm probably going to take it out."

"Oh, that would be a shame," I told him, and he lifted an eyebrow.

"It's not very useful."

"No," I said, "but it's fun."

He seemed nonplussed by that comment. "Well, go ahead and look around, and let me know if you think it will be safe for Rufus."

Clearly, Mr. Blake didn't want to discuss the possible fate of his backyard bar. Well, it was his property, so I knew I shouldn't be telling him what he could or couldn't do with it. I nodded, and began to walk along the back wall, looking for any obvious places where Rufus might be able to wriggle underneath. I didn't see any, though, and although the most determined dog could definitely dig his way below a wall if he really wanted to, I had a feeling that wasn't going to be a problem here. After all, would Rufus work that hard to get away from someone he so obviously wanted to be with?

"It looks fine," I said, after I'd made my way around the perimeter and had also ventured down the side yard to check the gate there. Its clearance was so low that I didn't think even a mouse could squeeze underneath, let alone a dog, and so I doubted Rufus could get out that way.

Benjamin nodded. "Good. Then why don't you go and fetch him? I assume you'll bring some food as well—I don't have anything I can feed a dog."

"Oh, I'll bring everything," I said, still with a sense of unreality floating through my head. Could it really have been this easy to get my prickly neighbor to watch my latest rescue?

Apparently, it was, because he walked me back inside and sent me home, telling me to knock when I returned. Feeling slightly dazed, I headed across the street and let myself in. Rufus started dancing around me, tail going a mile a minute. Usually, he wasn't quite that happy to see me. Could he smell that I'd been over at Benjamin Blake's house? That seemed to be the likeliest explanation for his current enthusiasm.

"Good news, baby," I told Rufus as I packed his food, including a baggie full of the dog treats I'd baked just the day before. "Your friend

Benjamin is going to watch you for a bit. Won't that be fun?"

I had my doubts as to how "fun" it actually would be, but as long as Rufus was happy, that was the important thing.

His tail was still going at light-speed, telling me he seemed pretty darn thrilled with the situation. I got his bed from the family room, and put it in a large shopping bag along with his leash and food. For a moment, I wondered whether I should give Benjamin the paperwork from the vet who'd examined Rufus and given him his shots and a clean bill of health, but then I decided I could hold on to those records for the time being. After all, the dog would only be across the street from me, and it was really his new owners who would want the vet records.

Once I had everything put together, I clipped the leash on Rufus's collar and grabbed the shopping bag with one hand and the dog with the other. "Be right back!" I called up the stairs to Frida. I didn't see any sign of her, which meant she'd probably stayed in her basket, resigned to lying low until I got the interloper out of her house.

With Rufus straining at the leash, I closed the front door behind me and let him pull me down the front path to the sidewalk. There, he had to sniff all around the patch of grass next to the street, stopping at last to relieve himself with an air of great gravity, as if that was the one and only piece of lawn in the world adequate to the task.

But after that, he tugged at the leash again, nose pointed toward Benjamin Blake's house. It seemed clear enough that he knew exactly where he was going.

I did my best to fix a pleasantly neutral expression on my face. Yes, I barely knew the guy, but I could already tell that he wasn't the sort of person who would have much patience for overly chirpy and cheerful behavior. Not that I tended to act that way normally; it was just that sometimes I had to assume that kind of demeanor with my dogs' foster parents, and I didn't want to let myself slip into that type of affect when I guessed my neighbor would not be appreciative...to put it mildly.

My finger hadn't even descended on the doorbell before the front door opened and he looked out at the two of us. At the sight of Benjamin Blake, Rufus's tail started wagging even harder, so much so that Benjamin looked vaguely alarmed.

"Is he always this hyperactive?"

"Oh, no," I assured him, even though that wasn't the exact truth. Rufus did have a lot of energy. However, he was just being extra lively at the moment because the situation was new. After a little time, he would calm down. "He's just happy to see you."

"Hmm."

However, even if Benjamin was having second thoughts, he didn't utter them aloud. Instead, he stepped out of the way so the dog and I could enter the foyer.

"Do you mind if I take him off his leash?" I asked.

"No," my neighbor replied. "I suppose he should be allowed to explore the house."

Murmuring a silent prayer that Rufus would be on his best behavior and wouldn't pee on Mr. Blake's expensive Persian rugs or decide to start nibbling on the leg of an antique chair, I bent down and unclipped the leash. At once, the dog dashed off into the living room, tail wagging so fast it was a blur, his pointed little snout poking into everything within reach so he could get his fill of all these new and exciting smells.

"He's totally house-trained," I said, noting the way Benjamin watched the dog's progress, body stiff and eyes narrowed, looking as if he was afraid to take a breath. "He'll be fine."

"I assume I can send you the cleaning bill if he is not."

For a second, I could only stare up into his face, unsure whether he was joking or not. I let out a chuckle that sounded as though it didn't quite know whether it should be amused, and said, "Oh, sure, if it's necessary."

Benjamin didn't hasten to tell me that of course, it really wasn't a problem. No, he just nodded faintly, then said, "And his food…?"

"I've got everything here," I replied, glad we'd moved on to a safer topic. "I keep my dog's bowls in the kitchen, so we might as well do the same thing here. Do you have an out-of-the-way spot where I can set them down?"

"In here."

He led me into the kitchen, which was just as spotless and magazine-perfect as it had been the day before. I had to wonder if he even used it. Maybe not; Naomi seemed to live on takeout when she wasn't going to some dinner party or another, so I knew it was entirely possible to have a fully equipped kitchen and still barely set foot in the place.

"Down there?" Benjamin asked, pointing at the spot underneath a cart that currently held one of those fancy convection toaster ovens.

It wouldn't have worked for a bigger dog, but since Rufus stood maybe eleven inches tall at best, he'd be able to eat out of bowls placed under the cart without any risk of banging his head. Also, there was probably less chance of Benjamin or anyone else accidentally kicking a bowl with them tucked out of the way down in the spot he'd suggested.

"Perfect," I told him. I got the bowls out of the shopping bag I'd used to carry them, then stuffed it into the back pocket of my jeans. "Is it okay if I go ahead and get these set up?"

"Be my guest."

I should have known he wouldn't have offered to do it himself. But I reminded myself that he was doing me a huge favor, and so I only smiled in reply and went ahead and filled one bowl with water. After setting it on the floor, I opened the bag of dog food and put in the precise quarter cup I fed him at each of his meals.

"He gets fed three times a day," I said. "A quarter-cup of dry food, and then he gets a treat after each of his walks. I walk him twice a day, but if you're busy, you can always let him out in the backyard."

Rufus came trotting in then; he'd obviously heard the familiar sound of his kibble hitting the metal bowl. I went ahead and put it on the floor next to the water, and he started eating right away, clearly not at all put off by his unfamiliar surroundings. Benjamin watched him silently, one eyebrow cocked at a faintly ironic angle. Since I didn't quite know what to make of his expression, I decided I'd better keep going.

"That's really about it," I said. "Since he's such

a recent rescue, it's not like we have any particular routines set up. If you're planning to be away for long periods—"

"I'm not," Benjamin cut in. "That is, I work from home."

His mouth shut tight after that comment, almost as if he was annoyed with himself for divulging even that much information. Because of course, as soon as he provided me with even that tiny tidbit, I started wondering what it was he did. Maybe he was a writer, or some kind of freelance computer programmer. Either occupation might go some way in explaining his antisocial attitude.

However, I knew it probably wasn't a good idea to ask any probing questions, and so I only said, "Well, I'm sure Rufus will appreciate that. It's always easier for a dog when there's someone around most of the time."

Benjamin gave an absent nod, attention still fixed on the dog. It was hard to say whether he was fascinated by the way Rufus was wolfing down his kibble...or whether he was inwardly berating himself for agreeing to this arrangement in the first place.

If it was the latter, then probably better for me to get the heck out of there before he started voicing any second thoughts. "And that's about it," I went on. "Really, he's a good dog, so I don't think you'll run into any problems. But if you do,

I'm just right across the street. Come over and get me if you need to."

"I doubt that will be necessary," he said, something in his tone seeming to indicate that he'd have to be in pretty dire straits before he lowered himself to ask for my help.

Irritation flared, but I reminded myself that he really was doing me a favor, and so I needed to do what I could to overlook his condescending attitude. "Thanks again for this, Benjamin," I said, and I thought I sounded sincere. I truly was, but something about him just rubbed me the wrong way.

I thought I caught a flicker in his hazel eyes then, although I couldn't say exactly what it was. "You can call me Ben," he said.

"Oh, okay," I replied. Was that his way of trying to seem a little friendlier? Hard to say. However, I had to admit to myself that "Ben" was a lot easier to manage than "Benjamin." "Then thanks, Ben. You have a good afternoon. And you, too," I added, then bent down to scratch Rufus behind his ears. "Be a good boy, and mind what Ben tells you to do."

Since the dog was busy crunching kibble, he didn't seem to pay me much mind. But that was okay—obviously, he was relaxed enough in his new surroundings, and that was the important thing.

Ben walked me to the door. I'd already thanked him twice, so doing it a third time would have been a little over the top. About all I could do was offer a smile and reiterate that he could come get me if he had any trouble with Rufus.

"And it's temporary," I added. "Just until I find a home for him."

"It's fine," Ben said, although, since he didn't smile, I couldn't tell for sure whether it really was fine or not. "Goodbye."

And he closed the door behind me. I stood on the front porch for a few seconds, wondering at the abrupt end to our meeting. But it seemed clear enough to me that—whoever he was and wherever he'd come from—Ben Blake didn't worry too much about social niceties.

I wouldn't allow myself to shrug, not since I didn't know for sure whether he was watching me through that beautiful amber-framed picture window in the living room. Instead, I flicked my hair over my shoulder and descended the porch steps, and forced myself not to look back.

For better or worse, Rufus would be staying with Ben.

INTERLUDE

Beelzebub sat in an armchair in his living room and stared at the dog. The dog stared back at him. Its tail gave a single wag and then went still, as if it didn't know for sure whether or not that had been the proper response.

To be honest, Beelzebub didn't know, either. He knew next to nothing about dogs. Or rather, of course he understood what they were and their place in the world and their role as humanity's companions, but spending millennia as one of Hell's gatekeepers didn't provide much opportunity for spending time with canines.

Actually, he was wondering why in the world he'd agreed to this arrangement in the first place. Surely there was no reason for him to do his new neighbor any favors. True, she'd been in something of a bind, but she could have kept Rufus with her if she had no other alternatives. Really, why in the world would Jillian choose to operate a chihuahua rescue in the first place if her own dog was so opposed to having more of those creatures in her house?

Crazy and contradictory, just like most human behavior.

Rufus blinked at him and began to pant a little, tail wagging a bit more.

Did the dog want to be petted?

Did he even want to pet the dog?

Gingerly, he reached out and began to pass his hand down the animal's back. Its fur was somehow both soft and coarse beneath his fingertips, the sensation oddly satisfying. Apparently, Rufus was enjoying this treatment as well, because he arched his back and pushed against Beelzebub's hand, insisting on more.

Maybe a little scratch, right there at the base of the dog's tail. Rufus wriggled in ecstasy, rump moving to and fro almost in time with the scratching movements of Beelzebub's fingers. It was strange to think that the animal could get so much pleasure from such a simple touch, but clearly, this was exactly what he'd wanted.

Or rather, it was a prelude to more petting, because—in a rather astonishing display of dexterity, considering how small the animal was—Rufus then jumped up into the armchair with his new friend and snuggled up against his shirt front, his little round head solid and insistent.

"All right," Beelzebub said, surprised to hear a note of actual warmth in his voice. Normally, he didn't sound quite so friendly. "You are a determined little beast, aren't you?"

And he scratched behind the dog's ears, then ran his hand down its back. At these ministrations, Rufus closed his eyes and panted away happily. It was quite obvious that he couldn't think of any place he would rather have been at that moment.

Odd how relaxing this was, to sit here and hold this small furry creature and know that it truly wanted to be with him. Perhaps that was why Beelzebub had consented to watch the dog in the first place.

It was the first time in his life he'd ever had a creature actually choose to spend time in his presence.

All right, he was talking about a dog and not a person, but still. He'd never had a friend; Asmodeus had been a co-worker and not much more. Honestly, Beelzebub couldn't quite think of why his fellow demon had been a constant companion during all the millennia they'd spent in Hell, but he had the sneaking suspicion that it was only because Asmodeus hadn't possessed any true alternatives.

At any rate, the effort the other demon had expended in making sure he was free of Hell—and therefore also free of Beelzebub's dubious company—seemed to indicate that he wasn't shedding any tears over the prospect of no longer being his friend. If he ever had been at all.

His hand stilled then, and Rufus stirred and looked up at him, then gave him another nudge with his nose, as if to say, *Don't even think you're going to stop that soon!*

"Very well," Beelzebub said, and stroked the dog's head again. Rufus settled back down, obviously ready to remain in his new master's lap for as long as possible.

Except that he wasn't the dog's new master, was he? A temporary babysitter and nothing more —an expediency Jillian Torres had exploited because she was in a bind and needed someone to help her out.

Then again....

He didn't know her well—and would only be able to get to know her in the normal, human way, since he no longer had the ability to possess humans and see exactly what was going on in their heads—but he could tell already that she was fiercely committed to this dog rescue endeavor of hers, silly as it might seem on the surface. If she was indiscriminate about who she chose to look after these creatures, then she wouldn't have been in her current bind in the first place. She simply would have placed Rufus with anyone who offered, regardless of whether or not she thought them suitable.

In which case...apparently, she believed he was suitable.

Beelzebub wasn't sure what to think about that.

Almost automatically, his hand continued to caress the tiny dog who nestled in his lap. Once again, Rufus's eyes were closed, and he appeared to be on the verge of falling asleep. Did that mean he expected Beelzebub to remain in the chair and continue to provide a warm place to slumber for the duration of his nap?

It certainly looked that way.

A stir of irritation moved through him. He had far more important things to do than sit there and be an animate dog bed. Why, he —

The thought broke off there as Beelzebub realized, with a strange surge of melancholy, that he honestly didn't have anything better to do with his time. The movers who had brought his things here —or, to be more accurate, the possessions God had deemed he should have, since Beelzebub hadn't chosen any of them—had done a thorough job, and his home required no further work to make it habitable. Likewise, the gardens that surrounded the house were immaculate and had no need of his attention…not that he would have known what to do with them even if they did.

This sensation of idleness was strange, and not particularly pleasant. He was used to being occupied at all times; having to oversee the countless millions of souls damned to Hell did tend to fill up one's day. Just exactly what did God think he was supposed to do with himself?

Anything he wanted, apparently.

For some reason, his thoughts strayed to Jillian Torres. What was she doing right now? If Rufus hadn't been snuggled in his lap with no apparent plans to move in the near future, Beelzebub might have gotten up from his chair and gone to the window to see if he could spy any signs of her. Which was foolish, for two reasons—partly because she probably had no reason to be outside at all, and partly because he shouldn't care what she was doing.

Still, she was the only person he'd had any meaningful interactions with since being condemned to this mortal existence. He supposed it wasn't so strange for him to wonder what she did to fill her days.

If nothing else, it might have given him some ideas as to what he should do with himself.

CHAPTER FOUR

You will not look over there, I told myself. *You will not.*

All right. One peek.

In most things, I had a modicum of self-control. When it came to my rescues...not so much.

I had a watering can in one hand, thus providing the excuse that I was only loitering by the front window in order to water the Boston fern that sat on a marble-topped plant stand nearby. However, although the fern needed some attention, I was really only there so I could take a quick glance across the street toward Ben's house.

What I thought I'd see, I had no idea. My neighbor and Rufus playing keep-away on the front lawn? Which reminded me that I hadn't told Ben how much the little dog loved playing with a tennis ball. I'd included one in the care package I'd sent over, but I'd completely forgotten to mention it.

Maybe I should go over and—

No. I stopped that thought before it could get up a good head of steam. He might not have been all that friendly, but Benjamin Blake wasn't stupid, either. If I went hurrying back to his house less than an hour after I'd dropped off the dog, my neighbor would be sure to wonder why I was so damn eager to stop by.

And I didn't have a very good reason, other than the tennis ball. Which no doubt Ben would figure out as soon as he went through the other items I'd brought over for Rufus. He didn't need a diagram.

Just let it go, I told myself.

Honestly, I didn't know for sure why my thoughts kept straying in Ben's direction. I wanted to believe it was only because of the dog, but I had a feeling that wasn't the whole story.

Face it, I thought then. *It's because he's hot, and you know it.*

All right, it would be difficult to deny that Benjamin Blake was an attractive man. Totally not my type, though. I'd never been into pretty boys. I liked men with chiseled features, men who had something interesting about their looks. Which was probably why I'd fallen for Tom Torres in the first place—he was your stereotypical tall, dark, and handsome guy, with deep-set eyes and strong cheekbones and sooty hair.

And maybe—just maybe—it was also because I knew that marrying a Latinx guy would piss off my conservative congressman father. Our relationship had always been contentious, part of the reason why I'd opted to go to school down in L.A., just about as far away from Redding as you could get while still remaining in the same state.

My marriage to Tom had upset my father, although he'd been more measured about the relationship than I'd expected. Anyway, what was that old saying about cutting off your nose to spite your face? That was pretty much what I'd done to myself, since I probably knew deep down that Tom was a player and not the kind of guy who was really willing to settle down with the white picket fence and everything else. The only big surprise about his infidelity was that he'd been dumb enough to get caught.

A knock sounded on the back door, saving me from further ruminations about my ex-husband and all the mistakes I'd made with him. Naomi's voice drifted through the house a moment later; clearly, the knock had only been a formality.

"Jillian?"

"In the living room," I called back.

She appeared almost as soon as I spoke. It

must have been a "studio" day, because her dark hair was styled into perfect glossy waves and her makeup was just as polished.

"Taping today?" I asked.

"Yep. I was doing a bunch of those little viewer question 'bites.'"

That was a tradition on her channel—she'd select questions from her viewers and then do short videos with her answers. They were good filler for in between the longer interviews, and I knew she generally filmed a bunch of them at once so she could release them as needed in the coming days and weeks.

She looked around, a slight frown pulling at her brows. "So, you got Rufus off to his foster okay?"

"Well, not exactly," I replied, then set the watering can down on the floor. Frida was currently curled up across the room next to the unlit fireplace, but she was a well-behaved dog; I didn't have to worry about her knocking over the watering can and spilling water everywhere. "It wouldn't have been a good place for him, so…he's staying at Ben's house right now."

That remark sent her perfect eyebrows shooting straight up. "Mr. Bangable? I thought you said he was a jerk."

"Well…."

"So, he's not a jerk?" Naomi's dark eyes lit up,

and I had to suppress an inner groan. I knew that look—it meant she expected me to dish, and dish good. "Obviously, I've missed a lot."

"Not really," I said quickly. "It's just—I could tell Rufus liked Ben, and so when the foster fell through, I went over and asked if he could help me out. And he said yes. That's all."

"'All'?" she repeated, clearly not buying my nonchalant tone for a second. "Taking a stray dog into your house is kind of a big deal. And if he's normally not that friendly...." She let the words trail off, but I could guess from the significant look she gave me exactly what she was going to say next. "He must like you."

"I doubt it," I said at once. Whatever else I did, I needed to disabuse her of the notion that there was even the faintest hint of attraction between Benjamin Blake and me. If forced to make the admission—like, by means of waterboarding or possibly shoving bamboo shoots under my fingernails—I might have reluctantly admitted that I thought he was good-looking. Sort of. But definitely not my type.

She came over to where I stood and peered out the window. "Is that—is he actually *playing* with Rufus?"

I spun around to look, any thoughts of trying to act nonchalant flying completely out of my head. Sure enough, there was Ben, tossing a neon-yellow tennis ball for Rufus. The dog was far too small to actually pick up a tennis ball in his mouth, but he'd pulled loose some threads so that he could grab those with his teeth and let the ball dangle below his mouth.

He got hold of the ball and trotted away, tail wagging. Ben seemed to understand that "keep away" was a big part of this particular game, because he feinted right and then went left, chasing the dog—but staying just far enough away that it wouldn't seem as if he'd have an easy time getting within reach of the ball. Rufus dodged him and circled back, tail still wagging furiously. Another feint, and then Ben had the ball and threw it across the yard, carefully, so it wouldn't go past the low fence that marked the edge of the property.

"They seem to be getting along pretty well," Naomi remarked, hands on her hips as she observed the spectacle. It was something of one, if for no other reason than you usually didn't see a guy in windowpane trousers, an immaculate white button-down shirt, and shiny brown lace-ups playing keep-away with a scruffy chihuahua mix. I hoped those shoes had good soles, because I didn't want to think what would happen to those expensive pants if Ben slipped and went down on the damp grass.

"It looks that way," I said, figuring that was a

safe enough reply. "Still think I'm crazy for asking Ben to foster Rufus?"

"Possibly a stroke of genius," she admitted, still watching the two of them. "Maybe you should just have him adopt the dog."

I thought it was way too early to ask him to make that kind of a commitment. Yes, man and dog seemed to have bonded really well, but I had no idea whether Ben was even open to the idea of having an animal around the house. If he was a dog kind of guy, you'd think he would have brought his pet with him when he moved here.

But maybe he'd had a dog and had lost it somehow—old age, disease, a terrible accident. Or maybe he'd shared a pet with his ex and had to leave the dog behind when the relationship broke up. That would also explain why he was such a prickly bastard.

Or maybe my imagination was running away with itself. I really needed to watch that—it could get me into trouble if I wasn't careful.

"We'll see," I said. "I think I'd rather wait and find out how he does in the interim before I start asking Ben to adopt the dog."

Naomi shrugged, and finally turned away from the window. "I suppose, but if you're already posting Rufus's info in the regular places, you may get people wanting to adopt him before too long.

It would be a shame to take him away from Ben without giving him first dibs."

She had a point there. Still, I figured we probably had a little time. People tended to be slower about adopting a pet these days, partly because of the expense, partly because it was harder and harder to find landlords who were okay with their tenants owning dogs. Rufus was adorable, and should have been the kind of dog to get snapped up quickly, but experience had taught me that what often seemed reasonable wasn't always the case.

I nodded but didn't reply, instead doing my best to change the subject. "How was the gallery opening?"

That question elicited a knowing smile, one that told me she guessed I wasn't really that interested in the opening...but very interested in moving the conversation away from Ben Blake.

"It was all right," she said. "The food was good, anyway. I don't know shit about art, so I mostly nodded and drank wine and ate cheese."

"I suppose there are worse ways to spend an evening," I replied, and she tossed a lock of glossy dark brown hair over one shoulder and shrugged.

"Maybe. I honestly didn't want to go, but Eloy said there were supposed to be some movers and shakers there, so I went."

"Ah." That was all I said, because I tried my

best to keep my lip zipped when it came to Eloy Esparza. It seemed he was always pushing her to go to these things in the name of making industry connections, but—at least, as far as I could tell— those so-called connections never seemed to go much of anywhere. Oh, I wouldn't deny that Naomi was very good at what she did, and extremely successful, and yet her situation also seemed stagnant, for lack of a better word. She hadn't yet been able to grow her online presence to a real-world one, even though I knew she was jonesing to get an actual TV show, something with a little more cachet than just a YouTube channel. But I supposed that she figured she needed to keep trying, and that was why she spent more nights out than in, going to all these parties and openings.

"Anyway," she went on, "enough about that. I'm free tonight—let's go do a girls' night out in Little Tokyo, get some sushi and sake. If you're not babysitting Rufus, then you don't have any reason to stay home, right?"

I didn't, of course; Frida was never terribly thrilled to be left alone, but I went out so infrequently that she couldn't really get her nose out of joint too much about being abandoned for one evening. Naomi loved sushi, while I was lukewarm on the topic. The evening still sounded like fun, though, if for no other reason than it would get me out of the house for a few hours.

"Sure," I said. "I might even put on some mascara."

"Good girl," she said approvingly. "Pick you up at seven?"

"Sounds like a plan."

"Great. Gotta head back—I still have five more Q&A segments to shoot. See you tonight."

She headed toward the back of the house after that, and a moment later, I heard the kitchen door close. Frida came into the living room and tilted her head at me, and I felt a pang of guilt. Only a small one, since I generally was home most of the time, but still.

"Looks like I'm going out tonight, kiddo," I told her. "Guess I'd better go and see if I have a clean pair of jeans."

Her ears twitched, and I could have sworn I saw a disapproving look pass over her pointed little face. Maybe I could appease her by bringing back a few morsels.

In the meantime, though, I needed to make sure I had something halfway decent to wear. Although I wasn't terribly invested in my wardrobe, I knew I had to make sure Naomi wouldn't be embarrassed to be seen with me. That was about the most I could hope for—I knew

better than to think I could ever look as effort-
lessly chic as my friend.

Actually, that was a good thing. If I was only
adequate, then I didn't have to worry about people
paying attention to me. I'd had enough of that
growing up as a congressman's daughter. These
days, I wanted to escape notice.

Life was just easier that way.

"You didn't tell me this was going to be a thing," I
muttered to Naomi, surveying the crowd of fash-
ionistas and entertainment industry types who'd
gathered at the sushi bar she'd chosen.

She assumed an expression of injured innocence. "This isn't a 'thing'—it's just a soft opening
for a restaurant."

"A restaurant run by the guy who used to be the
sous chef at Nobu," I shot back. Not that I would
know Nobu from a hole in the ground—I'd just
been reading the write-up on the back of the menu I
was handed as we walked into the place. But apparently Nobu was a big deal, a Hollywood restaurant
where some of the town's biggest names liked to
hang out. "You might have mentioned we were
going to an event and not just a quiet dinner out."

"If I'd told you that, you wouldn't have come,"

Naomi pointed out…which was pretty much the truth. I hated this sort of thing. "Anyway," she went on without allowing me a chance to respond, "you look great, so stop stressing. It's good to get out and have a life every once in a while."

Standing there and arguing with her would have only attracted attention, so I settled for giving her the stink-eye as we waited for our chance to be seated. And I didn't know if I agreed with her assessment that I looked "great," but at least I'd put on my best-fitting pair of jeans along with high-heeled boots, a white tank, and a black jacket, so I knew I was presentable enough. Some instinct had prompted me to put on actual makeup instead of the tinted lip balm that was the extent of my usual beauty routine, even though I could tell that a couple coats of mascara and a layer of a neutral brownish-pink lipstick wasn't quite enough to bring me up to the level of the women I saw around me. No, that would've required a few hours of airbrushing…and probably some plastic surgery as well.

To my relief, we were seated after not too long a wait, although I didn't like the location of our table—it was out in the middle of the restaurant's main room rather than tucked into a corner the way I would have preferred. Still, with as crazy crowded as the place was, I knew there was no point in asking for a different table; we were lucky to have gotten this one so promptly.

"Don't frown," Naomi said, eyes fixed on the menu. "Frowning causes lines."

"Life causes lines," I retorted. I didn't bother to ask her how she could tell I was frowning when she appeared to be studying the menu. She knew me well enough to realize a situation like this was bound to make me scowl.

Our waiter, an absolutely amazing-looking Asian guy probably a few years younger than either Naomi or I, stopped at our table then. "What are we drinking tonight?" he asked.

"Cloudy sake," she replied, without bothering to ask for my input. Not that it would have made much of a difference, since I didn't know a lot about sake. All right, I thought I remembered reading somewhere that you really weren't supposed to drink it hot, but I had no idea whether that particular rule applied to "cloudy sake"…whatever that was.

"Excellent," said the waiter, and wandered away toward the bar.

Naomi watched him go, mouth pursed a little. "Damn, that is one gorgeous man."

"I thought you were on a man cleanse," I told her.

"I can still look," she returned. "I just can't do

anything else." A pause, and then she inquired, "What about Ben Blake?"

"What about him?" I studied the offerings on the menu, trying to decide on something that sounded interesting without being too crazy. To tell the truth, I wasn't even in the mood for sushi, but this restaurant didn't offer anything except sushi and sashimi, so I couldn't take the coward's way out and order teriyaki and tempura instead.

"Well, you had all afternoon. You're telling me you didn't go over to his place and check on how Rufus was doing?"

Of course I hadn't—mainly because I'd done my best to quell the impulse to do that very thing. From what I'd seen of them playing keep-away on the lawn, Ben had things well in hand. Besides, how much help did a grown man need when it came to shepherding a five-pound chihuahua/terrier mix? It wasn't as though I'd dumped an English sheepdog or a Rottweiler in his lap.

"No," I said evenly, and put my menu down. "I don't want to create the wrong impression."

"And what impression would that be?"

"That I'm some divorced chick who's so desperate to have someone in her life that I'd use a dog to get close to him."

Naomi studied me for a moment, perfectly glossed lips pursed slightly. "I know you're not desperate. If you were, you would have been dating already."

Her comment should have mollified me, but I was still feeling a bit annoyed with her. Mostly for dragging me down to Little Tokyo on false pretenses...although I thought some of my current irritation stemmed from the realization that she didn't see anything wrong with her last comment. She seemed to think that the only reason I wasn't seeing someone was because I'd made the conscious decision to remain single. Well, all right, that was part of it; after my marriage collapsed so messily, I'd told myself that I wasn't going to wade back into that particular nightmare any time soon.

However, over the past few months or so, I'd found myself thinking that maybe it would be nice to start dating...only to realize there really wasn't anyone *to* date. That assessment might have sounded a bit melodramatic, but it was only the truth, or at least, the truth of my particular circumstances. Single men my age only seemed interested in hooking up, not having long-term relationships. Some might have called that a bit of an oversimplification, and yet it seemed to me the ones who'd wanted to settle down had already done that very thing. The guys who were left wanted a good time and not much more. I couldn't even blame them. So many people were saddled with debt or working multiple jobs or so exhausted from the long hours they had to spend at even the one job they had that it really wasn't any wonder they didn't have the energy left over for anything except some mindless sex and maybe dinner and a movie every once in a while. Or, more likely, Netflix, chill, and takeout...not necessarily in that order.

No wonder Naomi's bloodhound instincts had gone into overdrive when Ben moved into the neighborhood. Someone good-looking, rich, and apparently unattached didn't fall from the heavens every day.

Not that I thought Mr. Blake had come from any place quite so exalted. I had a feeling an angel wouldn't be quite so prickly.

"He's our neighbor," I said then, pointing out the patently obvious. "We could be living across the street from each other for a very long time. I'm not going to be his horny, desperate neighbor. I'm just not. Like I said before, it would be beyond awkward."

Naomi looked as though she was about to reply, but then our waiter returned with the bottle of sake and a couple of glasses. Thank God. I was definitely feeling as if I could use a drink.

But first he had to pour the sake for us, and then take our orders. Luckily, since I'd already glanced over the menu, I knew what I wanted. I ordered a simple tuna roll, while Naomi got something I didn't think I could even pronounce. Well, that figured. She was always far more adventurous in her food choices than I would ever be, and yet still always managed to remain a perfect size four.

Once the waiter was gone, she picked up her cup of sake. "So…what you're saying is that if you weren't worried about the whole thing going sideways, then you might want to make a play for him?"

"No, that is *not* what I'm saying," I replied, feeling suddenly tired. Maybe it was just the day catching up with me, but I was beginning to wonder if it had been such a good idea to go out to dinner after all. Not that I could do anything about the situation at that point, since we were already at the restaurant. "I'm just saying that sometimes it's okay if the good-looking guy is just your neighbor and nothing else. Not everything has to be hearts and roses."

"I never said that it did." Now Naomi sounded defensive, as if irritated that I'd assumed she was all about matchmaking and nothing else. And honestly, I knew she wasn't. Her mission in life was empowering people to be their best selves and to make good choices for what they wanted in their lives. At the same time, though, she probably didn't much like seeing me alone, especially since it had been a year since my divorce was finalized and she most likely thought it was time for me to get on with my life. "You're a good person, Jillian. I guess I just want you to have a little happiness of your own."

"I *am* happy," I said, although I wondered if that statement was the strict truth. All right, compared to a lot of people in this world, I had a very good life. I didn't have to worry about the roof over my head or whether I'd be able to pay the electric bill. I was able to work at doing something I loved—I didn't have a crappy commute or a shitty boss who made passes at me. So what if I was alone? A lot of people were. It wasn't the end of the world. Besides, I had Frida, and all the other sweet little souls who became a part of my life, if only temporarily. "Anyway," I went on, my mouth twisting in a wry grin, "if I'm trying to find happiness, I'm pretty sure Ben Blake isn't the solution. The guy isn't exactly what you could call easygoing, in case you hadn't noticed."

"Oh, I noticed," she said with a grin. "I guess I was thinking you could soften him up."

Not very likely. I wasn't sure if I'd ever before met a person so determined to be a curmudgeon. I still couldn't quite believe I'd gotten him to take Rufus. And if I hadn't seen him for myself, playing ball with a dog on his front lawn, I would never have believed him capable of participating in such an activity.

"I have enough projects in my life," I said. "I'll leave Ben Blake to some other enterprising soul."

"I guess I can see how you might feel that way." She lifted her cup of sake to her lips and took a sip…and then the grin she'd been wearing slipped away, face going almost blank. In an undertone, she said, "Oh, shit."

"'Oh, shit' what?" I asked. Her gaze seemed to be fixed on something or someone behind me, and I started to half turn in my seat to see what she was looking at.

"Stop!" she hissed. "Don't look. Just act calm."

Act calm? My gut clenched. Whenever someone told me to act calm, I tended to assume the worst. Before my mind could start manufacturing all sorts of worst-case scenarios, a shadow fell over the table Naomi and I shared.

"Hey, Jillian," said an all-too-familiar voice, and I felt my body go rigid. *Oh, shit* was right.

Standing next to me was Tom Torres, my ex-husband.

CHAPTER FIVE

IDIOTICALLY, THE FIRST THOUGHT THAT WENT through my head was, *Thank God I look halfway decent tonight.*

Which I knew was ridiculous. Tom and I were ancient history, and I honestly shouldn't have given two goddamns about what he thought of my appearance.

Except…he had his fiancée on his arm.

Antoinette Haskell, to be precise. Maybe I should have been slightly impressed that he possessed enough actual loyalty to have stuck with the woman he'd cheated on me with, but I had a feeling that was more because she was such a good catch than because theirs was a love for the ages or anything.

All right, maybe I was just a wee bit cynical about the whole situation.

However, my jaundiced view of their relationship didn't change the fact that she was a very rich divorcée. Her first husband had been in the shipping business or something, and was older... much older. But age didn't always confer wisdom, and there hadn't been a prenup. I didn't know all the details, but my general impression was that Ms. Haskell's net worth jumped way north of a hundred million dollars after her marriage ended. No wonder Tom had gone after her like a shark swimming toward an especially tempting batch of chum.

Antoinette was around my age but far more polished. Her auburn hair lay in perfect waves on her shoulders, and her pale skin was perfect and pore-less. I knew nothing about designer fashion, but even I could tell that the slim skirt and sleeveless blouse she wore had to have been hideously expensive.

"Oh, hi, Tom," I said, doing my best to sound careless and off-hand, although I wasn't sure whether I accomplished the airy unconcern I'd been striving for. "How have you been?"

"Great," he replied.

I hated to admit it, but he was definitely looking great, his olive skin bronzed by the sun, broad shoulders filling out the dark jacket he wore. No tie, but he still looked stylish and effortless, like some Hollywood star groomed for an appearance on a late night talk show. Sometimes I thought half his success in the courtroom stemmed from his looks; he always did better with juries that were more than fifty percent women.

He went on, "So, what are you doing here?"

His tone seemed to imply that the soft opening for a hip sushi bar in Little Tokyo was about the last place he would have expected to see me. I couldn't even argue with that, since I knew I wouldn't have come if Naomi had told me what kind of place this really was. However, I still found myself resenting his implication that I wasn't the type to attend this sort of event.

"Oh, just getting out," I said. "Naomi and I wanted to have a girls' night."

"How sweet," Antoinette put in. Her full mouth quirked a little, and I could tell she was amused that I quite clearly must still be single, or else I would surely have come here with a date.

Good thing that I really didn't care what she thought of me. Gorgeous Tom definitely was, but I had absolutely zero interest in getting back together with him. She was welcome to his cheating ass.

I couldn't help wondering what their prenup looked like, though.

"Getting together with friends is so important," Naomi put in. She was smiling, too, but I knew her well enough to see the tension behind her expression. If we'd been someplace a little less public, she might have let Antoinette know exactly what she thought of a woman low enough to sleep with her married divorce lawyer. "Hanging out with women gives you such a different perspective," she went on. "I find social-izing with only men can be kind of limiting."

Tom's jaw went tight. Like the rest of us, he knew better than to do or say anything that might cause a scene, but he'd obviously caught the insult in her words. Well, there was no love lost between the two of them. When Tom and I had first moved into the Carroll Avenue house, he'd encouraged my friendship with Naomi, since he was working long hours and he thought it would be good for me to have a neighbor who was also a friend. However, he'd probably kicked himself over that encouragement later, since it was Naomi who found my hungry and extremely talented divorce lawyer, thus resulting in my sole ownership of the house and spousal support for the next ten years, even though Tom and I had only been married for four, and therefore he shouldn't have been on the hook for support at all.

"It's a great restaurant," I said, which I realized as soon as I'd spoken was sort of an idiotic thing to say, since we hadn't gotten our food yet and so I could have no real idea of how good it was. "I mean," I added hastily, "the decor is really beautiful."

Antoinette gave me a contemptuous look, but Tom cut her off before she could say anything. "Well, we're meeting some friends here, so we won't keep you. Have a good evening."

"You too, Tom," I replied, my voice all sickly sweetness. Somehow, I managed to smile. "And you, Antoinette."

The corners of her mouth lifted ever so slightly. She didn't reply, however, but only looped her arm through Tom's and led him away through the crowd, toward the bar. Maybe that was where they were meeting their friends.

A silence fell. Naomi took a sip of her sake, then said, "Are you okay?"

"Of course, I'm okay," I replied. "It's no big deal—I was bound to run into him sometime."

Except that it kind of was a big deal. Once we'd signed the final papers, we'd had no further contact with each other. He'd removed his belongings from the house months and months before that, and so had absolutely no reason to come and see me. At the time, I was more angry on Frida's behalf than I was on my own—the little creature had adored Tom, and his leaving had been rough on her. She was just a dog; she didn't understand anything about divorce. No, she only knew that the person who used to play with her in the backyard and get her to dance for treats was no longer living with us, and the loss of someone who'd been such a big part of her world had been hard.

Anyway, I calculated that I hadn't seen my ex-husband for almost a year. It was a shock to lay eyes on him at the restaurant, mostly because I'd figured that in a town the size of L.A., it would be easy for us to continue to avoid one another.

Since Naomi was still staring at me, I made myself say again, "I'm fine. I've been over him for a long time."

"Good," she said. "That Antoinette is a piece of work, though. You'd think he'd have better taste than to get engaged to that bony bitch."

"Naomi!" She gazed back at me across the table, expression all innocence, and I asked, "Weren't you just saying the other day that words like that only continue to belittle and demean women, that we should just call people 'asshole' or whatever rather than use some kind of gendered insult?"

"There you go, throwing my wokeness right back in my face." Naomi let out a gust of a breath before drinking some more of her sake. "Okay, right, I did say that. And mostly I agree with it. But sometimes a woman comes along who really deserves that epithet."

Privately, I agreed with her. Maybe it was sour grapes, but Antoinette Haskell definitely didn't seem like a very nice person to me…in which case, I supposed that she and Tom deserved each other.

The waiter came by with our food then. Objectively, I could tell the sushi was very good, fresh and expertly presented, but I would have been a lot happier with some real comfort food —tacos, or my mother's homemade mac and cheese. Good thing I lived five hundred miles away, or I would have loaded up on that mac and cheese in the aftermath of my divorce and been a couple of sizes bigger than my current size six.

But I ate enough that Naomi couldn't take me to task for neglecting my meal, and we finished the small bottle of sake before getting her BMW back from the valet. It wasn't until we'd pulled out of the parking lot that she spoke.

"You're really okay?"

"Yes," I said, knowing I had to lie so she wouldn't feel completely awful about dragging me out to that particular restaurant on that particular night. "I'm just fine."

She'd suggested opening a bottle of wine once we were home and didn't have to drive anywhere, but I didn't feel like drinking anything else. Instead, I told her I was tired and planned to watch a little TV and then go to bed early.

While I could tell this excuse disappointed her, she didn't press the issue, only said good night and headed over to her house. I locked the doors and closed the curtains, lingering a bit at the front window.

The light in Ben Blake's front room was on. I supposed there wasn't anything terribly strange about that—I hadn't seen a TV in his living room, but maybe he was sitting in the armchair I'd spied there and reading a book. It seemed like something he would do.

Yes, reading a book, with Rufus curled up on the rug at his feet or possibly even asleep in his lap. It was a comforting mental image, and even though I knew it could be completely wrong, I still held it in my mind's eye as I went upstairs to get ready for bed. Frida dutifully followed me, although I could tell she was a little surprised that I'd be retiring to the bedroom for the evening when it was barely nine o'clock. I wasn't a night owl—my work kept me from being able stay in bed very late most days—but I still generally didn't go to sleep until ten-thirty or eleven.

What else did I have to do, though? I didn't want to watch TV or read. No, all I wanted was to go to sleep, to escape to a place where I wouldn't have to see Antoinette Haskell's mocking smile, or the possessive way her hand had slithered around Tom's arm.

Or the enormous diamond that had winked from the fourth finger of that hand. It was much bigger than the diamond he'd given me. Maybe she was the one who'd actually paid for that glittering rock. After all, Tom was successful, but her net worth was far greater than his.

It was stupid to be upset about such a thing, especially since the whole idea of an engagement ring and the machinations of the diamond industry involved in such notions were more than a little suspect. Manufactured scarcity so people would feel compelled to fork over the equivalent of months of their salary just to buy a piece of jewelry. Honestly, I should be laughing at Antoinette and my ex for falling prey to that unscrupulous manipulation.

Even so, I couldn't quite stamp out the jealousy that flared within me.

Once I'd hung up my clothes and changed into the oversized T-shirt I wore to sleep in, I found myself drawn to the window. I pushed the curtains aside, just the smallest bit, and found myself staring at Ben Blake's house. The light in his front window was still on; clearly, he wasn't planning an early evening like mine.

The thought danced through my head before I could stop it.

How would Tom have reacted if Ben had been my date at Hiro's, rather than Naomi? Would he have been as smooth and nonchalant? Or would he have been startled to find me out and about with a handsome, well-dressed companion?

It doesn't matter, I told myself firmly as I went over to my bed and pulled back the covers. *Because you know full well that there aren't any dates with Ben in your future.*

Or anyone else, at the rate I was going.

Scowling, I lay down and rested my head on the pillow. It was stupid to be so defeatist just because I'd had the bad luck to bump into my ex and his overpriced fiancée. Really, a lot of this was Naomi's fault—not for dragging me to Hiro's, but for putting it in my head that Ben was possible dating material. Otherwise, I probably wouldn't have even looked at him that way. I would have met him, thought, *Not my type,* and continued with my life, just as I had with the few likely men I'd met over the past six months or so. It was always easier to dismiss a person when your mind was already set in a certain groove.

Now, though....

He'd looked so damned cute playing with Rufus in his front yard. I'd been far enough away that I couldn't get a really good look at Ben's expression, but from what I'd been able to tell, he'd been focusing on the game almost fiercely, as if he'd never done such a thing before and wanted to make sure he got it right. Which seemed to shoot down my hypothesis that he'd had a dog before and that was why Rufus had warmed up to him so quickly, but that was okay. Sometimes an animal bonded with a person without any real explanation or justification.

I'd just shut my eyes when my phone buzzed. I always kept it on my nightstand in case some kind of emergency cropped up in the middle of the night, but right then, I was sorely tempted to ignore it. My evening had already been crappy enough—I didn't need any more complications.

However, habit won out, as it always did. Almost of its own volition, my hand reached for the phone and grabbed it, and held it to my ear. "Jillian Torres."

"Are you with the chihuahua rescue?" A woman's voice, sounding worried, although I was almost positive I'd never heard her before.

"Yes, I'm Jillian with Little Angels Chihuahua Rescue," I replied, and pushed myself up to a sitting position. "Is there a problem?"

A faint breathy sound that must have been a sigh, and the woman said, "I think so. My husband said I shouldn't get involved, but I can hear them crying over there, and—"

"Who's crying?" I asked, although I had a sinking feeling that I already knew.

"The puppies," the woman said. "At our neighbor's house. They have a bunch of chihuahuas—purebred, but one of them got pregnant by a neighborhood dog, and now the puppies are here and I think they're neglecting them or hurting them. I don't know for sure because I can't see into the yard. I just hear them crying."

My heart wanted to break, hearing the woman's story. True, I didn't have all the facts yet, but I'd encountered far too many situations where an unexpected pregnancy happened to a purebred dog and the owners callously discarded the resulting mixed-breed puppies. If they were lucky, they ended up in a shelter. But sometimes they were dumped on the street, or basically starved to death.

I couldn't let that happen. Not when this woman had summoned the courage to call a stranger and ask for help.

"Where are you?" I asked.

"In Monterey Park," she said. "Alhambra Avenue—number 418. The dogs are at number 416."

"Got it," I told her. It was a little bit of a drive, but not too far, maybe twenty minutes max. "Have you called animal control?"

"I tried that first," the woman replied. "They went over and checked, but they said the dogs were okay. My husband told me to let it go, but that was a week ago, and the crying has been so bad the past couple of days. I peeked over the fence and saw one of them—the poor thing was so skinny and scrawny, it could have been a rat. That was why I decided to call you."

My mind was already working furiously. I had to get those dogs out of there, no matter what else happened. "Are the owners home?"

"No. That's why I'm calling. They left a little while ago."

Well, that made things easier. Although I didn't want to trespass on someone else's property, I also had no intention of leaving those poor puppies to be neglected. I actually had an attorney on retainer, someone who could bail me out if things got dicey, but with any luck, I wouldn't even need to call Leslie. I could be in and out before the people in question returned home.

"Do you know where they went?" I asked as I rose from the bed. Holding the phone to my ear with one hand, I reached for the jeans I'd been wearing earlier that evening—they were lying across the foot of the bed, since I figured I'd wear them again the next day—then did my best to pull them on one-handed.

"To the movies. I know that because I heard them talking in the backyard this afternoon. They were arguing about what to go see."

That was some helpful intel. Even if they were only going to the movies and weren't planning to go out for a drink or a snack afterward, I'd still have a couple of hours to work with.

"Great," I said. "Um…can you tell me your name?"

"I'd rather not."

Fair enough. If this anonymous Good Samaritan had already called animal control on the people in question, they probably weren't on the best of terms anyway. Better not to make things worse by positively identifying herself as the one who'd contacted an animal rescue organization to jailbreak those neglected pups.

And honestly, this wasn't how I tended to operate. I worked directly with shelters, or people would contact me when they found a stray or—more rarely—had an animal they needed to rehome. In general, though, I didn't break into places and do a PETA impersonation by busting out neglected animals.

This case sounded like an extreme one, though, and I had a feeling the dogs in question didn't have time on their side. Hopefully, their owners would just be glad to have the unwanted puppies removed from their property and wouldn't ask too many questions.

"Okay," I said to the woman, still holding the phone to my ear as I jammed my feet into a pair of Keds. I figured the oversized T-shirt I wore was good enough for this particular errand, and I didn't see the point in wasting time putting on a bra. The important thing was to get out of my house as quickly as possible. "Any tips on how to get into their backyard?"

"That's easy," the woman replied. "There's a gate on the left side as you're looking at the house from the street. You can go in through there."

"Locked?"

"I don't know."

Oy. Well, I supposed I'd just have to hope for the best, since I didn't own a pair of bolt cutters. Worst-case scenario, I'd climb over the wall. It wouldn't be the first time.

"Okay, I'm heading out now," I said. I bent to pat Frida on the head, then hurried out of the bedroom and down the stairs. "I'll be there as fast as I can."

"Thank you," the woman said. Then she hung up.

In a way, I was relieved, since I was able to shove the phone into my pocket and reach out to grab the messenger bag I used for a purse from where it sat on a side table in the entry as I went flying past. Out the back door, pausing briefly to lock it, and then I hurried over to the garage, which was detached from the main house and was actually accessed from an alley.

I knew better than to exit the garage too quickly, since the alley was narrow and I never knew when one of my neighbors might be coming along, even though it was past nine by that point and most of them should have been long home from work. Anyway, a Prius wasn't really designed for high-speed reverse maneuvers, so, even though I could feel the urgency practically thrumming along my veins, I made myself back out carefully and then made my way along the alley to where it would dump me out on Douglas Street.

However, just as I started to make the turn, I had to hit the brakes, because my way was blocked by a man walking his dog.

Not just any man, though—it was Ben Blake, with Rufus prancing along at the end of the extendable leash I'd included with his "care package."

Ben stared at me for a second or two, and then recognition seemed to flare despite the dim illumination provided by the street lamp half a block away. He came around to the driver's side of the car, and I rolled down the window, so impatient that I didn't even care that I wasn't wearing a speck of makeup and my hair was pulled back into a sloppy ponytail.

"Going somewhere?" he asked. Naturally, he looked as dapper as ever, although now he wore a sleek brown leather jacket as protection against the cool, damp night air.

I wanted to ask him what the heck he was doing, walking Rufus at that hour of the night, but I really didn't have the time to waste in useless back-and-forths. "I have some puppies I need to rescue," I replied. "It's kind of an emergency."

His brows drew together. "So much of an emergency that you have to go now?"

"Yes," I said. "It's something that can't wait. But you have a good evening."

I put my finger on the button to roll the window back up, but for some reason, it wouldn't budge. As I stared down at it in consternation, wondering what was wrong, Ben spoke again.

"Do you need help?"

For a second, all I could do was blink at him. Ben Blake seemed like about the last person who would ever willingly offer assistance to someone else. But maybe I was judging him unfairly. True, he wasn't exactly Mr. Congeniality. On the other hand, he'd taken in Rufus when he could have easily turned down my request.

And truthfully, I could use some help. Not that I wanted to get Ben in trouble, but I didn't know how many puppies were going to need rescuing, and an extra set of hands could come in, well, handy. Still, he needed to know what he was getting himself into.

"Um…what I'm doing *might* be borderline illegal," I told him.

To my surprise, he gave an approving nod. "Even better," he said. He bent down and picked up Rufus, who looked a little startled but didn't try to get out of Ben's arms. "Unlock the door— I'm coming with you."

CHAPTER SIX

S<small>ILENCE REIGNED INSIDE THE</small> P<small>RIUS</small>—<small>UNTIL</small> I got on the 101 Freeway headed south so I could merge onto the 10. As the car picked up speed, Ben finally spoke.

"What is this rescue mission, exactly?"

Funny how he hadn't seemed too curious a few minutes earlier. But maybe he'd been waiting until I was off surface streets and onto the relatively less crowded freeway before he distracted me with questions about exactly what I was up to.

Briefly, I explained about the phone call I'd gotten and how I really didn't have any choice but to extricate those helpless puppies from a less than desirable situation. "So, there'll probably be some trespassing involved," I concluded. "But don't worry—I have a good attorney on retainer for just these sorts of situations."

One corner of his mouth lifted slightly. "If your occupation requires you to have an attorney on retainer, possibly it's time to rethink your choice of careers."

His tone was so dry that I guessed he was teasing me. Or at least, I hoped he was. "Occupational hazard," I responded, my tone deliberately light. Besides, running Little Angels was much more than a career—it was a vocation, a mission. A few fines and a couple of misdemeanors on my record were a small price to pay for making sure those helpless animals were safe.

Besides, I'd never actually gotten arrested for anything. I'd come close once or twice, but so far, I'd had people dismiss me as a crazy dog lady and let the matter go.

Claws scritched on the plastic of the door, and I glanced back to see Rufus standing on his hind legs and doing his best to look out the window. Because he was so small, he could just barely get his snout up to the level of the sill, but he was trying his hardest. Anyway, his tail wagged like crazy, which told me he was having fun with this unexpected interruption in his evening walk.

"You were walking Rufus awfully late," I remarked then. Maybe the slightest accusatory note had crept into my tone, although I didn't really mean it. Mostly, I was just wondering why Ben had taken the dog for a walk after nine o'clock at night instead of closer to six like I'd recommended.

"The evening got away from me," Ben replied. He was staring forward through the windshield, face in profile to me, so I couldn't get a very good read on his expression. Actually, his face was almost blank; if he was annoyed at me for making the comment in the first place, I didn't see any sign of it. He added, "I'd say it must have been luck, because if I'd walked him earlier in the evening, I wouldn't have bumped into you."

That was one way of looking at the situation. As we got closer to Monterey Park, I began to question the wisdom of bringing him along on this errand, but it was too late to do anything about it now.

"True," I said. My car's nav directed me to get off the freeway at Garfield Avenue, so I didn't say anything else as I guided the Prius in the indicated direction. When I turned onto Alhambra, I told Ben, "I'm going to go around the block once just to get the lay of the land. The house we're looking for is number 416."

He nodded. "I'll keep an eye out."

I cruised through the neighborhood, one of modest but well-kept homes, most of them probably built in the late 1940s or early '50s in the postwar boom that had brought so many people to Southern California. The house at 416

Alhambra Avenue was no different, a one-story Spanish-style home with a low cinder-block wall topped by wrought-iron fencing in the front, and a higher block wall enclosing the backyard. Just as the woman on the phone had said, there was a large gate on the left-hand side of the property, actually big enough for someone to pull a boat or an RV through there if they wanted to park it in the backyard. I considered briefly whether I should call her to double-check that we were in the right place, but I discarded that idea. There was no guarantee she would even pick up, and I didn't want to waste any time.

"It doesn't look as if anyone is home," Ben said, eyes scanning our surroundings.

That was my assessment as well—I couldn't see any cars parked in the driveway, and although one light appeared to have been left on in the front room, the rest of the house was dark. So far, it seemed as though the anonymous caller had given me some useful information. "That's what I was hoping for," I replied. "Since they're only one house away from the end of the street, I'm going to park around the corner—that should make us a little bit less conspicuous."

"We'd have a faster getaway if you parked in the driveway," he pointed out, but I shook my head.

"True, but even if no one is home, the neighbors might notice a strange car in their driveway."

"I suppose so."

From his tone, it sounded as if he would have liked to argue the point a bit more, but to my relief, he didn't say anything else. Instead, he was silent as I guided the Prius around the corner and then parked and turned off the lights. In the back seat, Rufus regarded the two of us with bright, interested eyes, but he stayed put as I took off my seat belt and climbed out of the car and Ben did the same.

I went around to the hatch and got out two of the backpacks I carried with me in the car at all times. They had soft blankets placed inside and were a perfect size for transporting chihuahuas. I gave one of them to Ben, saying, "We can put the puppies in these. I don't know how many there are, but most chis only have around three to five pups in a litter at the most, so we should be okay."

He took the backpack from me and glanced inside. "What's the plan?"

"I don't have much of one," I said. "I ran out the door as soon as I could since I knew I wouldn't have a lot of time to play with. But basically—go through the gate, grab the puppies, come back to the car, and get the hell out of here."

"And if the gate is locked?"

"Then you can give me a leg up, and I'll get the puppies and hand them over the wall to you."

His eyes narrowed slightly at this contingency plan, but to my relief, he didn't argue or try to convince me that he should be the one who went over the wall. It just made more sense for me to do it—I was smaller and probably more agile... and I wasn't wearing expensive wool windowpane plaid pants. I had to wonder if the guy even owned a pair of jeans. "All right," he said.

We walked as casually as we could to the corner and turned onto Alhambra Avenue. While we were doing our best to look nonchalant, I knew we probably would have made an odd-looking pair to anyone who saw us, him in his designer clothes and me in jeans, Keds, and a T-shirt three sizes too big with the logo of a brewing company in Pasadena emblazoned on the back. However, I had to hope that the street lighting was dim enough that no one would be able to make out too many details of our appearance... although I knew that my long blonde hair tended to be an attention-getter, even when it was sloppily pulled back into a scrunchie the way it was that evening.

A tree obscured part of the line of sight between the house and the driveway. Even better. While I assumed no one was home, even if someone had been inside, they probably wouldn't have been able to catch a clear view of the two of us.

Once we got to the gate, I reached over the top and fumbled for the latch. A padlock met my searching fingers, and I muttered a curse under my breath.

"It's locked," I said.

"Let me see," Ben said, and presumably did the same thing I just had—reached down to touch the latch and found a padlock holding it shut. However, just a second or two later, he pulled his hand away.

The padlock lay in his palm.

"How did you do that?" I asked, staring down at it, astounded.

"It hadn't caught all the way," he replied calmly. As he spoke, he pulled a handkerchief out of his pocket and used it to wipe down the surface —to remove the fingerprints, I assumed.

Maybe I'd underestimated Mr. Blake. Maybe he was an international jewel thief or something.

"Go on," he added. "We don't know when the people who live here are coming back."

Right. I pulled the gate open just wide enough that we could slip into the yard, but not so wide that anyone passing by on the street would notice anything amiss. Once we were inside, I paused to take a quick note of my surroundings. The side yard held a few rusty, discarded wheels, yellowed grass, and not much else.

Then I heard it—a weak set of cries coming from the back of the house. I ran toward a covered porch and saw a thin, soiled blanket pushed into the far corner. On that blanket lay three little pups, each of them smaller than my hand, burrowed into each other for warmth. Their piteous whines seemed to tear at my ears.

"Over here."

Not waiting for Ben, I crouched down and reached toward the closest pup. It flinched, and my blood boiled with anger. An animal that young shouldn't have had any fear of humans yet, but I could tell it was afraid.

"It's all right, it's all right," I half-whispered, half-crooned, and touched its velvety little head with my finger. The poor thing was shivering—it shouldn't have been outside on a cool night like this.

No sign of the dogs' mother. I guessed she was probably inside; my anonymous caller had said the mother was a purebred, and so I assumed she was being taken care of.

"How many?" Ben asked.

"Three," I said. "I'll take this one—the other two look a little bigger and stronger. Can you get them?"

He didn't ask why I was so focused on the tiny

creature I was petting. Maybe he could tell that it was the most in need. Anyway, he bent and picked up the other two puppies and gently put them in the backpack, then straightened. "We should go."

I nodded, and scooped up the little dog who'd claimed my attention. As I took her away from the blanket, I realized there was a fourth puppy, its fur so dark that it almost blended in with the rough gray wool of the blanket they'd been sleeping on.

It wasn't moving.

No…please, no, I thought, and reached with my free hand for the tiny shape. It was cold and stiff under my fingers. A little sob escaped my lips, and Ben looked down at me in alarm.

"What's the matter?"

I didn't think I could speak. I shook my head, and he bent and saw the source of my distress. The lighting in the yard wasn't very good—they had some solar landscape lights planted here and there around the border of the lawn, and that was it—but I thought I saw his jaw tighten.

"It's dead," he said quietly. "You can't do anything for it. But these other ones—you can still help them. We need to go."

While some part of me understood the logic of what he was saying, I couldn't allow myself to leave that poor thing behind. Anyone monstrous enough to leave these little dogs to fend for themselves in the cold and the dark would probably throw that puppy's body in the trash and think nothing more of it.

I didn't reply to Ben, only lifted the lifeless puppy from the blanket and carefully placed it in the backpack I carried. The other one was still curled up in my hand, and I held it gently against my body as I stood up.

Tears burned in my eyes as we hurried away from the covered porch and went back out through the gate. Ben was just replacing the padlock when a pair of headlights raked across the driveway, catching us in their glare.

A man's voice shouted, "Hey!"

My feet responded, even though the rest of my body felt as if it wanted to freeze in terror. Still holding the puppy cradled against me, I bolted across the narrow strip of grass separating the driveway from the neighbor's yard. Ben ran, too, his long legs easily outpacing mine, although I noticed he held the backpack out in one hand, as if he realized that slinging it over his shoulder would have jostled the precious cargo he carried.

He was definitely going to get to the car first. I reached into my jeans pocket with my free hand and punched the remote to unlock the vehicle. "You drive!" I yelled at him.

For a second, his eyes widened, and then I thought I saw him nod. He headed for the driver's side of my Prius and slid in, quickly adjusting the driver's seat so his knees wouldn't be smashed up against his chest, then put the backpack on the back seat. That same rough man's voice was yelling at me to stop, but I had absolutely no intention of obeying his commands. No, I tore across the corner lot and threw open the car door and got in the passenger seat. As soon as I shut the door, Ben jammed his foot on the gas and sent the car leaping forward—no mean feat, since Priuses generally weren't known for their acceleration.

The little dog I held let out a single meeping cry, although there was something almost questioning about the sound, as if she didn't quite know what to make of all these goings-on.

"It's all right, baby," I crooned, even as I leaned over into the back seat so I could reach into the backpack and pet the two dogs inside. Their cold little noses touched me, sniffing, and I let out a sigh of relief. At least they seemed as if they would be okay.

And then Rufus sniffed at the backpack as well, and nudged it. Cautiously, the puppies poked their heads out, and Rufus touched his nose to theirs, as if to let them know they were in a safe place.

"Turn around and put your seatbelt on," Ben said, sounding as testy as a grandpa driving his unruly grandchildren to school. "That's not safe."

No, it wasn't. I petted the puppies one more time, and then settled myself in the passenger seat and did my best to fasten the safety belt while still holding my tiny charge in my right hand. She was barely moving, although I felt her little tongue pass over my skin. Poor thing was starving.

"We'll get you some food when we get home," I promised her, then gulped in a breath of air and tried to blink away the tears that still burned in my eyes.

Ben sent me a curious look. "Why so upset? We got the dogs away."

"But we couldn't save all of them," I replied, my voice cracking on the last syllable.

"You saved three."

He sounded so calm and matter-of-fact. How could he not have been moved by the sight of that poor little puppy's lifeless body?

"I should have been able to save them all," I said. "I could have, if she'd only called me a little earlier."

"It's not your fault," he said, tone still reasonable.

I knew that intellectually. But it still hurt. "I don't understand how anyone could be so cruel to helpless little animals like that."

"Humans are cruel," Ben observed. From the way he spoke, you would have thought he was talking about a species he had absolutely no connection to.

"They can be," I allowed. That was about as far as I was willing to go. I ran my hand over the tiny little girl I held, doing my best to send her wordless reassurance that she was now safe, that the worst was behind her. I added, not sure why I felt compelled to defend humanity, "But they are also capable of great compassion."

Ben didn't seem to have an answer to that remark, because he gave a small lift of his shoulders and then returned his focus to the road. Although he had to be unfamiliar with the car, he drove quite expertly, and I found myself relaxing a little as the miles slipped under the tires and the house in Monterey Park slid farther and farther behind us.

In less than twenty minutes, he was pulling into the alleyway behind my house, and then we were in the garage. He opened the rear door and coaxed Rufus out—the dog seemed to want to stay and keep watch over the puppies—and then carefully lifted the backpack from the seat. At the same time, I got out, my own little one still cradled against my body, and took my backpack with its grim cargo from where it had been resting on the floor.

"What are you going to do with it?" Ben asked.

"Bury it," I replied. "The poor thing deserves that much. Probably under the willow tree in the far corner—that seems like a nice restful spot."

He was silent for a second or two. Then he said, "Do you need me to help you?"

Despite the sad circumstances, I couldn't quite prevent myself from experiencing a rush of warmth, of relief, at his offer. It was definitely not something I would have expected him to say, and I wondered whether I'd misjudged him.

"Thank you," I said. "I'd really appreciate that. But," I went on, making myself sound brisk and together, and not like a woman who'd spent the better part of the trip between Angelino Heights and Monterey Park sniffing back tears, "the most important thing right now is to get these puppies situated and some formula in them."

"You have puppy formula?"

"Of course," I said as we left the garage and headed along the path that led to the back door. "It's in powdered form, so I just have to mix it up. These puppies look like they're about two weeks old, so in another few weeks, I can start weaning them off it and get them on solid food, but they're going to need a lot of pampering between now and then."

"Ah."

He didn't ask for any more details after that, and I got the impression that, although he'd helped me out this far, it was probably better if I didn't ask him to take on puppy-sitting duties. Not that I would do such a thing; puppies were very time-intensive, and I didn't expect him to drop everything to spend hours at my house bottle-feeding the little creatures.

I let us into the kitchen, where Frida was waiting for us, ears cocked at an inquisitive angle. "It's okay," I told her. "We're just going to have some guests staying with us for a while." I turned toward Ben and said, "I have extra blankets and dog beds in the storage area on the service porch. Can you stay here and watch the puppies while I get everything set up?"

"Of course," he replied, although he now looked almost impatient, as if he was wondering how much more of his time I was going to require before he could take Rufus with him back to his house and wash his hands of the whole matter.

You're the one who wanted to come along on this little adventure, I thought, but I did my best to brush my irritation aside. After all, he had done an awful lot for me, and it was getting late.

I took Ben's backpack from him and scooped out the two puppies and the blanket it had held, letting them all settle down in a corner of the kitchen floor near the stove. Once they were situated, I carefully put the puppy I held on the blanket next to her two brothers. The backpack with their poor lost sibling I put on one of the kitchen chairs, figuring I'd deal with that in the morning when I was feeling a little more emotionally stable.

With Ben standing silent guard, I went into the service porch and rummaged through the cupboards, getting out the softest of my spare dog beds, along with several fleecy blankets and a couple of heating pads. I used the dog bed as a sort of basket to hold the can of formula and bottles I scrounged from another cabinet, leftovers from the last time I'd had to caretake a litter of puppies.

Thus laden, I returned to the kitchen...and stopped dead in surprise. Ben still stood there, but now he held a tiny bundle of dark fur in his hands —a bundle of fur that shivered and shook and stared at me with frightened black eyes, but one that was unquestionably alive.

"How...?" I began, and stopped there, not even sure what I'd meant to ask.

"She's fine," he said. "You left the room, and I thought I saw the backpack move, so I reached inside. I lifted her out and saw that she was breathing. She must have been so cold, you thought she was dead."

That had to be the only plausible explanation, and yet...was it possible? Maybe. Back at the house in Monterey Park, I'd been upset and in a hurry, and that was the sort of combination that made people make mistakes.

"Well, thank God," I said, and Ben's mouth twisted.

"If you must."

I brushed aside the odd comment and went to take the puppy from him. Sure enough, she trembled in my hands, but she was alive and breathing and even had a little glint in her round dark eyes. A fighter, this one.

"Good girl," I murmured, and set her down with her siblings. They immediately pressed up against her, all of them snuggling into the blanket I'd provided. Still, they were going to be much more comfortable in just a few moments.

"Let's put them in the family room," I told Ben. "It has pocket doors, so I can close it off from the rest of the house. That's probably the safest place. Do you mind setting up the bed in there while I mix up their formula? The wall by the sofa would be best—there's an outlet you can use to plug in the heating pads."

"No, I don't mind getting it set up," he replied, although something in the resigned tone in which he gave that answer told me he did mind, only he didn't want to upset me by saying no. If the situation had been any different, I would have told him I'd handle it and that he could go on home. That night, though, I needed him to keep an eye on the puppies while I worked —they seemed so fragile that I didn't want to take the risk of leaving them alone for even a few minutes.

Once I'd put the formula and the bottles on the counter, he gathered up the bed and its accompanying blankets and heating pads, and took the bundle out of the kitchen. I moved quickly, measuring the dry formula mix and water, and then pouring the milk replacement into four small baby bottles. Good thing the litter I'd rescued a few years back had been a big one, five puppies in all, which was why I had so many bottles on hand. Otherwise, I would have had to either make the puppies share, or entreat Ben to run to the closest grocery store and buy me a couple more.

He'd been very helpful so far, but I had a feeling that would have been asking a bit much.

Armed with the bottles of formula, I headed down the hall to the family room. It was a cozy space with a bay window that looked out on the backyard, dark wainscoting, and the home's second fireplace, this one with a rosy marble surround and a mahogany mantel. To my surprise, Ben had a fire going in there, its heat already reaching out to warm up the space.

"That was fast work," I said, nodding toward the hearth.

A shrug. "You already had the wood in the grate. It didn't take that much effort."

Yes, there had been several logs sitting on the metal grate, left over from the holidays, when I'd planned to have a fire on New Year's but had never gotten around to it. Even with everything set up, though, I didn't quite see how he could have gotten a fire burning so quickly.

But I had other, far more important things to worry about right then. Ben had placed the dog bed on the floor next to the sofa, just as I'd requested, and the heating pad was plugged in and covered by one of the blankets. The little pups were already snuggled up on it, their eyes half closed in pleasure. They probably hadn't been that warm since they were born; late January in Southern California of course wasn't as cold as it could be in other parts of the country, but neither was it all eighty-degree weather and sunshine.

I extended two of the bottles toward Ben. "One last favor? I want to get these little guys all fed as quickly as possible, and it'll go a lot faster if you help. After they eat, they'll sleep, and then they should be okay for a while."

A very short while—dogs as young as these ones needed to be fed every couple of hours. Another part of the reason why I'd decided to set them up in the family room was that I could bring some bedding down to the couch and spend the night there, keeping an eye on my new charges. My bedroom was sort of Frida's sanctum, and I thought it better to have them someplace she considered more neutral ground. Anyway, I knew I was going to be feeding them frequently, so it was better to be as close to them as possible.

A very brief hesitation, and then Ben came over and took the bottles from me. He looked down at them uncertainly, a frown puckering his brows. "I've never done anything like this before."

"Nothing to it," I said stoutly. "They want to eat. Just cradle them like this"—I paused to pick up the little dark pup who'd been so close to death, and held her nestled against my side. With my other hand, I held the bottle up against her mouth. She nudged against it, then made a little squeak of a sound before she fastened on the rubber nipple and began to drink. "See? Easy. When they're full, just put them back in their bed and feed the next one."

He still didn't look entirely convinced about the ease of the operation, but he didn't protest, either, only knelt down on the faded Persian rug, expression grim, and picked up one of the other puppies, this one a warm caramel color. Ben hardly needed to do anything—as soon as the bottle got within an inch of its mouth, the pup began to suckle, greedily drinking down the formula. The worried look left his face, and instead my companion appeared almost startled, as if he couldn't quite believe he had to do anything except kneel there and let the dog drink its fill.

The puppy I held made short work of the formula I'd given her, so I gently put her back in the bed and picked up her brother. He drank quickly as well, then fell asleep almost as soon as I set him down. The other puppies looked as though they were about to pass out, too—not that I could blame them.

Right then, Frida appeared at the doorway to the family room. She'd stayed out of the way during the previous operations, but now she moved forward and went straight toward the puppies. I held my breath, waiting to see whether I'd have to intervene in some way. She was a good dog, but she didn't always play nicely with others.

To my surprise, she climbed into the bed and nudged a couple of the puppies with her snout, pushing them closer to her. Instinctually, they snuggled in, knowing they were supposed to have a mama dog looking after them, even if they'd been deprived of their own mother. Frida looked past their little sleeping forms, something in her dark gaze even, calm, as if to tell me, *I've got this.*

"I'll be damned," I breathed.

Ben was looking a little startled as well. "Is it normal for them to do that?"

I pushed myself to my feet and brushed at the knees of my jeans. "Well, there are plenty of instances where dogs have sort of 'adopted' litters of abandoned puppies, but Frida's never been that good with other dogs. So…I'm kind of surprised. But glad."

"This should make things a little easier for you, I would think," Ben observed.

"Maybe," I replied. Obviously, Frida couldn't feed the puppies—she wasn't their mother, and had been spayed as soon as she was old enough—but she could snuggle with them and help keep them warm, and maybe she would also assist me in keeping them clean and watching over them in other ways. Since I hadn't been expecting her to do much of anything with the puppies except keep a wary distance, I'd have to wait and see how things developed. "I know it's going to be good for the puppies—they won't feel so abandoned if they have a mother figure around, even if it isn't their own mother." I pushed back the long tail of hair that fell over my shoulder, belatedly realizing that it was a ragged mess and I'd been doing all this in a baggy T-shirt with no bra underneath. That thought made me want to cross my arms to hide my breasts, but I had a feeling doing so would only call attention to my chest…not that Ben had sent a single look in its direction the entire night.

"Well, then," he said.

"Thank you," I told him. If he were someone I knew better, I would have given him a quick hug to let him know how grateful I was for his help. However, considering we were barely acquaintances—and the girls were a little unfettered for a casual hug—I remained where I was and hoped he'd be able to see from my expression how glad I was of his assistance. "Really. I don't know if I could have managed all this without you."

"It's nothing," Ben said quickly. He shifted his weight, looking like someone on the verge of bolting from the room.

I didn't know him very well—or at all, really —but I still had the impression he was someone who liked to ignore emotions, whether his own or other people's. Most likely, my open gratitude embarrassed him.

"Well, I don't think it's nothing," I said. "But I know I've taken enough of your evening. Have a good night, Ben."

He didn't even bid me a good evening of my own, only inclined his head slightly, then left the room. Outside in the hall, I could hear him call to Rufus, followed by the clicking of the dog's toenails on the wooden floor. A moment later, the front door shut, and I was left alone in the house.

Alone, except for Frida and a newly acquired litter of puppies. I went and sat down on the sofa, and let out a breath. It would be nice to think that the hardest part was over, but I still had four puppies to take care of, little creatures who would be utterly dependent on me for the next few weeks.

Or rather, dependent on us. I looked down to where my dog lay with our newest rescues snuggled up against her, and realized I wasn't as alone in this as I'd thought.

"You're a good girl, Frida," I said, and her tail thumped gently against the dog bed.

We got this, I thought.

INTERLUDE

Was it possible for someone to be so…good?

Beelzebub wasn't sure. Certainly, those individuals who overflowed with altruistic motivations were not the sort to end up in Hell, and so he had to admit to himself that his experience wasn't all that large. When Jillian had first told him about her dog-rescue operation, he'd naturally assumed she must have some sort of selfish reason for taking on such an endeavor. Now, though, after seeing the tears in her eyes when she thought the little dark-furred puppy was dead, seeing her utter fearlessness in trespassing to get the animals away from their abusive owners, he was experiencing some doubts. Nothing she'd done had been for any reason except to make sure the puppies were safe. That was why he hadn't even hesitated when she left the room, had reached in the backpack and pulled out the little dead dog. It hadn't been gone from this world for very long, which was why it had been so easy for him to reawaken the spark within its fragile body. Such a simple thing, really, although never before had he used his powers to bring life to something. It had felt good, for reasons he wasn't sure he wanted to analyze too closely.

Anyway, if this had all been some sort of elaborate charade to get him to spend more time in her company, Jillian certainly could have done better than to look as if she'd rolled out of bed before embarking on her rescue mission. No makeup, hair pulled back in a mess of a ponytail, baggy clothes? Not exactly the sort of outfit most women would have employed to attract male attention.

Well, except that she quite obviously hadn't been wearing any support garments underneath her oversized T-shirt. That T-shirt had hidden most of the telltales…but not all.

Beelzebub wasn't quite sure what to make of the way his mind kept dwelling on that one particular detail, on the way her breasts had bounced as she ran across the neighbor's yard to get to her car. Never in the past had he ever spent any amount of time thinking about human women's physiques, except possibly to wonder if it was burdensome to have those appendages hanging off one's body. If nothing else, they had to get in the way.

But now he couldn't seem to get the image out of his mind…and he couldn't quite ignore the way this human body he wore wanted to react to that image. Ridiculous, really. God might have forced him into a mortal existence, to have to suffer all the indignities of biology that went along with inhabiting a human form, but surely he should have been able to escape the final humiliation of experiencing lust.

Judging by the way he currently felt, apparently not.

He stared up at the ceiling of his bedroom, at the faint glow from the streetlights that painted dappled shadows on the smooth plaster surface. At the foot of the bed, Rufus slept in a tight little ball. The dog had jumped up on the bed as soon as Beelzebub sat down on it, and although he supposed he could have shooed the animal away, he decided to let the matter go. After all, he was a very small creature. How much of a disturbance could he cause, sleeping several feet away on the king-size mattress?

Maybe thinking about the dog would help make the raging erection Beelzebub was currently suffering go away.

He knew better than to touch the offending member. No, all he could do was force his thoughts elsewhere, anywhere except the swell of Jillian Torres' bosom.

Unfortunately, the more he tried to think about something else, the more he kept thinking about her. For a woman who seemed to care very little about her appearance, she had an uncanny ability to attract a man's eye.

No, this was ridiculous. He would not be attracted to her. Absolutely not. If Lucifer and Asmodeus wanted to lose themselves in a human female's arms, that was their prerogative. A foolish one, and a stupid waste of their abilities, but they had freedom of choice, and apparently that was the choice they had made. He, Beelzebub, was made of sterner stuff.

Or at least, he'd thought he was.

I suppose You think You're so very clever, he thought. *I suppose You put me in this house just so I would meet Jillian Torres and fall in love. Well, I won't. And there's nothing You can do about it.*

Beelzebub scowled and crossed his arms over his chest, gaze still fixed on the ceiling. He might have been pulled from Hell and made to live as a human, but that didn't make him a human.

And even the most distracting female in the world wouldn't alter his resolve.

CHAPTER SEVEN

THE PUPPIES SLEPT AFTER THEIR LATEST feeding, so I'd allowed myself a quick shower and the chance to sit down at the table in the kitchen to have a cup of coffee. I needed it after being up and down with them all night long. Yes, I'd gone through much the same thing with my previous litter of abandoned puppies, but they'd been a little older, a little more self-sufficient. These poor things were going to need constant attention for at least another week.

Thank God for Frida—she'd slept with them all night, and didn't even want to go on a walk the next morning, only asked to be let out in the backyard so she could do her business before returning to the family room to snuggle with the puppies. They already looked worlds better, eyes bright and their bodies somehow rounder, as if they'd managed to put on a little weight overnight.

Or maybe it was just that they'd realized they were now in a safe place, and could allow themselves to blossom.

I knew I hadn't weathered the night quite as well—my eyes were shadowed and I didn't have a lot of color—but that didn't matter so much. It wasn't as if I planned on going anywhere that day; by some stroke of luck, I didn't have any meetings or foster visits or anything else on the calendar for Friday. So I could definitely stay home and watch the puppies, and do my best to keep myself from thinking about Ben Blake. He'd really surprised me the night before. I honestly hadn't thought he was the type to flout the law by trespassing on a stranger's property to steal a litter of neglected puppies, or to stay on afterward and bottle-feed those same pups.

Appearances often deceived. They'd just done so spectacularly when it came to my neighbor.

A knock came at the kitchen door, and my heart speeded up a little as a pulse of excitement went through me. Could Ben be coming over to check on the dogs?

But then I heard Naomi's voice call, "Hey!", and I realized I was being silly if I thought Ben would drop everything to show up at 9 a.m. at a neighbor's house to get a look at a bunch of puppies that weren't even his. No, he'd probably slept the sleep of the just, and was now going to do what he could to stay out of my orbit in case I sucked him into any other illegal activities.

"Hey," I called back, and remained sitting at the table as she let herself in and closed the door behind her. The weather was gray and gloomy and looked as if it wanted to rain, even though it hadn't started yet. A good kind of day to stay inside, which, luckily, was exactly what I planned to do. "Coffee?"

"Love some," Naomi said. She went over to the stainless-steel monstrosity that sat on the counter—I'd gotten the expensive Italian espresso machine in the divorce—and poured herself a cup. After seating herself at the table across from me, she asked, "Are you going to tell me why Ben Blake was leaving your house at ten o'clock last night?"

"It was because we were having hot monkey sex," I replied, deadpan, and she stared at me for a moment before she chuckled and shook her head.

"As much as I'd like to believe that, I'm pretty sure that's not what was going on."

Unfortunately, no. I had to stop myself there, however. Did I even want to have hot monkey sex with Ben? I was finding myself liking him more and more—and all my protests that he wasn't my type were beginning to ring increasingly hollow—

but I didn't think I'd taken quite that mental leap. Not yet, anyway.

On the other hand, I couldn't deny that I would have liked it to be him sitting across the table from me and having coffee that gray January morning.

"He helped me with a dog rescue last night," I said calmly, and Naomi's dark eyes widened.

"He what?"

"You heard me."

She lifted her cup of coffee and took a sip, leaving a dark red lip print on the rim of the biscuit-colored stoneware. "He doesn't seem like the 'dog rescue' type to me."

"Well, he kind of fell into it, I guess. I was leaving to get the dogs and bumped into him, and he sort of invited himself along."

A brief silence as she absorbed that information. Then she said, "He likes you."

I waved dismissively with one hand, but Naomi shook her head.

"I mean it. No guy is going to 'invite himself along' on an outing like that unless he's doing it in order to spend time with you."

"Or maybe he just cares about dogs," I said. "I mean, he did take Rufus."

"He probably did that to impress you, too."

That wasn't the feeling I'd gotten. To tell the truth, I still didn't quite know why Ben had agreed to foster the dog, except that maybe he'd been feeling a little lonely in that big house and had made a spur-of-the-moment decision to have a pet, if only a temporary one.

I sipped from my own coffee, reveling in the sensation of the much-needed caffeine making its way along my weary veins. "You know, Naomi, not everything is about men and women. Sometimes people do stuff because it's the right thing to do, with no other motivation involved."

Her eyes crinkled at the corners. "If you say so."

There probably wasn't much point in arguing with her, so I just shrugged and continued to drink coffee. After a few moments, though, I said, "Do you want to see the puppies?"

"Sure," she replied, although I had the feeling she'd answered that way only to humor me. "Are they cute, or are they still in the 'drowned rat' stage?"

"They're cute," I said severely. All right, I knew she was teasing me...sort of. She wasn't a dog person, and I knew that she still didn't quite get my chihuahua obsession.

Which was okay. A lot of people didn't under-stand my love for the diminutive breed, but I just adored how tough and scrappy and smart they were, how they mostly didn't even seem to realize how small they were. They were fighters, and I admired that.

We got up from the kitchen table and went down the hall to the family room. The puppies were just starting to wake up from their latest milk nap, and were stretching and yawning while Frida looked at them with indulgent eyes.

Naomi surveyed this scene and glanced over at me, surprise clear in her face. "You got Frida to babysit the puppies?"

"I didn't 'get' her to do anything. She went to them of her own volition. But they're all getting along great."

She moved a little closer and stared down at the puppies. Each one of them was its own little individual—the dark one who'd had such a close brush with death, one all caramel color, one tricolor, while the last was dark brown with a white chest and paws. Now that they'd been cleaned up and were already beginning to fill out, I could see how the fur around their ears and tails was starting to wisp out and get fuller. It was hard to say what they'd been mixed with—I'd probably need a vet to make that determination—but I had a feeling they were at least part Pomeranian. They were going to be adorable little dogs.

"They are kind of cute," Naomi admitted.

"Want one?" I asked, teasing her.

"No!" she responded immediately, then gave

me a sideways glare. "But if I wanted a dog, I'd be tempted. They're way too young for that, though, aren't they?"

"Oh, yes," I said, and went down on my knees next to their bed so I could pick up the dark one and pet her. They were all sweet, but that little girl had already claimed a piece of my heart. "They won't be ready to be adopted until they're at least ten weeks old. I think they're only about two weeks right now, so we've got a ways to go. I called the vet and made an appointment to have them all checked out—we're supposed to be there at ten-thirty."

This announcement made a slight flicker of worry come and go in my friend's eyes. "You don't need help, do you?"

"No," I told her, trying not to smile. "I know better than to draft you for a project like that. I'll put them in the dog carrier—they're so tiny, they'll fit in the spare one."

"Good," she said, then added hastily, "I mean, I would if you really needed me to, except that would be cutting it pretty close, since I have a meeting downtown at noon."

And the thing was, I knew she would have helped me out if I'd needed someone to accompany me to the vet. But the puppies were doing fine, and I'd bring Frida along so they wouldn't get worried or nervous. Luckily, my vet was just down the road in Echo Park, so we wouldn't have very far to go.

The doorbell rang then, and I glanced down the hall toward the front door, startled. It was only a little past nine, so even if the unlikely had occurred and Ben really had decided to come by to visit the puppies, I doubted he would have done so quite that early.

Then again, even though I did my best to keep my home address a secret and used a mail drop for all official Little Angels business, there had still been a few times when I'd opened the door to find an abandoned dog on my doorstep. Word got out, no matter how careful you were.

Right then, I wasn't sure if I could accommodate any more dogs. My hands were pretty full... but I knew I would never turn away a dog in need.

"I'd better see who's there," I said.

"Okay," Naomi responded. "I'll stay here and hold down the fort."

Actually, I thought it was really Frida who was holding down the fort, but I only flashed my friend a smile and headed down the hallway to the front door. When I opened it, my heart seemed to jump straight up and lodge somewhere in my throat.

Standing on the front porch was a police officer in a dark blue uniform. He was probably about ten years older than I, Hispanic, and wearing a stern expression. "Jillian Torres?"

"Y-yes," I said. Even though I could guess at his answer before I even asked the question, I still had to inquire, "What's this about?"

"Do you drive a white 2017 Toyota Prius, license number 8PLT009?"

How had they seen my license number? The guy chasing me off his property had been yards away, and the street hadn't been that well lit. I swallowed and said, "Yes, that's my car."

Without blinking, he said, "I'm afraid you're under arrest for trespassing and suspected burglary."

Naomi came into the foyer then, expression shocked. "What's going on?"

"I'm getting arrested," I said wearily. "Can you get someone to watch the dogs?"

"I—"

The officer said, "I'm taking her to the police facility in Monterey Park. You can talk to her there after she's booked."

"But—"

"Come along," the policeman told me. His hand rested at his hip, near the handcuffs that dangled there. He hadn't made any mention of cuffing me, but the implication was clear enough —I needed to shut up and get moving, or I'd have the dubious pleasure of treating my neighbors to the sight of me getting hauled away in handcuffs.

I didn't have any time to waste. "Naomi, please!"

"All right, all right." Her face was white, but she looked more angry on my behalf than truly worried. "I'll take care of the dogs, and I'll call your lawyer."

"And the vet," I said as the officer took me by the arm and began to lead me down the porch steps. "You'll need to cancel my appointment."

And that was all I had a chance to say, because then he was pulling me along the front walk to where his squad car was parked out in front. I didn't dare risk his ire by looking back over my shoulder to see what Naomi was doing, but I assumed she would get it together and start making the necessary phone calls.

I was silent as the policeman put me in the back seat of his car and then went to climb in the driver's seat. He hadn't read me my Miranda rights, but maybe he didn't have to do that right away. I honestly couldn't remember how that all worked.

Good thing it was after nine o'clock, and so most people who lived on the street had already left for work and weren't around to witness my shame. I balled my hands in my lap as I watched the scenery flow past outside the car window, and forced myself to take a breath. This was no big deal. They didn't have any real evidence—Ben had wiped his fingerprints off the padlock, and I didn't think prints would have transferred to the fabric of the dirty blanket where the puppies had been sleeping.

Besides, this was why I had an attorney on retainer in the first place. Leslie would get it all straightened out. Besides, once I explained why I had entered that yard and taken the dogs in the first place, I was sure any charges would be dropped. If anything, charges should be filed against the homeowner for criminal neglect and cruelty to animals.

And so on. I let those reassuring thoughts run through my mind during the trip to Monterey Park, even though the whole time, I could feel the knot of dread in my stomach pulling tighter and tighter. What if my father's political opponents got wind of my arrest and tried to use it against him? It was an election year, and although my father had held the same seat in Congress for ten consecutive terms, maybe this would be the one thing that would get enough of his supporters to drop him so he'd lose.

No, that was silly. No one in his district probably gave a good goddamn what I did—well, as long as I didn't come out as gay or something. It was a pretty conservative bunch up in California's First District.

Eventually, we got to the police station, a nondescript dark beige block of a building that seemed to share a parking lot with city hall. The officer—who'd never given me his name—came and got me out of the back of the car, then made me do the perp walk through the entrance and into booking. There, I had to get fingerprinted and photographed, and fill out some paperwork before being placed in a holding cell with a couple of other women. None of them looked very happy to be there.

I could totally understand that.

They kept giving me sideways glances, probably because I really didn't look like I belonged there. Two of the women were dressed in a way that told me exactly why they'd been arrested, and the others looked pale and thin, and were probably in for some kind of drug charges. While I hadn't made any special effort with my appearance that morning, I was wearing nice jeans and a gray V-neck sweater with a tank top under it, and flats instead of tennis shoes, just because I'd been planning to go to the vet later and didn't want to look like a slob. The conservative ensemble made me stick out like a sore thumb.

A while later—it felt like an eternity but was more like forty-five minutes or so—a female officer came and fetched me, and took me to a small room with a table and some chairs. Presumably, this was where they planned to interrogate me.

"Doesn't someone have to read me my rights?" I asked, but she only shook her head.

"This isn't an interrogation. A detective will be in to talk with you shortly."

And she went out without giving me a chance to respond.

Irritated, I went ahead and sat down on one of the chairs, since I didn't know what else to do. I supposed it was marginally better that I hadn't been left in the holding cell, but I still would have liked to know what was going on.

In the next moment, though, the door opened, and several men entered. The one in the lead was probably the detective—he wore a dress shirt and a tie, and was slim and looked like he was somewhere in his late forties. The man immediately behind him was around the same age, but bulky and unshaven, forehead creased in a perpetual scowl, his jeans faded with ragged hems.

The third man was Benjamin Blake.

I sat upright in my chair, eyes widening. What the hell was *he* doing here? I supposed that he might have somehow caught wind of what had happened to me, but I didn't see why in the world he would have come down to the police station...

especially when he'd been an accessory to the breaking and entering. You'd think he'd want to stay as far away as possible.

"Jillian Torres?" the man in the lead inquired. "I'm Detective Sorenson."

I managed a smile at him, although I knew it was pretty wavery. "What's going on?"

His expression remained serious, but I saw the way his gaze shifted sideways toward Ben and the other man, who I guessed had to be the owner of the house where we'd rescued the puppies. "Ms. Torres, this is a little irregular, but there may be a way to handle this without charges being formally brought against you."

"Oh?" I said, trying to look interested without also appearing that I was guilty as sin, and therefore in need of some alternative arrangement. Then I added, "I'm not sure I should talk to you without my attorney present."

The detective frowned, and the other man said, "Yeah, we can wait for your fancy lawyer—or you can make this all go away."

Ben spoke for the first time then, sounding supremely bored. "Name your price."

"Mr. Blake—" Detective Sorenson began, but he lifted a hand.

"We know that's what all this is about, don't we?" Ben said. His gaze flicked to the homeowner, taking in the gray stubble on his chin and his unkempt clothing with a single dismissive glance. As usual, Ben himself looked like he'd walked out of a department store window, that day in brown herringbone trousers and a matching vest, a fine cream linen shirt underneath. "I think we all have an interest in making this go away."

About all I could do was nod. Of course, I'd much prefer to sweep the whole incident under the rug and go on with my life, but Ben's comment about naming a price worried me. It wasn't as though I was sitting on stacks of cash; I had about ten grand in my savings account, a few more thousand dollars in checking, and that was about it for personal operating expenses. There was also a chunk of change in the Little Angels business account, but that money was set aside for pet supplies, vet visits, and the like; I would never consider dipping into it to cover my legal expenses. Yes, if I ran into a dire enough emergency, I could always appeal to my parents for help, but asking them for money would be excruciatingly embarrassing, and definitely something I'd prefer to avoid.

Ben looked over at me and paused; I couldn't quite tell what was going on behind those hazel eyes…mostly because I didn't know him well enough to begin to guess what he was planning, or even how he'd managed to insinuate himself into the situation. Had Naomi called him? Had he seen the police car pull up to my house, and then drawn the obvious conclusions? Either possibility made some sense, although I supposed it really didn't matter at the moment.

"Those were valuable dogs," the homeowner said. No one had mentioned his name, and I wasn't going to ask.

Scowling at him, I said, "If they were so valuable, then why did you leave them out in the cold to die?"

"They weren't going to die," he shot back. "They were sheltered, they had a blanket—"

"Mr. Caruso," Detective Sorenson said. "You may want to be careful about what you say."

The man subsided, but continued to glare at me out of narrowed dark eyes. Not that I cared what he thought—I knew he was a despicable human being, since no decent person with a shred of feelings could have treated helpless little puppies in such a way.

"Anyway," I went on, directing my words toward the detective, since I could tell Mr. Caruso was a lost cause, "they're mixed-breed puppies. Adorable, but not valuable in the same way purebred dogs would be."

"Not true," Mr. Caruso said. "They're Pomchis. Lot of demand for designer dogs like that."

Ah, so my guess that they were part

Pomeranian had been correct. And all right, Pomchis had a following. Maybe not as big as Labradoodles or Pomskis—Pomeranian/husky mixes—but enough that they might be worth more than a run-of-the-mill mutt. Still, that fact certainly didn't get the man off the hook for his treatment of the dogs in his care.

"How much?" Ben asked, still looking as if he couldn't care less what the dogs in question actually were.

"Six hundred, six-fifty each, easy," Mr. Caruso responded.

That was a bit of a stretch, since even a pure-bred chi generally wasn't worth that much unless it came from an award-winning bloodline, or was the coveted teacup variety. However, Ben didn't seem to recognize this highway robbery for what it was, because he only reached into the interior pocket of his vest and produced a slim checkbook. "Let's say three thousand even, shall we? That should take care of any…pain and suffering…this incident might have caused."

"That's ridiculous!" I protested. Three thousand dollars was crazy. Yes, I had that much on hand, but paying Ben back was going to take a huge chunk out of my savings account. I'd rather have the asshole press charges and fight him in court.

Of course, the legal battle would probably end

up costing me more than the three thousand Ben was offering. However, there were principles involved here.

Mr. Caruso seemed to be of a similar mind, because he sneered at me and said, "Fine. Then I'll see you in court."

"Not necessary," Ben put in. He extracted a gold pen from the same pocket that had held the checkbook, then set it down on the table and began filling out a check. "First name?"

"Charles," Mr. Caruso responded, dark eyes beginning to look greedy.

"Excellent." Ben finished writing out the check, then briskly tore it off its pad and held it out to the man standing next to him. Before he could take it, Ben added, "No charges filed, correct?"

"Consider the matter dropped." Mr. Caruso plucked the check from between Ben's fingers, studied it, and then folded it up and placed it in his wallet.

"Then we're done here," Detective Sorenson said. He looked as if he wanted nothing more than to get all of us out of the building. I supposed I couldn't blame him—I kind of doubted that kidnapped dogs, even with an accompanying charge of trespassing, were very high on the Monterey Park P.D.'s list of priorities.

I got up from my chair and walked over

toward Ben, since I didn't know quite else what to do. As I went, the detective spoke again.

"And Ms. Torres—while I admire your crusading instincts, try to remember that laws regarding private property exist for a reason."

"I will," I said, even though I knew I wouldn't hesitate to do the exact same thing if similar circumstances ever presented themselves.

Then Ben and I left the room, and followed the signs down to the front desk. Since I hadn't been formally charged with anything, the paperwork was minimal—it wasn't as if he had to post bail for me or something—but we still had to wait for the officer on duty to fetch my personal belongings. They weren't much, just my cell phone and the silver hoop earrings I'd been wearing, since the officer who'd come to my house had taken me away before I could even grab my purse. However, I definitely wasn't leaving without that phone.

But the item in question was returned without incident, along with my earrings, and in less than ten minutes, I was following Ben out the front door and to the parking lot. My mind was so full of questions, I didn't even know which one to ask first.

Those questions took a back seat to the one that rose to my lips when he paused next to a perfectly restored British racing green '60s-vintage Jaguar convertible. "This is your car?" I blurted.

"Yes," he said calmly as he unlocked the passenger door. "Do you have a problem with it?"

"No," I replied right away. "It's...it's gorgeous."

Which it was. Because the day was gray and cool, he had the top up, but that didn't take anything away from the car's inherent beauty. I didn't pretend to be an expert on cars, and yet some vehicles were so classic that you didn't need to know much about them to know they were perfect. And, as I sat down and breathed in the scent of expensive luggage-tan leather, I thought this car matched Ben perfectly, went with his somewhat retro wardrobe and vintage house.

He came around to the driver's side and got in, then started the engine. It had a wicked rumble that told me it was probably very fast, although he certainly drove sedately enough as he backed out of the parking space and headed north on Garfield Avenue so he could get on the 10 Freeway headed west toward downtown.

"How did you know where I was?" I asked once we were on the freeway.

His shoulders lifted slightly. I noticed that he didn't look away from the road, kept his gaze fixed firmly ahead, although I didn't know for sure if that was because he wasn't familiar with the area and therefore didn't want to take any chances…or because he didn't want to glance over at me and see the gratitude in my expression.

"I saw the police car pull up in front of your house and the officer get out. It didn't require too great a leap of logic to figure out what had happened. Once the police car had left, I went over to your house and told your friend Naomi that I would go bail you out, since I'd been your partner in crime in our little escapade the evening before."

I could only imagine her expression as he made the offer. "What did she say?"

"She said that was very nice of me, but that you'd already asked her to call your lawyer. I said I didn't think that would be necessary. I knew we could handle this without getting lawyers involved."

If I'd been thinking a little more clearly, I supposed I should have wondered what had happened to Leslie, why she hadn't come to the police station while I was waiting in the holding cell. But it seemed that Ben had intervened, and I had to be grateful for that. Even a simple trip down to the police station would have started to seriously eat into my retainer.

"Naomi is watching the dogs," Ben went on. "I asked her to do that, since she was already there. I hope you don't mind."

"No, I don't mind," I said faintly. On the other hand, I was pretty sure Naomi minded, although she clearly hadn't told him no. All the more reason to get back home as quickly as possible so I could relieve her of dog-sitting duty and she could go on with her day.

"At any rate," he said, "I don't think you need to worry about Mr. Caruso."

No, but I had to worry about the three grand Ben had given the jerk. "I'll pay you back as soon as I can."

The offer only made him lift an eyebrow. "Not necessary."

"It's necessary to me," I said firmly. "I dragged you into this mess, but I certainly don't expect you to pay for it on top of everything else."

His fingers tapped on the steering wheel in some impatience. "Jillian, I won't even miss that three thousand dollars. Can you say the same?"

Of course, I couldn't. Yes, maybe it was crazy to be so cash-poor while living in a house worth well north of a million, but those were my circumstances. I released a breath and realized a few spatters of rain were beginning to hit the windshield. "No, I can't."

"Well, then."

His tone made it seem as if that was the end of the discussion. However, I wasn't sure I could let it go that easily. "That's a lot of money to give someone who's practically a stranger."

Another shrug. "We're neighbors."

As if that was enough of a reason to hand over several grand without blinking. Feeling desperate, I said, "Well, you need to let me do something for you to say thanks. Why don't you come over tonight and let me make you dinner?"

At last, he looked over at me, although as usual, his expression was inscrutable. "You consider that a fair trade?"

"No, of course not," I replied, feeling the familiar stir of irritation despite my gratitude to him for springing me out of jail. "It's just a little way of saying thank-you."

"Ah." A long pause, during which I wondered if I really had lost my mind. Not that I was terribly worried about making dinner—I actually was a decent cook, and I could go online and order whatever I needed from Safeway and have it delivered to the house—but that I thought Ben might be receptive to such a gesture.

"Or not," I said hastily. "We can think of something else. Just don't ask me to paint your house—I'm afraid of heights."

That comment actually elicited a chuckle. "No, I wouldn't make such a request of you. And…." He paused there, as though weighing whether to continue or not. Then he said, "I think I would like to come to dinner."

And I didn't know whether to be relieved…or alarmed.

What had I just gotten myself into?

CHAPTER EIGHT

AFTER THE MORNING I'D HAD, PROBABLY THE last person I wanted showing up in my kitchen after I got home from my stint at the Monterey Park police station was Eloy Esparza, Naomi's assistant…or manager…or stylist. He was actually a bewildering combination of all three, depending on what was going on in Naomi's life at any particular moment. At any rate, I was feeling a little fried, and I would have preferred to not have him descend.

Unfortunately, it was pretty obvious that the universe had decided to ignore my wishes.

He gave a peremptory knock at the back door and then came sailing in, black hair impossibly sleek despite the damp day outside. Actually, it had stopped raining for a little bit, and I had the uncharitable thought that he'd waited for a break in the weather before coming over to my place so he wouldn't damage his coiffure.

"What's up, Eloy?" I asked as I chopped some fresh rosemary from the bush growing on my windowsill. Because I didn't want Ben to think I was going out of my way to do something fancy, I'd decided on roast chicken and potatoes for dinner, with a salad and grilled asparagus on the side.

Eloy paused by the sink and put his hands on his hips, a scowl pulling at his black brows. "I hope you're not going to get up to any more shenanigans that involve getting bailed out of police custody, because Naomi doesn't have time for that kind of nonsense."

Because I'd had previous dealings with Eloy, my brain was able to follow that somewhat convoluted logic. "Um, it wasn't Naomi who bailed me out. It was Ben Blake."

"Whatever." Eloy waved a hand somewhere toward Ben's house—or maybe just the universe in general. It was difficult to say for sure. "Naomi still had to stay here and watch those puppies—and she had to cancel her lunch engagement. That does not look good, you know."

"Oh, I'm sorry," I responded immediately. A rush of contrition went over me—Naomi hadn't said word one about missing her lunch date when I got back to the house. "In all the craziness, I just forgot. She didn't say anything when I came home."

"Well, of course, she didn't, because she wouldn't want you to worry. But if word gets out that Naomi Klein is a flake who can't be trusted to keep her appointments…well, you can see how that would be a problem."

"I totally understand," I said. "And you really don't have to worry, Eloy—even if I wanted to get into trouble, I'm going to be stuck here babysitting a litter of puppies for the foreseeable future."

His eyes narrowed, telling me that he really didn't trust me to do the right thing. Honestly, I didn't know what I could say to him to let him know this had been a one-off occurrence, since it seemed clear he thought I would go off half-cocked again if the opportunity presented itself. I supposed that was the downside of being the neighborhood's crazy dog lady; people tended to think the worst…or the best, depending on how you looked at it.

I had to do what I could to repair the situation, though. "Really," I continued. "I know how hard you two have been working to level up, so to speak. I don't want to get in the way of that. Naomi's kind-hearted, and the last thing I'd ever want to do is take advantage of that and interfere with her work."

Those words seemed to have been the right ones to say, because Eloy's expression softened slightly. Looking at him then, I once again got the impression that he cared about her a lot more than a mere manager/client relationship would indicate. Maybe he was bisexual.

Not that I would ever have the nerve to ask.

"She does put herself out there for people," he said. "That's why she's so good at what she does… and why we're working so hard to try to get her message out to an even bigger audience."

I nodded. "You're doing a great job," I told him. "But now…." I let the words trail off, and pointed the tip of my knife toward the pile of chopped rosemary and the lemons waiting their turn to be cut up so they could get stuffed inside the chicken. "I really need to keep going with this, or dinner won't be ready at seven."

His dark eyes gleamed. I could tell he was ready for a little gossip—and a change of topic. "Big date?"

"Not a date at all," I said calmly. "I just asked Ben over for dinner to say thank-you for springing me out of the slammer today."

"Right." One corner of Eloy's lip curled, and he added, "You can call it whatever you like, honey. Sure sounds like a date to me."

Having made that pronouncement, he let himself out the back door—and let in a little burst of cold, moist air. I shivered, even as I told myself he didn't know what he was talking about.

Date, indeed.

I did my best to look casual and unconcerned as I welcomed Ben to the house and led him to the dining room, but I wasn't sure how successful I was. Although I'd tried to dismiss Eloy's comment about a "date" from my mind as I prepped dinner and set the table, I hadn't done a very good job of it, because once the chicken and potatoes were in the oven and the table was ready, I hurried upstairs and brushed my hair multiple times, then took the unprecedented step of actually applying mascara and berry-hued lip stain before changing into a dark rose-colored cardigan.

Was it too much? I couldn't say for sure, because Ben didn't seem to take any note of my appearance at all. No, he just took the seat at the head of the table—at my urging, but he didn't try to demur, either—and looked around in some interest.

"No dogs?" he asked, and I had to smile.

"They've all been fed and are snuggled up against Frida in the family room," I replied. "Since it's such a wet evening, I lit another fire. I don't think the dogs are going anywhere."

"Probably not." His gaze strayed to the bottle of pinot noir I had sitting in a wine coaster on the table. It was still unopened, with a wine key lying next to it; I might have possessed a number of useful talents, but opening a wine bottle without mangling the cork wasn't one of them. "Should I?" he asked.

"Yes, please," I said, thankful that he'd gotten the hint and I hadn't been forced to ask him outright to open the bottle.

He picked up both items and proceeded to remove the cork with the kind of economy of movement one would normally expect from a sommelier, or at least a waiter in a high-end restaurant. If it had been anyone else, I might have speculated that he'd once worked as a waiter, except that I knew anyone with his temperament wouldn't have lasted five minutes waiting on tables.

"I hope chicken and potatoes are okay," I said as he poured a measure of wine into each of our glasses. "I suppose I should have asked if you had any dietary restrictions."

"No, that's fine," he said. Then his hazel eyes took on a sly glint. "Although there are some who would say pinot noir is a daring choice for chicken."

"I didn't have any rosé, and it's too cold and damp for white wine," I responded blithely. If that was taking the bait, so be it. I didn't want him to think I was completely uninformed, although Tom had been the one who was the wine expert in our relationship. "It's not a heavy pinot, so I think it should be fine."

His eyes still held that glint. "What if I told you I didn't drink?"

"Then I'd have a glass and cork up the bottle, and drink it with Naomi sometime," I said, and allowed myself a grin. "But I'd be surprised that someone who could open a wine bottle that neatly didn't drink."

"Betrayed by my own skill." A corner of his mouth quirked, and he picked up his napkin and put it in his lap. He was wearing the clothes he'd had on earlier that day, although for his walk over to my house, he'd protected the ensemble with a full-length raincoat and an umbrella. I couldn't even remember the last time I'd seen a man my age wearing an actual raincoat. But then, it seemed clear enough to me that Benjamin Blake walked to his own drummer. "You would be right to be surprised. I do like wine, actually."

"Good." The timer on the oven went off then, and I said, "Just give me a couple of minutes to get everything served up, and then we'll be ready to get started."

I wasn't surprised that he didn't offer to help—I would have been much more startled to see him get up from the table in order to lend his assistance in the kitchen. No, wherever he'd come from, it seemed to me that he was used to people waiting on him. Maybe he was some sort of trust fund baby. That would explain the house and the car and the clothes—and the way he'd acted as if paying three grand to get rid of Mr. Caruso was on a par with paying for dinner and a movie.

Well, if that turned out to be the case, I'd try not to hold it against him. It wasn't as if I came from a working-class background, either; my father's family had been in the cattle business for several generations, and although he divested himself of his interests in the Cunningham family ranches and packing houses, the money he'd put in trusts had kept us all quite comfortable. More than once, he'd offered to give me an allowance, and yet I'd always refused. It was one thing to take spousal support from Tom—he'd dug his own grave on that particular point—but no way was I going to be a grown-ass woman going on thirty and still taking money from her parents.

I'd already set out all the serving pieces, so it didn't take me very long to get the chicken transferred from its roasting pan to the platter I used for chicken and roasts, and the potatoes and veggies and salad in their respective bowls. Two trips were required to get everything into the dining room, but in less than five minutes, I was sitting back down at the table. I raised my glass to Ben.

"To getting busted out of jail," I said.

He looked slightly confused. "I wouldn't call that 'busted out.' We negotiated a settlement and walked away."

"Okay, true, but I still feel like we got away with something."

A small shrug. "If that's how you want to look at it."

We clinked glasses and each took a sip of wine. It wasn't anything pretentious, just an inexpensive import from Oregon that I'd bought at the local Safeway, but I thought it would do. And since Ben gave the faintest of nods before he took a second sip, it seemed the wine had passed muster.

Then I reached for the carving knife and fork, and glanced over at him. "Breast or thigh?"

He blinked. "Excuse me?"

"Do you want a piece of the breast, or are you more of a leg man?"

Another blink. "Breast is fine."

I got to work. Maybe I wasn't very good at opening a bottle of wine, but my father had made sure his only daughter knew how to carve a bird. And barbecue, and shoot a gun and ride a horse.

However, none of those skills would be of much use on a rainy January night in Los Angeles, so I settled for giving Ben the choicest piece of breast, laying a perfectly cut slice on his plate.

"There you go."

Good thing I wasn't expecting to impress him. He only nodded, and began helping himself to the side dishes while I cut myself a slice of breast as well. I supposed I should have been glad that he didn't offer to carve the chicken, because I doubted he could have done as good a job of it. However, as before, he seemed content to be waited on. In someone else, I might have found that kind of attitude annoying. But since he'd definitely done me a solid earlier that day, I decided to give his slightly high-handed behavior a pass…for the moment, anyway.

We were quiet for a few minutes as we got started on our food. Although he didn't comment on it, I could tell by the way he ate that he must be enjoying the meal. When he slowed down a little, I asked, "How's Rufus doing?"

"Fine," Ben said, then reached for his glass of wine. "Possibly a little annoyed that I didn't bring him along with me."

"You could have, you know," I told him. "We could have put him in with Frida and the puppies, since they all seem to get along so well."

Ben shook his head. "No, he would have

gotten wet. I wouldn't want him to track mud all over your floors."

It was debatable how much mud one small dog could track into a house—especially since there really wasn't much in the way of mud between Ben's house and mine—but I didn't protest. There would be plenty of time for Rufus to have a play date with Frida and the puppies, since they would be with us for at least the next six or seven weeks, possibly longer.

"It's interesting what you've done with the house," Ben went on.

I lifted my glass of wine and took a sip. Still holding it near my mouth, I said, "'Interesting' in that you actually find it interesting, or 'interesting' in the way that people say 'interesting' when they can't really find anything to compliment?"

His head tilted slightly as he appeared to contemplate the question, but he didn't seem to take offense. I wasn't even sure why I'd asked him that, except I honestly was curious. I figured if nothing else, he would tell me the truth. He didn't seem the type to hold much back.

"The first kind, I suppose," he said. "You've tried to stay true to the bones of the house, but it is definitely not decorated the way it would have been when it was first built."

That was for sure. While I loved these old houses, I found Victorian interior design to be way too fussy for my own personal taste, even though I also appreciated it when other people stayed truer to the spirit of the period with their own interior decorating. For myself, I thought it was easier to appreciate the lines of those houses and their architectural detail when there wasn't a lot of clutter to interfere. However, I wasn't sure of the best way to express my thoughts without having it sound as if I was criticizing Ben's home, which could almost have been a time capsule from 1895, except for the updated kitchen. Well, and the bathrooms; although I hadn't actually seen any of them, I had to assume they'd been modernized, too.

"No, that was something Tom and I went back and forth on," I said. When Ben's eyebrows lifted in question, I explained, "My ex-husband. He actually wasn't all that into Victorian style, but—"

Ben cut in there. "Why would you buy a house here if it wasn't to his taste?"

Good question. I'd been enchanted by Carroll Avenue since the first time I drove through the neighborhood and got a good look at all those lovingly restored Victorian homes. Back then, I was still in college and wasn't doing much more than sightseeing, trying to familiarize myself as much as I could with L.A.'s various neighborhoods. But when Tom and I were newly married and starting to house-hunt—and knowing how lucky we were to be in a position to do so, thanks to the high six figures he was already earning at a prestigious downtown law firm—he got advance notice that the house was going on the market, and we went and took a look and made an offer that same day. For him, it was more the cachet of living in Angelino Heights…and the home's convenient location so close to downtown…than because he loved the house.

I had fallen in love, though. Yes, the house needed a lot of work, since the people selling it had lived there for more than thirty years, and they hadn't done anything to update the place, but that was all cosmetic stuff. Its bones were good, and I adored the turret on the front of the house and the curved windows with their accompanying window seats in the living room. I loved the stained glass in the windows that were set in the wall next to the staircase, and the big backyard with its boxwood hedges and old, rustling oaks and willows and sycamores. It felt completely permanent, sturdy and safe. I'd thought Tom and I could make a life there. I'd been completely wrong about that, but at least I got to stay in the house, to continue to love it and make sure it would survive another hundred years.

However, I couldn't tell Ben all that. He'd probably think I was completely sentimental, and he'd probably be right. I still didn't know why he'd decided to live here on Carroll Avenue, but I had a feeling his motivations were probably closer to those of my ex than my own.

"It was a great investment," I said, then took a sip of wine. My glass was almost empty, so I reached for the bottle of wine, thinking it was time for a refill.

Apparently, Ben had been thinking the same thing, because he extended a hand toward the bottle as well. Before I knew what was happening, our fingers had brushed against one another.

Almost at once, he jerked his hand away as if my touch had scalded him. Was he a germaphobe, or did he have a phobia about touching other people?

Or was there another, more personal reason why he didn't think it was a good idea to touch me?

Right then, I could see the wisdom in avoiding such contact, because an unwelcome rush of heat went through me. My body felt far more alive than it had a moment earlier, and I really didn't want to acknowledge what my reaction might mean.

"Oops," I said, with a not-very-convincing chuckle. "Great minds think alike, I guess. Let me refill yours, too."

And I poured some wine into each of our

glasses, then took mine and sipped from it. Something about Ben's posture seemed to relax slightly, and he followed suit, lifting his glass so he could take a swallow.

"Yes," he said, apparently intent on picking up the thread of our conversation so he could ignore that awkward little pause. "The houses in this neighborhood tend to appreciate faster than they do in other parts of Los Angeles."

"And most of L.A. does pretty well for itself, so that should tell you something," I said, even as I heaved an inner sigh of relief. Yes, that had been weird, but we both seemed to have moved past our inadvertent contact. "But anyway, I suppose it was because Tom wasn't really that invested in the house that he didn't fight too hard to hang on to it. When it came time to remodel, though, he wanted it to look like something out of *Victorian Home* magazine, while I wanted to be a little more relaxed about the whole thing. Since I was the one doing most of the work, he decided to let me make the design choices."

Ben glanced around the room, at the gleaming crown molding and the rich dark red on the walls. "You restored this house by yourself?"

"Well, not completely by myself," I replied. "I mean, we hired contractors to redo the kitchen and bathrooms and paint the exterior, and to update the wiring and the plumbing. But I did all the interior painting, and I resanded and refinished the floors, and landscaped the backyard."

Put that way, it did sound like a lot. I supposed while I was doing the work, I wasn't really thinking about all the effort I was putting into the house, only that I wanted to do what I could to hold up my end of things since Tom was the one making all the money. I hadn't really thought all that much about what I wanted to do after college, but when we crunched the numbers, it made much more sense—and was more cost-effective—for me to stay at home and work on the house rather than take some twenty-bucks-an-hour admin job somewhere.

Ben was staring at me as if I'd sprouted an extra head. Was it so far outside his experience that a woman might take on all those tasks, and actually enjoy herself in the process? Maybe. He did seem sort of sheltered in a lot of ways.

When he spoke, though, his question was one I hadn't been expecting. "Where did you find time in all that to start rescuing chihuahuas?"

I shrugged. "Oh, it wasn't anything I really planned. The house was mostly finished, and Tom and I had gotten Frida as a rescue about a year earlier, and one of the people at the shelter contacted me to see if I'd be interested in adopting another dog. I wasn't sure, but then they mentioned fostering, so I took in the dog—

ChiChi—and watched her for a few weeks until she was adopted by another family. I started doing some research, though, and realized how over-crowded the city's shelters were, how many dogs were being euthanized...." I let the words trail off there, because I could tell from the way Ben shifted uncomfortably in his chair that he didn't want to listen to a rant about the shortcomings of the city's animal-control department. "Anyway," I went on, "I learned how chihuahuas can really have a tough time in that kind of environment, and I read about other small-dog rescue organiza-tions in other parts of the state. So...I started networking, and here we are."

I reached for my glass of wine and took a large swallow, mouth a little dry after that long speech. In the beginning, I hadn't thought Little Angels would turn into anything formal, would just be a way for a group of people who were willing to foster chihuahuas to keep in contact. But it kept growing, so one of the attorneys at Tom's firm had walked me through applying for 501(c) nonprofit status, and it all sort of ended up as a real thing. I supposed my efforts had amused him more than anything else, although he did like the idea of having a wife who ran a not-for-profit dog rescue, just because it was the sort of thing that gave him fodder for conversation at cocktail parties.

Ben seemed to consider what I'd said, then

picked up his fork and took the last few bites of chicken on his plate. Once he was done, he pushed the plate away and set his fork down on top of it. "Why chihuahuas?"

That was like asking someone why they preferred chocolate ice cream to strawberry. We'd always had dogs at my house when I was growing up, but they were big, rambunctious types—lab mixes, mostly. But my best friend in grades three through six had a chihuahua, and I'd always been fascinated by the little guy…Bugsy, a long-haired chi who seemed to have no idea he was only eleven inches from forehead to paw. He was smart and fierce and utterly adorable, and I'd told myself that one day I'd have a dog like that of my own.

And now I did…well, five at the moment. The current situation wasn't permanent, of course, but those puppies would be calling this house home for the foreseeable future.

"I've just always liked them," I said. "And it seemed as though they needed someone to have their back, so to speak. They're so little."

"Well, that's true." He reached for his glass of wine and drank some more; there was still some left in the bottle, so he could help himself if he was so inclined. After two glasses, I knew I was done. I still didn't quite know what to do about that odd little moment of connection we'd shared when our fingers had brushed against one another, but I figured it was probably safer to avoid getting anywhere close to tipsy.

"Speaking of which," I added, thinking it was a good idea to change up the scenery, so to speak, "I should probably go check on the puppies. It's been a while since I looked in on them."

"I'd like to see them," Ben said, surprising me again. I'd sort of gotten the impression that he'd considered himself done with them once they were safely set up in my family room, but maybe I'd misjudged him.

"Sure. Do you want a glass of water or anything before we head over there?"

For just the briefest second, his eyes narrowed, and I saw his gaze track to the bottle of wine, which clearly had at least a glass's worth left in it, if not more. But he only replied, "That sounds like a good idea."

Relieved that he hadn't made an issue out of finishing the bottle—I knew I'd had enough—I got up from the table and went into the kitchen, where I poured us both glasses of water. Then I headed back to the dining room and handed him his glass. "Let's head on over to Puppy Central."

He followed me to the family room, where I paused to push open the pocket doors that kept the dogs inside from wandering around the house. It was fairly warm in there, thanks to the fire I'd left burning in the hearth, although it had settled down a bit and wasn't much more than glowing coals and one log that still flicked fitfully.

The puppies had wandered away from their bed and were lying on the rug in front of the fire, with Frida a few paces away, keeping a watchful eye on the gang. Two of them were dozing, while the little black-furred one who'd already stolen my heart and one of her brothers, the tricolor pup, were butting against each other, trying to gnaw on each other's ears.

"They look very well," Ben observed. He'd quietly pulled the pocket doors closed behind him, probably so the pups wouldn't have a chance to make an escape. Not that they looked at all inclined to do such a thing—they had a nice, warm, quiet spot to call their own, and so were probably in doggy heaven.

"They've definitely perked up," I agreed. "They just needed to feel warm and cared for."

As if responding to my voice, the little black-furred girl let out a little *yip* and came trundling over to me. I bent down and petted her, could feel the wisps of her fur soft and crisp against my fingertips. "I think I'm going to call this one Boudicca."

"After the British warrior queen?" Ben asked, sounding amused.

I supposed I shouldn't have been surprised

that he would know the reference. "Exactly. Because she's a fighter, this one."

"She does seem to be quite adaptable." He went over to the armchair and sat down, gaze taking in the puppy I was petting, her brothers and sister luxuriating in the warmth from the hearth. For a second, I thought I saw something flicker in his eyes, although I couldn't say exactly what it was. Not amusement, or at least, that wasn't all.

But because I wasn't about to make a fool of myself by staring at him and trying to decipher his expression, I made myself focus on Boudicca, on the way she pushed back against me, as if testing her weight. Then her tiny mouth fastened on my finger, and I realized she was probably hungry again. It had been several hours since their last feeding.

I lifted her up and put her back in her bed, then turned toward Ben. "I need to feed them. Want to help?"

He looked somewhat taken aback. "I—" A pause, and then he said, sounding resigned, "I suppose so. At least I already know what to do."

"Oh, you're a pro," I assured him. "Just give me a minute to get the formula mixed up."

I left him sitting in the chair, watching the dogs, while I went back to the kitchen and got out the bottles and formula, and put together a batch for that evening's feeding. This task didn't take very long, and I was back in the family room in less than five minutes. Nothing much had changed, except the puppies had all gathered together in their bed, smashed up against Frida.

Part of me hated to disturb them, but they'd probably be even more cranky about going hungry than they would be about getting moved from the bed. I picked up one of the males and handed him and a bottle to Ben, who accepted them in silence and then placed the bottle's nipple up to the puppy's mouth. He started feeding at once, so I gathered up Boudicca and sat down with her to give her a bottle as well.

For a minute or two, all was silent, the only sound the faint crackles that came from the dying fire, and a soft whisper of wind and rain from beyond the window. It was so cozy and somehow soothing to be there like that, with the hungry dog in my arms and Ben a few feet away in the armchair. It had been Tom's favorite place to sit as well, although I really couldn't imagine two men who were more different from one another.

And that was a good thing. I didn't want Ben to be at all like Tom.

I wanted…I didn't know what I wanted.

You don't have to want anything, I told myself, doing my best to concentrate on Boudicca and the formula she was greedily slurping down. *You just have to be.*

But as my gaze rested on Ben, who was similarly focused on the dog he held, I realized I probably wanted a little more than that.

I just didn't know what to do about it.

INTERLUDE

Rain fell, and Beelzebub scowled at the streaks it made on his bedroom window. Wasn't it supposed not to rain in Los Angeles?

If that was the case, then apparently someone hadn't gotten the memo.

He closed the drapes and turned away from the window to see Rufus watching him, one ear cocked while the other drooped downward. The dog clearly hadn't been happy to be abandoned for the evening, especially when Ben returned to the house smelling of other dogs and, no doubt, the chicken dinner he'd just consumed.

"Next time," he said as he went to the closet and began to unbutton his vest.

Of course, that off-hand comment made him frown even more. It assumed that there would be a next time he dined at Jillian Torres's house, and he wasn't sure whether he wanted to commit to such a thing or not.

Not because she couldn't cook. The meal had actually been excellent, if the fare simple. He'd been a little surprised by her expertise in the kitchen. Something about her overly casual mode of dress and off-hand manner had made him assume she didn't have the sort of focus required to be a good cook, but his assumption had been wrong.

No, it was because....

He let the thought trail off because he wasn't sure it was entirely wise to entertain it. Even as he tried to dismiss the ridiculous notion from his mind, however, it popped up again.

It was because he didn't know whether he trusted himself around her.

Which he knew was ridiculous. So what if their fingers had accidentally touched when they both reached for the bottle of wine at the same time? It was such a trifling matter, he shouldn't allow it to occupy any space in his mind. Unfortunately, the more he tried not to think about it, the more his mind wanted to dwell on that split-second of contact.

Something had passed through him as they touched. A thrill, a...a spasm. No, that was the wrong word. He just knew that this human body of his had reacted to her, and probably the best way to avoid a repeat of that unfortunate incident was to do whatever was necessary to avoid being alone with her.

That might be difficult. She did her best to act as if she could manage everything on her own—and he had to admit that the work she'd put into her house was impressive, if what she'd told him was true—and yet he couldn't help thinking that she enjoyed having him help her with the puppies. Not in a way where she expected him to be there for her all the time, but rather that she'd feel somewhat let down if he didn't occasionally pitch in.

The sad thing was, he rather enjoyed it as well. There was something about being around those small, helpless animals that moved him in a way he'd never expected. Oh, he could only imagine how Asmodeus would laugh at him if he ever confessed such a thing. Luckily, Beelzebub's former compatriot was off living the high life in his Hollywood Hills home with his new wife at his side—they'd gotten married at the house just a week prior—and therefore would never have to find out how low Lucifer's former lieutenant had fallen.

Puppies, indeed.

Then again, in all his long, long existence, he'd never had any reason to spend time around dogs. After all, it had been his job to oversee Hell's prisoners, and there were no dogs in the underworld. As the saying went, all dogs went to Heaven...or at least, the canine version of it.

But no, there had been that one moment in Jillian's family room, while she played with Boudicca—ridiculous name—and he'd sat in the armchair and watched them, and he'd felt curiously content. More than content, really, as the low firelight caught warm flickers in her pale hair, and painted the smooth curve of her cheek in golden light.

He'd been happy.

And that was impossible. Beelzebub, Lord of the Flies, guardian of Hell, was many things, but happy surely wasn't one of them. He had not been made for happiness, or joy, or....

His mind shied away from the word before he would even allow himself to think it. That was not what he had felt. He would admit to the very slightest ease in her company, and that was all. Anything more was madness.

Beelzebub put his shirt in the hamper and climbed out of his trousers, then hung them back up. He could have closed his eyes and been undressed in a split-second, but something in the ritual of removing his clothes and putting them away soothed him, made him resent this human existence just a little less.

Actually, after the evening he'd just spent, he

wasn't sure if he truly resented it at all. There could be those moments of quiet beauty, small slivers of time that made him think there might be more to this kind of life than he'd believed.

If that wasn't simply the wine talking. This was a mortal body, and so it wasn't immune to the effects of alcohol, even if he would have to consume far more than a normal human being to feel truly intoxicated. Even so, Beelzebub thought he would rather believe he was a bit tipsy than think he was getting soft in his old age.

Yes, it had to have been the wine, and possibly the effect of playing nursemaid to the puppies. The combination had made him sloppy and sentimental.

It had absolutely nothing to do with Jillian Torres.

Nothing at all.

CHAPTER NINE

I'D HALFWAY EXPECTED TO HAVE NAOMI POP into my kitchen and demand to hear all the details about my dinner with Ben Blake, but apparently she hadn't noticed his comings and goings, or she'd been out for the evening and had missed the whole thing. Either way, I wasn't going to mention it to her. Neither would I bring up Eloy's little visit and the warnings he'd given me. I didn't much care for the way he'd said it, but I under-stood the warning. Naomi was my friend, and I didn't want to do anything that might hinder her career. She texted me later that day to let me know she had a bunch of meetings and then had to tape some shows, so she would be slammed for the next few days. I told her I totally understood and that I had my hands full with the puppies anyway.

That wasn't even a lie. Looking after them

took up huge chunks of my days, even with Frida acting as their surrogate mother. In between feedings and cleanings and training them to use the puppy pads I put out on the family room floor, I barely had enough time to keep up with my team of foster dog parents and the constant stream of inquiries I got either via the contact form on my website or by phone.

Ben actually came over several times, ostensibly to let Rufus hang with Frida and the pups... not that Ben would ever lower himself to use slang like "hang," not with the carefully precise way he spoke. No accent that I could detect, but I still got the feeling he hadn't grown up in California.

I did my best not to act self-conscious around him, partly because nothing had really happened between us, and partly because he was my neighbor and I knew it would be awful to have strained relations with someone who might be living across the street from me for years or even decades. After all, when people got to Carroll Avenue, they tended to stay put.

So I talked about the puppies and about Little Angels, and he talked about his plans to renovate the backyard when the weather got a little better —January had gone out in rain, and February was coming in the same way—and we fed the dogs and watched them grow bigger as each day passed. Simple, casual talk, the sort of conversation a pair of neighbors would have. I supposed that was good, except each time I watched him walk away from the house, Rufus dancing at the end of his leash, white-tipped tail flying like a flag, I wondered if there was something I could have said to make Ben stay a little longer, or maybe something he might have been trying to tell me and which I, in my utter cluelessness, had missed.

Or maybe there was nothing to miss, because even though I knew I was crushing on him in a way I hadn't thought was possible for a divorced woman about to hit thirty in the next few months, I had absolutely no evidence to prove that he felt the same way about me. Or felt anything at all, really, except a sort of generalized friendliness.

I knew I should have been putting out feelers for fosters or forever homes for my rescued puppies, but I wasn't quite ready to make that commitment. They still had several weeks before placing them elsewhere would even be feasible, although it also wasn't the sort of thing I could put off until the last minute. I honestly didn't know whether I'd be able to part with Boudicca, and Frida got along with her well enough that it probably wouldn't be an issue for her to stay with us permanently.

No one had approached me about Rufus, either, although I didn't feel too bad about that.

He seemed perfectly happy with Ben, and I kept hoping that one of the times my neighbor came over for a visit, he would ask me if he could go ahead and keep Rufus on a permanent basis.

That happy event hadn't yet occurred, though, and I wasn't about to broach the subject. I thought it better to skate along and allow the status quo to remain in place.

Actually, that mindset—if a little cowardly—worked just as well for the situation with me and Ben, come to think of it.

I was at the mailbox on our first sunny morning in some time, sorting through my mail, when I found myself suddenly scowling as I stared down at the envelope in my hand. It was a letter from the county assessor's office with an angry red "past due" stamped on it.

What the hell?

I'd gotten ownership of the house, but, as part of our divorce settlement, it was Tom's responsibility to pay the property taxes. He was supposed to make the payment as a one-time lump sum rather than have the taxes included as part of the mortgage, but it looked as though he'd conveniently allowed that particular line item in his budget to slide.

Bastard.

I stalked up the front walk and back into the house, muttering curses under my breath. Right then, I was glad I hadn't seen Ben that morning, because I wasn't sure whether I could have contained my ire around him, and I sure as hell didn't want to tell him what had me so upset. Not that I expected him to offer to pay my delinquent property taxes, but ever since the three grand he'd laid out to get Mr. Caruso off my back about the puppies we'd "liberated," I'd wondered if Ben would somehow feel compelled to come to my rescue if another such emergency reared its head.

Well, this was definitely an emergency. Or rather, it would be if this "oversight" was something a little more than a simple mistake. The county wanted twelve grand by the end of the month, and I didn't have it. Okay, technically, I had twelve grand if I emptied both my checking and savings accounts and scrounged every last quarter out of the couch cushions, but doing so would leave me in an extremely precarious position.

I went in the family room and checked on the puppies, but they were fine—rolling around on the rug, playing and biting and chasing each other's tails. Since I didn't want to bring any negative energy into such a happy space, I went into the kitchen and sat down at the table there, cell phone in hand.

And there I remained, staring at the entry for my ex-husband in my contacts list. I really didn't want to call Tom. *Really* didn't. The best way for me to deal with the destruction of my marriage had been to put him severely behind me, and so I'd done whatever I could to avoid any kind of contact, whether on the phone or in person. That was why bumping into him at that damn sushi restaurant in Little Tokyo had been so unnerving. The last thing I'd wanted him to think was that I'd shown up there in the hope that I might run into him. All right, probably he hadn't thought such a thing at all, but I didn't want there to be even the *possibility* that the idea might have crossed his mind.

So I sat and stared at my phone, and listened to the happy yips from the puppies in the other room, and watched the digital clock on the microwave move from 10:15 to 10:16 and finally to 10:17.

This was ridiculous. I was a grown-ass woman, not some scared high school kid afraid to call her crush and ask about their homework assignment.

I took a breath, and pushed the entry for Tom's cell. If he didn't pick up, I'd have to call the office and talk to his assistant Lora, but I'd really prefer to avoid that particular contact as well. She seemed like a nice enough person, except that I always caught a pitying tone in her voice when she talked to me, as though she thought I had to be something of a screw-up, or

I would have managed to hang on to my husband.

No, sweetheart, that was all his fault for not being able to keep it in his pants.

However, I was already angry enough with my ex. I didn't need to get myself worked up even more by dwelling on his transgressions.

His cell phone rang once, twice. I held back a curse and waited for it to roll over into voicemail, but to my surprise, he actually picked up on the third ring.

"Tom Torres."

He sounded slick and professional. Had he not glanced at his phone's screen, or was he simply pretending that he didn't recognize my number?

"Tom, it's Jillian," I said, doing my best to keep the irritation I was feeling from seeping into my voice. As angry as I was with him, I didn't want him to know how much he'd pissed me off.

"Jillian!" he said, his tone one of surprise. That could have been an act, though. He always had been pretty good at putting on a false face to present to the world. "What's up? It was really nice seeing you last week."

Bullshit, I thought, but if that was how he wanted to play it, fine. "Sorry to bother you at work," I said, "but I just got a late notice from the assessor's office saying that the property taxes hadn't been paid."

"Oh. Oh, shit."

Oh, shit, indeed. "I'm sure it's just a mistake," I went on, "but I wanted to let you know. We're going to start racking up some serious fees if it's not paid by the end of the month."

A pause, and then he said, "I'm really sorry about that. I had a reminder set on my calendar, but I must have missed it. Tell you what—I can drop by after work tonight and bring you a check."

Having my ex-husband "drop by" the house was probably pretty high up on the list of scenarios I would have preferred to avoid. "That's not necessary," I told him. "All you have to do is go online and pay it there."

For a few seconds, he didn't say anything. When he spoke again, his tone was almost sooth-ing…always a bad sign. Every time he'd adopted that tone in the past, it was because he knew he could use it to coax something out of me.

"I'd rather come over," he said. "I haven't seen the house in months, and I'd like to check on things."

"There's no need for you to 'check' on anything," I said crisply. "It's not your house anymore, remember?"

I couldn't see his face, of course, and yet I thought I could guess what his expression must have looked like in that moment—still smoothly handsome, but with a certain tension to his jaw. If he was annoyed enough, sometimes a tic would show in his cheek. It was the sort of thing he could mostly control when he was in the courtroom, since he didn't want opposing counsel to pick up on any of his tells, but he hadn't been able to completely hide it from me.

"I know that," he said, an edge to his voice. "It's hard to forget when I have that place blowing a hole in my checking account every month."

Voice sweet, I responded, "Don't do the crime if you can't do the time."

"Are we going to get into that again?"

Actually, I had no intention of rehashing one of our old arguments. But there was something about him that tended to goad me into doing or saying the wrong thing, which was why I did my best to make sure our orbits never intersected. "I was just pointing out that it's not my fault this isn't your house anymore."

"Right," he ground out, not bothering to hide his annoyance. "But if you want the money, then you're going to let me come over there and give it to you in person. Otherwise, you can pay the property taxes yourself."

"Careful," I said. "That sort of comment could land you back in court."

"Maybe. I doubt you have the cash reserves for that sort of thing, though."

Of course, I didn't, and he knew that as well as I did. And in the meantime, the fees at the assessor's office would be stacking up, and at some point they'd put a lien on the property if the taxes weren't paid. My hands were full enough as it was; I didn't have the time or energy to get into a legal dispute with someone who could get pro bono work from another attorney at his firm.

"Fine," I snapped. "Come over and drop off the damn check. Don't expect me to feed you doughnuts and coffee, though."

"It'll be after five, so a martini and some mixed nuts would be more appropriate."

"Not happening," I said, and ended the call. As I shoved the phone back into my pocket, I halfway expected Tom to call back, but apparently he was satisfied with the way he'd gotten the upper hand in that particular exchange and had decided to quit while he was ahead.

Jackass. That had been half the problem in our relationship—he was almost always able to argue rings around me. Which made sense, I supposed, since he was a lawyer and I wasn't. But it had annoyed the hell out of me when we were together, and it annoyed me even more now that we were divorced.

And as I gazed around the kitchen, I realized he'd screwed me over in yet another way. I'd let the house go this past week, preoccupied with the puppies, and it was something of a disaster. Personal pride wouldn't allow me to have Tom over with the place looking like a bomb had hit it, and so I was going to have to spend the rest of my day tidying and cleaning up. Good thing I didn't have any meetings planned, or I would have had to cancel them all.

"Asshole," I muttered, and made myself get to work.

My mood had recovered somewhat by the late afternoon, mostly because it did feel better to have the house clean again, even if my reasons for that day's frenzy of housework weren't exactly ones I would have chosen for myself. Although I'd begun to allow the puppies to roam throughout the ground floor of the house, I shut them back up in the family room again so they wouldn't make a mess of my clean floors. Frida went in with them, looking a little resigned. The weather had turned fair, and she probably would have preferred to have free rein to go in and out through the doggy door in the kitchen so she could enjoy the last bits of sunshine before the day ended.

But she didn't protest, and as I closed the pocket doors, I hoped Tom wouldn't want to poke around in the family room. I was under no obligation to explain myself to him, of course, and whether I had one litter of puppies or ten cooped up in there was my own business. However, he always had been far better at getting information out of me than I would have liked to admit, and I didn't want to be put in the position of dancing around his questions as to the puppies' origins.

Tom texted me as he was leaving the office, so I knew he'd be over a little after six, depending on traffic. By that time, dusk had fallen; I'd spotted Ben walking Rufus about an hour earlier and had waved as they went by, but he didn't make any overtures, and I was glad. Things were complicated enough without having Tom and Ben meet face to face. Of course, there wasn't anything going on between Ben and me, but there were some weird subtextual vibes to our relationship, and I definitely didn't want my ex-husband to pick up on any of that. No, he could stop by with the check, poke around and reassure himself that the house hadn't burned to the ground or been completely repainted dusty mauve or something like that, and then head off to a cozy evening with Antoinette in their glitzy Hancock Park home. At least, I assumed it was glitzy; I couldn't really imagine Antoinette living in a house that didn't look like something out of *Architectural Digest.*

I did my best to push her out of my head. She'd already occupied enough space there rent-free these past couple of years, and I was tired of her. Of the both of them, really. If Tom and I hadn't bought this house together, then I probably could have completely excised him from my life. It wasn't as though we'd had kids or anything—I'd tried to discuss the topic with him a few times, but he'd always put me off, saying he was focused on his career and that we'd have plenty of time for a family later. With hindsight, I probably should have taken his demurral as a warning sign, although at the time, I'd done my best to feel reassured that he was so intent on earning a good living, all the while telling myself that we still had years to worry about that sort of thing.

Anyway, Tom had already used up his allotment of my mental energy. All the same, I found myself smoothing my hair and putting on a fresh coat of tinted lip balm as the time for his arrival approached, even though I knew it was stupid of me to think he would even notice my appearance...and even more foolish for me to care what he thought.

The doorbell rang at ten minutes after six. The traffic must have been especially bad that night, since normally it wouldn't have taken him quite that long to get from the law firm's offices downtown to the house on Carroll Avenue. In fact, when I opened the door, I saw that he was frowning faintly, although his expression cleared just as soon as he saw me.

"Hey," he said. "Sorry about the time—there was an accident on Flower Street."

"It's all right," I replied automatically. I wouldn't bother to point out to him that I didn't have anything going on, that my dinner plans involved the excitement of reheating some Thai takeout and nothing more. "Come on in."

I stepped out of the way so he could come inside. Right away, I noticed how his gaze took in the gleaming floors, the vase full of inexpensive alstroemeria from the grocery store, yellow and cheerful against the dark green walls of the foyer. In the winter when the garden wasn't blooming, I liked to get fresh flowers when I could. It always helped to cheer up the place and remind me spring was on the way.

"The house looks good," Tom said.

"Thanks." *It damn well should look good, after the work I did today,* I thought, although of course I would never confess to my ex exactly how much effort I'd put in that afternoon to make sure everything was in order. "Do you want some water?" I added, trying to be somewhat hospitable.

His dark eyes glinted down at me. "Got anything a bit higher octane than that?"

"No," I replied primly. "I don't keep much alcohol in the house."

"Water, then," he said, looking somehow amused and resigned at the same time.

I led him into the kitchen and poured him some water from the pitcher I kept in the fridge. He took the glass from me and glanced around, and I had the urge to ask him if he'd brought his white gloves along for this inspection but somehow managed to hold my tongue.

"You can use the kitchen table to write the check," I told him.

Subtle? No, but I didn't want him hanging around any longer than necessary.

"Actually, it's already made out." He patted the breast pocket of his expensive suit jacket; although he'd loosened his tie a little, otherwise he looked immaculate. I would have guessed that he'd been in court that day, except he dressed like that all the time. Antoinette's inherited millions would definitely go a long way in keeping him in designer Italian suits. Reaching into his pocket, he added, "Here you go."

I took the check from him, glanced down at it, and frowned. "This is made out to me and not the assessor's office."

"Oh, I figured it would be easier that way. You can deposit the check in your account and then pay online, rather than having to mail it in or take it to a county office."

And also make me wait several days for the check to clear, since I knew my bank would sit on anything more than a couple of thousand dollars. Yes, I had until the end of the month to get all this straightened out, but I still didn't like the thought of such a delay.

If I pointed any of this out, however, I would only let Tom know how stressed I was about the situation. Better to just take the money, deposit the check the next day, and then make the online payment as soon as the funds had cleared.

"Thanks," I said, then folded up the check and stuck it in my jeans pocket, making a mental note to take it out before I deposited the pants in the hamper when I got undressed later that night. The last thing I wanted was to send the damn thing through the wash after having to suffer my ex-husband's company in order to get it. Since he just stood there, watching me, I felt compelled to add, "Anything else? Want to see the upstairs and make sure I haven't turned it into an S&M club or something?"

He chuckled. "No, I'm pretty sure you wouldn't do anything like that to the house." A certain light I remembered all too well entered his dark eyes. "You look good, Jillian. Kind of glowing. Anything you want to tell me about?"

"I'm trying a new moisturizer Naomi gave me," I said. If it had been anyone else, I might have been flattered...except I knew he had only made the compliment to see if it put me off balance. He didn't really care what I looked like, not when he had someone waiting for him who was infinitely more polished and glamorous than I would ever be. I pushed my glasses up on my nose, and he frowned ever so slightly. He'd always disliked those glasses and had encouraged me to wear contact lenses all the time. Honestly, I liked how I looked without them, too, but a lot of the time, I just didn't feel like fussing with contacts. And anyway, whether or not to wear glasses was my decision, and not something anyone else should have commented on.

At least he had the sense not to say anything about my glasses. He probably knew the remark about the moisturizer had been made as a joke, and so he replied, "Well, it seems to be working."

The time to be paying me compliments was long past, and so I didn't quite know what his game was. Probably just messing with me. He always had to feel as if he was in control of a situation, no matter what.

"Well, if there isn't anything else...." I began, and let the words trail off, hoping he'd get the hint.

Tom tilted his head slightly. "Big plans tonight?"

"Oh, sure," I lied. "Another girls' night out with Naomi."

He gave the briefest of nods to my reply. Maybe he'd been fishing to see if I had a date or something.

There was a joke.

"Then I'll be on my way," he said. "Sorry about the mixup, but you'll have everything sorted out soon enough."

No thanks to you, I thought, but I somehow managed to smile. "Yes—good thing I have until the end of the month."

We walked back to the entry. Just as Tom was reaching for the door to open it, the doorbell rang. I paused for a moment, wondering who in the world would be on my doorstep at six-thirty on a weeknight. Then I realized it could be someone dropping off a dog rescue, and I immediately grabbed the knob and opened the door.

Standing outside was Ben Blake. His usual smoothly relaxed expression had been replaced by one of almost panic. Not even glancing at Tom, he said, "Jillian, I need you to come over. There's something wrong with Rufus."

"Who's Rufus?" Tom asked, and Ben shot him an annoyed look.

"Who are *you?*"

"Ben, this is Tom…my ex," I said, then added hastily, "He came by to drop something off for me. What's the matter with Rufus?"

"He just threw up," Ben told me. "He hasn't eaten anything unusual, so I don't know what could be wrong. Can you come over and take a look at him?"

"Of course," I said. I looked up at Tom. "I really need to go. Have a safe drive home."

"Sure," he responded, his expression a little startled, as though he hadn't been expecting such an abrupt dismissal. Almost immediately, though, his eyes narrowed as he surveyed Ben, sizing him up, trying to ascertain where he fit in my life.

Well, there's a good question, I thought. *If you get it figured out, please let me know.*

But at least he stepped outside, and I was able to close the door, tell him a hasty goodbye, and then follow Ben down the front walk. We passed Tom's shiny new BMW 8-series sedan as we hurried across the street, but Ben didn't give it even the barest glance. Clearly, he had far more important matters on his mind.

For myself, I wasn't too worried…yet. Dogs had an uncanny ability to get into things they shouldn't eat, and considering Rufus's propensity for poking his nose everywhere and anywhere, I thought it fairly likely that this was just a temporary indisposition. I'd had the vet check him out as soon as he came into my care, and she hadn't found anything wrong with him. He'd been vaccinated, and Angelino Heights wasn't exactly a hotbed of tick activity.

However, even though I didn't think we had much to worry about, I was still grateful to Ben for showing up and forcing an end to my meeting with Tom. While I would have preferred that the two men never met at all, at least their introduction had been so hasty that I didn't think any lasting impressions had been involved.

We went inside Ben's house, and he led me down the center hall to a room off to the left, one with another fireplace and a flat-screen TV mounted to the wall above the hearth. Rufus lay on the rug, shivering.

"Has he thrown up more than once?" I asked, going over to where the dog waited so I could kneel down next to him.

"Not unless he vomited while I was out."

I looked around but didn't see any evidence of the dog being sick again—good thing, since the rug where I currently knelt looked like the real deal and not a modern Chinese knock-off of an antique Persian carpet. "Hey, buddy," I said, stroking Rufus behind the ears. "What's going on?"

The dog looked up at me with worried dark eyes. I moved my hands so I could stroke him along the belly and see if he was tender in any particular spot. He lay quietly, letting me perform a cursory examination, and he didn't whimper or wince or try to snap at me. Those all seemed like good signs, because if he'd been in any kind of pain, he wouldn't have been so patient. Ben stood a few feet away, brow furrowed, although he seemed content to remain silent until I rendered my judgment.

"I think he's all right," I said after a moment. "His belly doesn't seem sore, and he only vomited the one time. I have a feeling his body just wanted to get rid of something that didn't agree with him. But if he throws up again, or if he seems lethargic and doesn't want to eat, then you'll need to take him to the vet. I'll give you Rosalie's number—she's great."

Something in the taut set of Ben's shoulders seemed to relax just the slightest amount. "You're sure?"

I pushed myself to my feet. "I'm not a vet, Ben. But I've cared for a lot of dogs, and I have a feeling there's nothing seriously wrong with Rufus. You're new to all this, so I can see why you might have been alarmed."

"I wasn't alarmed," he returned immediately, chin lifted. "Concerned...yes, although he isn't really my dog."

"No, but you've given him a temporary home,

and you want to make sure he's okay." I decided I'd better leave it there, since I could tell Ben was feeling touchy about his momentary loss of control. God forbid he should show even the slightest sign of a human emotion.

No, that wasn't fair. He had emotions, even if he did seem to hold them in fairly tight check. Why, I didn't know, and I had a feeling he wasn't going to tell me any time soon. He certainly hadn't revealed anything about his background— no mention of where he'd lived before he came to Carroll Avenue, not even the slightest hint about friends or family or ex-girlfriends…or boyfriends, although I didn't really get that vibe from him. There weren't any family photos in the house, nothing to show he who he was or where he came from.

Once or twice, I'd wondered quite un-ironically whether he was in the witness protection program or something, except that I didn't think the U.S. government was in the habit of buying million-dollar-plus houses for the people it was protecting, or providing them with mint-condition vintage cars that looked as though they should be on the show circuit. However, it did feel to me as if he was hiding from something.

Maybe just himself.

"I suppose so," Ben allowed. He went over to Rufus and knelt down next to him, gently touching the sensitive skin behind the dog's ears. "Is there anything I should do?"

It was the care with which he treated Rufus that convinced me my neighbor wasn't completely devoid of compassion or concern. For some reason, though, it was much easier for him to connect with a dog than with a human being.

Actually, I could kind of sympathize with that sort of attitude.

"Just keep an eye on him," I said. "See if he drinks his water, if he's interested in food. Maybe try a treat first, see how that goes. But, like I said, if he throws up again or seems listless as time goes on, then call Rosalie. Tell her Jillian sent you."

"And her number?" he asked, pulling a slim black iPhone out of the breast pocket of his jacket. Apparently, he'd backtracked on his whole "no cellphone" policy, but I decided not to say anything.

I gave him the vet's phone number, then said, "Well, I need to get back. It's about time for the puppies' dinnertime feeding." About time for my dinner, too, but I left out that part. I didn't want Ben to think I was fishing for an invitation to stay at his place for dinner.

He surprised me, though. Expression diffident, he ventured, "Would you come back, though, once you're done feeding the puppies? I'd feel better if you were here for a while to keep an eye on Rufus. I can order in something—anything you like."

For just a moment, I hesitated. I didn't want to send the wrong message. Then again, he was asking me on Rufus's behalf. This wasn't a date or anything, just a friend doing a favor for a friend.

"Sure," I replied, and was relieved to see his face brighten. "I'll be back in about fifteen minutes."

"Thank you," he said.

"Not a problem," I told him.

And I sincerely hoped it wouldn't be.

CHAPTER TEN

WHEN I RETURNED, BEN TOLD ME THAT Rufus had eaten a dog treat and then promptly fell asleep.

"Although I'm sure he'll wake up as soon as our food arrives," he said, just the faintest hint of a smile touching the corners of his mouth. "I'm fairly certain that dog can hear me opening the refrigerator door from the other side of the house."

"It's a talent all dogs have," I replied with a grin. "Didn't you know that?"

"I'm finding out." We sat in the formal dining room, the long table covered with a fine white cloth as we ate Chinese takeout. Since Chinatown was less than a mile away, it was easy to get awesome Chinese delivery in our neighborhood.

No wine, though; evidently, Ben didn't want to risk even the faintest hint of intimacy with this meal. Just as well probably, since I was still feeling a little off-balance after my meeting with Tom. Why, I wasn't entirely sure, as nothing terrible had really happened. However, I couldn't help wondering whether he'd manufactured the whole crisis with the property tax payment as an excuse to see me. Again, I couldn't see any real reason why he would do such a thing, except as a petty way of messing with my head.

"So…that was your ex-husband?" Ben asked, and I raised surprised eyes from my plate of orange chicken.

"Yes, Tom," I replied, wondering why my neighbor had broached the subject. Surely, discussing my ex-husband wasn't the wisest thing to do if we really were trying to keep the conversation away from personal topics. "We had a little business to handle, so he swung by after work."

"He works downtown?"

"Yes. He's at Pierce, Morrow, and Levitt—they're one of L.A.'s biggest law firms."

"Partner?"

Again, I had to wonder what the point was of the third degree. But since none of this was exactly a state secret, I decided to go along…for the moment. "Yes, he made partner two years ago." And good thing he was already a partner when his affair with Antoinette Haskell was found out, or I had a feeling his bosses wouldn't have worked so hard to sweep the thing under the rug and do whatever they could to keep me happy so I wouldn't go blabbing about Tom's indiscretions to the California Bar Association. Having a partner disbarred was never a good look.

Ben picked up a piece of dim sum with some tongs and set it on his plate. His brows were pulled together, which seemed to indicate he wasn't entirely happy with my answers. I had no idea why. Did it really matter whether Tom was a partner at his law firm or not?

Well, not unless....

No, that was silly...unless it wasn't.

Could it be that Ben was asking all these questions about Tom because he was jealous?

Don't flatter yourself, I thought as I speared a piece of orange chicken, chewed, and then swallowed. *There could be all kinds of reasons why Ben might want to know about your ex.*

Except he hadn't asked any questions until he'd actually met Tom, had seen him in person. Even I had to admit that Tom cut a striking figure wherever he went. Feature for feature, he probably wasn't as handsome as Ben, but I supposed I could see how it would be difficult to find out that the woman you were interested in had a handsome, wealthy lawyer ex-husband…especially if said ex-husband had popped up out of nowhere to pay a surprise visit.

Put that way, the scenario I'd manufactured didn't seem quite so ludicrous. Or at least, it wouldn't have seemed ludicrous if someone other than me had been involved. I didn't think I quite measured up as the object of Ben Blake's infatuation. If that was what was even going on here.

"Is Rufus still over by you?" I asked. A clumsy way to change the subject, but I really didn't want to talk about Tom anymore.

The small frown that had puckered Ben's forehead disappeared, and he suddenly looked amused and indulgent. "Yes, he's sitting next to my chair and watching every morsel that goes in my mouth."

"Do you feed him from the table?"

Ben set down his fork and tilted an eyebrow at me. "Am I not supposed to?"

I shrugged. "Some would say you shouldn't feed dogs people food. I'm completely guilty of feeding my dog scraps—I'm just careful about how much I give her. But if you've been giving Rufus morsels from your dinner, then of course he's going to hang out at the table and beg."

"Guilty as charged." He glanced down at his

Mongolian beef. "This might be too rich for him, though."

"Especially after having an upset tummy," I said. "You should probably hold off on giving him any table scraps for a few days. Rufus won't like it, but better to be safe until he's completely out of the woods."

Ben nodded, and we continued with our meal. After a time, the dog came over to beg by my chair, since he'd obviously figured out that his master had no plans to be forthcoming with any table scraps, but I hardened my heart and did my best to ignore his importuning.

And when we were done, I bent down and patted Rufus and told him he was a good boy, just so he'd know it was nothing personal, only that he needed to watch his tummy for a bit until we knew he was completely well.

"Thank you for dinner," I said to Ben as he walked me to the door. "I was only going to have leftovers, so takeout from Jade Dragon was a nice treat."

"It's the least I could do to thank you for helping me with Rufus," he replied. "Although he seems to be quite recovered now."

Yes, he was—the dog had followed us down the hall and was still scampering around our legs, maybe hoping one of us would part with a last-minute fortune cookie or something.

"Dogs are resilient," I said. "Maybe a lot more so than people."

Ben paused, eyes scanning my face for a few seconds. I didn't know what he was looking for, or what he saw—maybe some evidence that I wasn't as over my ex-husband as I wanted people to believe. When he spoke, his tone was curiously soft...for him. "Sometimes people can surprise you."

I looked up at him, trying to seem friendly but neutral, and not like a woman who'd secretly wondered what it would feel like if he bent down and pressed his mouth against hers. "Yes," I said lightly, "sometimes they can."

And I made myself turn away from him and walk down the porch steps. Whatever was going on between us, I knew it wasn't time for a kiss. Not that night.

Maybe not ever.

Then again, who knew what would happen? After all, I'd been dreading seeing Tom again, and yet his presence at my house seemed to have changed something in Ben, or at least woken him up to something he hadn't wanted to acknowledge.

I'd just have to wait and see whether that change meant anything.

The next morning, I was surprised by a knock at my door at exactly 10 a.m. Considering the last time I'd had an unexpected caller, the person on my doorstep had been a cop, trepidation tickled its way along my nerve endings when I went to open the door. However, the woman who waited outside definitely wasn't a cop…even if her presence there was almost as much of a surprise.

"Hi, Janine," I said, wondering what in the world had prompted Janine Widawsky, who lived next door and had studiously avoided me ever since the incident with the first litter of puppies I'd rescued, to show up at my house early on a Saturday morning.

"Sorry to bother you," she said. Her eyes wouldn't quite meet mine, and I wondered if she was now regretting the way she'd sicced animal control on me for "disturbing the peace." Actually, I had a feeling the complaint had mostly originated with Alton, her extremely successful but supremely uptight mortgage broker husband, but that Janine had been forced to play bad cop. She extended an envelope toward me, and I took it, somewhat mystified. "The mailman put this in our mailbox a while back, and I kept meaning to bring it over. I just found it again today when I was going through our bills."

Since her tone was halfway contrite, I decided not to give her any grief over ignoring the neglected piece of mail for what sounded like an appreciable amount of time. It wasn't as if I got a lot of important mail anyway…the overdue bill from the county assessor's office notwithstanding. "Thanks," I said. "And don't worry about it—I doubt it's anything important."

"I hope not," she replied. "Anyway, have a good Saturday."

And she all but fled down the porch steps, walking quickly so I wouldn't have a chance to attempt something neighborly, like inviting her inside for a cup of coffee. Not that I would have made such an overture, since it was pretty clear what she and her husband thought of me. They didn't like the revolving dog door at my house, and they probably thought I brought down their property values by driving a three-year-old Prius and wearing faded jeans and Keds and Tom's old cast-off plaid shirts when I worked in the yard. Or maybe they disliked the very notion of me doing my own yard work, rather than hiring a land-scaping company the way everyone else on the street seemed to.

With a small shake of my head, I closed the front door and looked down at the envelope I held. It was heavy cream-colored paper, not your usual businesslike white. The return address was for an organization I'd never heard of.

The South Coast Foundation.

Hmm.

I peeked into the family room to check on the puppies—they seemed to like hanging out in there, even though I generally left the door open so they could come and go as they pleased—but they were sleeping, probably tired out from their breakfast. Frida wasn't there, though. I went into the kitchen and spied her having a drink of water, so I waited until she was done and then bent down and petted her sleek brown head.

"You've been doing a great job, sweetie," I told her. "I need to figure out something to do for you that's a special treat."

At the word "treat," her ears perked up, and I grinned.

"Okay," I said. "Just don't tell anyone I've been giving you off-schedule treats."

I set the envelope down on the counter so I could get her one of my homemade dog biscuits. She took it and then settled herself down on the rug in front of the sink so she could chew it in peace. That was one of her quirks—she always wanted to be on a soft surface of some sort when she was eating, which was why her food and water bowls were set on a cute red bone-shaped rug.

Smiling, I picked up the envelope and opened it, figuring it was some kind of business solicitation; since I had a registered nonprofit, I got a lot of mail from accountants and tax preparers and document-shredding services and the like. However, I had a mailbox at the local UPS store for my business correspondence, so it was a little strange for something like that to come directly to the house.

However, as I began to read the letter the envelope had contained, I realized this was something very different.

On behalf of the South Coast Foundation, I'd like to congratulate you on being chosen as one of L.A.'s top ten nonprofits. We would like to honor you at a banquet and awards ceremony to be held on Saturday, February 13th. Please call 323-555-3030 to confirm your attendance. All of our honorees are welcome to bring a plus-one.

Thank you for your valuable contribution to our city!

The letter was signed by someone named Luke Nicolini. Of course, I'd never heard of him, but I assumed he was the person who ran the South Coast Foundation.

And then the date clicked in my head.

Today was Saturday, February 13th. I'd probably been doing my best to ignore the whole thing, since Valentine's Day was looming, and I hated that goddamn holiday with a passion. Tom had proposed to me on Valentine's Day, and ever since our breakup, I'd done my best to pretend— like him—that it didn't exist.

Well, obviously, there was no way I could go. I felt awful for blowing off the foundation—and this Luke Nicolini person—but I didn't see how I could possibly call at the eleventh hour and say, *Oh, hey, I decided to show up to your little gala after all.*

Very bad form, even if none of this was my fault.

Thanks, Janine, I thought sourly, even as I told myself to look on the bright side. It wasn't as if I had anything to wear to a fancy banquet. And as for a "plus-one"? Yeah, right.

"Knock-knock," Naomi said right then, sticking her head in past the kitchen door. She must have gotten a good look at my expression, because she added, "What's wrong?"

"This," I replied, and held the letter out toward her.

She came inside and closed the door behind her. Frida, done with her dog cookie, came over for her usual pat on the head. Naomi wasn't dog crazy like I was, but she at least appreciated my pup's overwhelming awesomeness.

Doggy protocol observed, she directed her attention to the letter I'd handed her. I could tell when she got to the pertinent part, because her brows drew together and she looked up at me. "The thirteenth? That's today."

"I know," I said glumly. "The letter got misdirected, and Janine just brought it over this morning."

"How nice of her to sit on it for…." Naomi's words trailed off as she came over to where I stood, picked up the envelope from the counter behind me, and read the postmark. "…nearly two weeks."

"She said she kept meaning to bring it over, but she forgot."

"Uh-huh." My friend set the envelope back down, and then planted her hands on her hips as she sent an evil glare in the direction of Janine's house next door. "How very convenient."

I tilted my head at Naomi. "Oh, come on. I don't think it's anything she did on purpose. How could she even have known what the letter inside that envelope said?"

"I don't know," Naomi replied. "But I still think it's a little fishy."

"Well, that's your prerogative," I said, my tone mild. "Anyway, done is done. The event is tonight, so I've missed my chance."

"Not necessarily. Why don't you try calling and letting them know what happened?"

I stared at her, wondering if she'd taken leave of her senses. "Naomi, it's Saturday morning. I'm sure that's a business number. No one's going to be there answering phone calls."

"Maybe not," she allowed. Obviously, she

wasn't about to let it go, however, because she added, "But I don't see the harm in trying."

"And what if someone answers and says it's okay?" I asked. "I haven't got anything to wear—I don't have a date—"

"Oh, stop being a Debbie Downer," Naomi cut in. "We're practically the same size—you can borrow something of mine. As for a date"—she paused, dark eyes glinting with mischief—"you can ask Ben to come with you."

"I will not," I said. As much as part of me thought it might be pretty amazing to have Ben accompany me to some fancy gala banquet, I knew he would be utterly mortified if I inquired whether he'd want to be my plus-one for that sort of function. And what about the humiliation if he said no?

"Fine," Naomi said airily. "I'll ask him for you. But this is all academic if it's too late to even go, so call." Her gaze flicked to my cell phone, which I'd left lying on the kitchen counter earlier that morning. "Go on. Do it."

Oh, this was all crazy. But I knew I couldn't wriggle my way out of this one, not unless I wanted to have Naomi give me crap about my cowardice for at least the next six months. Holding back a sigh, I picked up the phone, then entered the phone number from the letter.

Please go to voicemail, I prayed. *Please go to voicemail.*

Of course, it didn't. "South Coast Foundation," a woman's voice said.

"Oh, hi," I faltered. "Um, I know this is extremely late notice, but I actually just got your letter about the gala today—it was delivered to a neighbor's house by mistake—and I was wondering if there was any way I could still attend the event tonight."

"And you're with which nonprofit?" the woman asked.

"Little Angels Chihuahua Rescue."

A brief silence on the other end of the line, making me think she was looking it up on her computer. "Oh, yes," the woman said. "Jillian Torres?"

"Yes, that's me."

"We'd love to have you, Jillian. Seven o'clock in the Crystal Ballroom at the Biltmore. Have you been there before?"

"Yes," I replied. No way in the world would I admit that my wedding reception had been held there. Not in the Crystal Ballroom—that space had been beyond even the fairly lavish budget Tom and I had set for the event—but despite that, I was all too familiar with the venue. "I know it pretty well."

"Wonderful," the woman said. "Then we'll see

you—and your guest—tonight at seven. Have a lovely day!"

She hung up then, and I pulled the phone away from my ear and met Naomi's expectant gaze. "It's a go," I said.

"Yay!" My friend clapped her hands like a little kid getting ready to open presents on Christmas morning. Not that Naomi celebrated Christmas—she was Jewish—but still, I knew she was probably thrilled at the chance to play evening gown Barbie with me. She always bemoaned the way I dressed like such a schlump when I apparently had such "good material" to work with. I didn't know about that, but I did know I would be in good hands with her. "I'm so glad I don't have anything on the schedule today. That means Eloy and I can devote all our energy to making you perfect."

"There's no need to drag Eloy into this—" I began, but she shook her head.

"Sweetie, he's a hair and makeup genius. Of course, I'm going to drag him into this. How else do you think I look so flawless all the time?"

I thought she might have been indulging in a bit of hyperbole, since I thought she looked fine even on the days when she did her own hair, but I had to admit that she looked perfect whenever she was on camera. "All right," I said reluctantly.

"Great." She was beaming as she reached into

her pocket and pulled out her iPhone. "I'll call him and tell him that he needs to come over this afternoon. Now, you scram—you need to go over and ask Ben if he'll go with you to the gala."

"He's going to say no," I told her, figuring I might as well set myself up for disappointment in advance.

She lifted a skeptical eyebrow. "You don't know that for sure. And if he is stupid enough to turn you down, well, I'll be your date instead."

Actually, that sounded like a great idea. Showing up with my YouTube celeb bestie would probably score me a few bonus points, and would also allow me to avoid the humiliation of having Ben give me one of his patented *are you insane?* looks when I asked him to be my date. "Can't we just make that the plan?"

"No," Naomi said firmly. "Don't be a coward —and don't think I haven't noticed the way you two have been dancing around each other for the past week and a half."

"We have not—"

"Oh, yes, you have. It's so obvious you're into each other, even if both of you are too chickenshit to admit it. This will give you an excuse to have a proper date. So get your ass over there already, or I'll go and ask Ben for you."

"You wouldn't," I said, even though I feared she probably would, if pressed.

All she had to do was cross her arms and lift another eyebrow at me in reply.

"All right, all right," I said, knowing resistance was futile…and also realizing that if I pushed her about being my date instead of Ben, she'd only tell me hell, no, and push me out the door anyway. Better to think that was the real reason for my capitulation, rather than admit I actually did want to go to a fancy party with Benjamin Blake. "I'm going. Just hang around until I get back—I don't like leaving the puppies all alone."

"I'm not going anywhere," she told me. "In fact, I'll even dog-sit for you tonight. How's that for an added incentive?"

All right, that helped a little, although I didn't know if free dog-sitting was still enough to compensate me for having to go across the street and ask Ben Blake out on a date. No, that was the wrong way to frame the situation. This was just a friend helping out a friend. After all, he'd already come to my rescue once, so why wouldn't he do the same this time? Maybe accompanying me to a black tie gala wasn't quite the same thing as being my accomplice as we stole a litter of neglected puppies from a Monterey Park backyard, but still….

"Sounds good," I managed, and then forced myself to leave the kitchen and march out the front door. It was a pretty day, with a fresh sea breeze and a few puffy clouds dotting a sky that looked bluer than any sky in Los Angeles had a right to be. I chose to take the good weather as a positive sign. If this had been a doomed venture, it would have been raining buckets, right?

I paused to look from side to side before I crossed the street. Carroll Avenue wasn't overly busy most of the time, but on Saturdays we often got tours from local conservancy groups coming through, and I figured it was better to be safe. Getting run over by a tour van would definitely not be a good omen.

But the street was clear, and so I was able to hasten across without incident. Forcing myself up the front steps to Ben's house required a little more effort, but soon enough, I found myself standing there, staring at the doorbell and wondering how long it would take me to work up the nerve to push it.

Fate seemed to solve that particular conundrum for me, because in the next moment, the door opened and I found myself staring up into Ben's face. He took a step backward, clearly startled, and then recovered himself enough to say, "Good morning, Jillian. To what do I owe this pleasure?"

I realized then that he held a leash in his hand, and Rufus was straining at the end of that leash, obviously raring to go on his morning walk. As usual, my timing was impeccable.

"Oh, I just wanted to ask you something," I said, knowing I needed to force out the words or I'd never have the courage to do this.

"Ask me what?" His grip tightened on the leash, since Rufus was doing his best to push past me and get down to that oh-so-inviting grass in the front yard.

"Well, it's—" I pulled in a breath and went on, "That is, I've been invited to a gala for local nonprofits at the Biltmore downtown tonight, and I was wondering if you were free. To go with me, I mean."

He stared at me as if I'd just asked him to buy a Winnebago and tour the country with me and the dogs. "On a date?" he asked in incredulous tones.

"Not a date," I said quickly. "Just…as a way to help me out. You see, the invitation says I can bring a plus-one, and I thought, well, if you weren't busy…."

A very long pause. Then he said, "This is very short notice."

"I know," I replied. "I actually just found out about it—the letter went in my next door neighbor's mailbox instead of mine, and she just passed it along to me this morning."

"Ah." Another one of those unnerving pauses, followed by, "Is this a formal event?"

"Well, it's a gala," I said. "I assume that means it's at least semiformal. You'd need to wear a suit, I think." As if that would be a problem for him. The man dressed like he was modeling for *Town & Country* magazine or something.

Ben nodded, and actually looked a little pleased. Maybe he was glad to have the chance to dress up for something. "What time?"

"It starts at seven, so I supposed we'd need to leave around six-thirty."

"All right," he said. "I'll pick you up at six-thirty—in my car," he added severely. "I certainly don't want to go to the Biltmore in that electrified tin can of yours."

"Sure," I replied, relief surging through me. And honestly, I thought I liked the idea of showing up in his vintage Jag. It was definitely a lot classier than my Prius. "Thank you so much, Ben. Oh, and Naomi can watch Rufus. She's already offered to dog-sit the puppies."

"Well, that's a relief," Ben said, his tone dry, as if he wasn't sure that having free dog-sitting thrown into the equation made it all better. "But speaking of Rufus, I've really kept him long enough from his walk. I'll see you at six-thirty."

"Yes, see you then." I flashed a smile at him

and then hurried down the steps so I was out of the way.

For some reason, that smile remained plastered on my face as I crossed the street back to my house. I would never have believed it if someone had told me such a thing even an hour earlier, but I was actually going on a date with Benjamin Blake...even if he didn't quite know it.

CHAPTER ELEVEN

"Stop blinking," Eloy told me in severe tones while also rolling his eyes at Naomi, who sat on a stool nearby so she wouldn't miss out on any of the preparations.

"Sorry," I said. "I'm not used to someone coming at my eyeball with tweezers."

"You didn't wear false eyelashes at your wedding?" Naomi asked, looking almost scandalized.

"Of course not," I snapped. "Tom knew what I looked like—I didn't see the need to put on a big show."

Well, maybe that was a slight exaggeration. I'd had my hair and makeup professionally done for the wedding, of course, but I'd told the makeup artist that I didn't want anything over the top. She knew what she was doing—somehow she'd managed to make my lashes look twice as thick and long as they actually were, all without the help of false eyelashes, which had suited me just fine.

"And I don't need to go all crazy now," I went on. "Look, Eloy, I appreciate what you're trying to do, but I honestly think false eyelashes are a bit much. This is just an awards dinner, not the Academy Awards or something."

Instead of mollifying him, my comment seemed to make him appear even more appalled. "Honey, did you know the Crystal Ballroom at the Biltmore is where the Oscars started all those years ago? Show a little respect."

I actually did know that little factoid, probably because I'd read it on the hotel's website when Tom and I were researching venues for our wedding reception. However, I decided this was one hill I probably didn't need to die on. "Fine," I sighed. "Bring on the eyelashes."

"Praise the Lord," Eloy said, and went at it. I did my best to hold still while he pressed the damn things against my eyelids, even though my own lashes wanted to flutter like frantic butterflies in an effort to keep him away.

And I sat quietly as he applied shadow and liner and did some sort of complicated thing he called contouring, which seemed to be a careful application of shadows and highlights to my cheekbones and jaw and brow bones. Honestly, even though I watched him as he worked—and thought idly that he smelled really good, of some sort of cologne that was almost vanilla-ish but in a masculine way—I really couldn't tell exactly what he was doing. The one thing I did know was that I'd never be able to duplicate the effect on my own, not in a million years.

But somehow he'd managed to make my cheekbones look higher and fuller, my nose slimmer and my jaw line sleek and defined. I still looked like me—well, except for those damn false eyelashes, I supposed—but a far better-looking "me" than I'd ever seen before.

"You are a wizard, Eloy," I said as he packed up his makeup kit and got to work on my hair. We'd decided to leave it mostly down, but he had insisted on using a big-barrel curling iron to set soft waves in my waist-length locks.

"I know," he replied with a grin, while Naomi rolled her eyes. "This is fun, though. I've been itching to get my hands on you for months."

"I bet you say that to all the girls," I returned, and he chuckled while Naomi let out a peal of laughter. At the same time, though, I noticed how he sent a quick sideways glance at her, as if to gauge how she'd reacted to my quip.

Interesting.

And once my hair was done, all smooth and

gleaming and falling in perfect waves over my shoulders, it was time to shoo Eloy away—we'd been working in the dressing area of Naomi's bedroom, which had a real, honest-to-God Holly-wood-style mirror framed in lights and a marble counter beneath large enough to accommodate even all of Eloy's beauty tools—so I could get out of the robe I was wearing and into the dress Naomi had chosen for me.

I'd thought she'd put me in something simple, probably black, since it seemed the standard choice of evening wear. However, she'd talked me into a cobalt-blue strapless dress whose floaty, filmy skirt contrasted with its structured bodice, although it didn't fight it. I had to admit the color looked gorgeous with my light blonde hair and dark blue eyes, even if I wasn't sure whether I really wanted to go out in public with quite so much cleavage on display.

"It's a little boobalicious, don't you think?" I asked, doing my best to haul the bodice up another inch or so.

"No, it's perfect," she said severely. "It actually fits you better than it fits me. I'm not even sure why I bought it, except that I probably didn't want to pass up a genuine Vera Wang for seventy percent off."

Even at that big a discount, the gown had probably set her back a fair bit, but I didn't comment. Naomi went to enough fancy events that she could justify the expense—for all I knew, she could write off large chunks of her wardrobe as a business expense—and I had to count myself lucky that she had something I could use.

"And big earrings, I think," she went on. "No necklace. Try these."

She handed me some gorgeous dangles of engraved silver and what looked like cabochon sapphires. They could have been costume; they could have been real. With Naomi, sometimes it was hard to know, because she mixed things as her style dictated and never seemed to care how much something was worth, only whether it looked good or not.

I put on the earrings and had to admit they worked perfectly with the gown. They were my only adornment, since she didn't offer any bracelets or rings, and I knew I didn't have anything of my own that would have worked. She slipped a silvery gray pashmina shawl over one arm and handed me a silver-beaded evening purse, big enough for lipstick and cash and maybe my house key.

"Okay, you're perfect, Cinderella," she said, after stepping away so she could survey me from head to toe—the silver sandals I wore under the gown's voluminous skirt were also hers, of course—and then give an approving nod. "Let's get you over to your place so you won't be late for Prince Charming."

"Ben is *not* Prince Charming," I protested, and she grinned.

"Well, okay, I'm not going to argue with that. But he is your date, and you don't want to make him wait."

I decided not to argue with that comment—not when she'd made a rhyme and everything—and so we went downstairs and collected Eloy, who was going to hang out with Naomi at my place so they could both watch the dogs. He also looked impressed by my appearance.

"You should wear that color more often," he told me, and I murmured that I'd think about it.

To tell the truth, though, I wasn't sure whether I'd feel comfortable wearing such an eye-catching hue on a daily basis. It was one thing when I was getting dressed up for a special evening out, and quite another when contemplating clothes that I'd wear to walk the dog or go to the grocery store or mow the lawn.

But I could worry about all that later. We hurried out the back door of Naomi's house, went through the gate that separated our two properties, and then climbed the stairs on the back porch to come in through my kitchen. From there, the two of them went into the family room to turn on the TV and hang with the puppies, while I went to the front of the house to wait for Ben. In a way, I sort of did feel like a princess in her tower room, waiting for her prince to come to her, just because of the turret that was the main architectural feature of the living room. However, I had to admit that Ben Blake wasn't exactly your stereotypical prince.

At a little before six-thirty, I saw a pair of headlights pull up to the curb in front of the house, and a moment later, the doorbell rang. I got up to open it…and stood there, astonished.

The man looked damn good in a tuxedo.

I realized he was gaping at me in roughly the same way I was staring at him, and so I said quickly, "Hi, Ben. Go ahead and take Rufus into the family room."

Because he had the dog with him, just as I'd suggested. Ben recovered himself enough to reply, "Yes, of course," and then led Rufus into the room where Naomi and Eloy and the rest of the dogs were waiting. I heard him offer a muffled greeting, followed by a reply from Naomi, and then Ben came back out to the entry where I was waiting.

"All set?" I asked, and he nodded.

"Yes—we'd better get going."

It was probably silly of me to think he was going to offer his arm. Instead, he went out the front door and down the steps, and I followed him, doing my best to hold up my skirts so they wouldn't pick up any stray bits of grass or other yard detritus from the front walk.

At least he did open the passenger door for me, and waited until I'd gotten my voluminous skirts scrunched into the footwell before he closed the door and went around to the driver's side. A moment later, we were pulling out from the curb and were on our way.

It wasn't until we'd gotten on the 101 Freeway to make the short hop to the Temple Street exit that he spoke. "You look…different…tonight."

"Oh, well," I said as I pulled the shawl a little closer around my bare shoulders. "Naomi and Eloy couldn't resist the opportunity to play dress-up with me. This is all Naomi's stuff—I just borrowed it."

"Ah." Ben hesitated, then said, "It looks nice."

"Thank you," I replied, glad that the interior of the car was fairly dark and he wouldn't be able to see the way I was blushing. All right, in the grand scheme of compliments, "nice" was pretty lackluster. Still, I was surprised he'd said even that much.

A little while later, we were pulling up in front of the Biltmore Hotel, where a valet came around to take the car. I could tell that Ben wasn't terribly thrilled to hand over his keys to a stranger, but the only other option would have been to park in the public underground lot a block away at Pershing

Square, and wandering around downtown L.A. in an evening gown and heels was not exactly how I wanted to spend my Saturday night.

Since I really wasn't expecting Ben to offer me his arm, I wasn't disappointed as he strode into the foyer of the hotel a pace or two ahead of me. I did my best to keep up, but I wasn't used to wearing high heels—even though Naomi had taken pity on me and given me a pair of beautiful ankle-strap kitten-heel sandals instead of some of the four-inch stilettos she owned. Two steps in those, and I probably would have pitched right over on my face.

The Crystal Ballroom was one level up and to the right. The beautiful double staircase with the little balcony that overlooked the lobby had been featured in countless films and television shows; if my dress had been white and not bright blue, I might have been tempted to pause there and have an "Evita" moment as I gazed down at the people below. As it was, I followed Ben up the stairs and then waited in a short line as a pretty blonde woman in a black short-sleeved cocktail dress checked the people ahead of us off a list she held on a clipboard.

"Jillian Torres and guest," I told her, and she smiled.

"I'm so glad you could make it," she said, her voice somehow familiar. Then it clicked.

"Oh—was it you I spoke to on the phone?"

"Yes," she replied. "I'm Lindsay Johnson, Mr. Nicolini's assistant. You're at table 3A—it's a little to the left, up toward the front. You'll find place cards there."

"Thank you so much," I replied, and began to head in the direction she'd indicated.

Next to me, Ben looked positively thunderous, although there certainly wasn't anything in what Lindsay Johnson had told us that should have evoked such a response. Voice almost a growl, he said, "You didn't say anything about Luke Nicolini being involved with this event."

"Does it matter?" I responded, a little startled. Eyes narrowing, I asked, "Why, do you know him?"

"We've had…business dealings," Ben said. His mouth shut tight after that comment, as if he had no intention of providing any further information.

If the expression on his face was any indication, those "business dealings" hadn't worked out particularly well for Ben. Which was unfortunate, but since we were here, there wasn't much I could do to remedy the situation except hope the two men would be able to stay out of one another's orbits. I figured that probably shouldn't be too difficult; it looked as though there were close to a hundred people in attendance at the gala already, and no doubt Mr. Nicolini had plenty to keep him occupied.

"Sorry," I murmured. "It just never occurred to me that you might be acquainted with the organizer of the event." Some impulse prompted me to add, "Maybe if you'd told me even a little bit about yourself, I would have known who to avoid."

Ben's mouth tightened, but then he gave a shrug that didn't fool me for a second and said, "It's not an issue. I'm sure Mr. Nicolini will be so busy this evening that he won't even notice I'm here. Drink?"

This last question was tacked on to his comment in an off-hand tone, as if he really didn't care one way or another whether I had one. However, considering that this evening hadn't exactly gotten off to an auspicious start, I thought it was probably a good idea to have a drink to take the edge off, so to speak.

"A glass of white wine would be great," I said, and he didn't reply, only gave me a curt nod and threaded his way through the crowd toward the opposite side of the room, where an open bar had been set up.

Holding back a sigh, I sat down at our table and managed to smile at the people seated there. I guessed they were probably other honorees, since they wore their "dress-up" clothes a bit awkwardly, as if they weren't really used to putting on fine feathers and going out to black tie events.

You and me both, I thought, although I knew I was pulling it off a bit better, thanks to Eloy and Naomi's expert assistance. If I'd had to dress myself and do my own hair and makeup, I doubt I would have looked even a quarter as good as I currently did.

I smiled at them and introduced myself, while they told me their names and organizations—one a food bank, another a shelter for trans youth, yet another a foundation that provided counseling and professional clothing for homeless women trying to reenter the workforce. Those all sounded like extremely noble causes, making me wonder if my little chi rescue outfit was a bit frivolous in contrast.

But before any of us had to try to make more small talk, Ben came back to the table, a glass of white wine in either hand. Even though he still didn't appear precisely thrilled to be there, I had to admit that he looked amazing in his tuxedo, like a movie star who'd deigned to come slumming with the *hoi polloi* for the evening. If it had been anyone else, I might have wondered why he had a tuxedo as part of his wardrobe, but my neighbor was something of a peacock.

"Thank you," I said when he handed me one of the glasses of wine.

He didn't reply, only inclined his head slightly as he took the only unoccupied seat at the table. Still without speaking, he lifted his wine and took a sip, his gaze roving the crowd—looking for Luke Nicolini, I assumed.

Because I was watching Ben closely, I could see the precise moment when he caught sight of the man in question. The flickering movements of his eyes halted abruptly, and his lips—lips that were way more sensual than they had any right to be—thinned.

I followed his gaze and saw a tall, dark-haired man in an impeccably cut tuxedo standing next to an extremely pretty woman around my age, maybe a little younger, with brown hair and big brown eyes. She wore a red beaded gown and appeared to be laughing at something her companion had just said. As far as I could tell, he was older than she, maybe in his late thirties or early forties, handsome and with striking blue eyes. Another couple stood with them, an attractive sandy-haired man in his middle thirties and a beautiful woman with coppery red hair who also looked younger than her companion.

As far as I could tell, they all seemed to be enjoying themselves, talking with animated hand gestures, laughing from time to time. If the tall man with the near-black hair really was Luke Nicolini, he didn't exactly look like the sort of person who would be involved with anything nefarious. How could he be, if he was the sort of philanthropist who threw parties like this to honor local charities?

Unfortunately, since Ben and I were in a public place, I couldn't ask him point-blank what his history with Luke Nicolini actually was. About all I could do was comment on the wine, and ask Ben if he'd ever been to the Biltmore before.

"Once," he said, his tone almost absent, as if he was thinking about something else entirely. "A long time ago."

I would have asked for more details, except I was pretty sure he wouldn't provide any. So far, he'd been awfully good at keeping silent on the subject of his past, and this definitely wasn't the place for any attempts at getting him to open up.

All right. I'd just have to try some other topic of conversation. No way was I going to sit there silently next to him, not when I'd noticed one of the other honorees, a thin woman in her late forties or early fifties, giving Ben and me a quizzical look, as if she couldn't quite figure out what the two of us were doing together.

You're not the only one, I thought. While it was getting harder and harder to ignore my physical attraction to Ben, I had to admit that he was an odd duck, prickly and almost impossible to get to know.

Except...there had been those few rare moments when he'd let his guard down, when he'd smiled at me or unbent enough to chase Rufus around the yard, playing keep-away with a ball, that told me there was something within him that was worth waiting for. Was worth working hard for, even if I couldn't be sure whether Ben wanted me to make the effort.

To my relief, the lights flickered slightly, giving the signal that the open "social" part of the evening was now ending, and dinner would start to be served. Even as the banquet staff began to come around with the salad course, Luke Nicolini left the little group he'd been standing with and went up to the small dais that had been constructed at the front of the room. On the dais was a podium flanked by several lovely arrangements of lilies and roses, and it was there that he stood.

"Welcome to the South Coast Foundation's first annual celebration of local nonprofits," he said. He had a nice voice, cultured and deep. I wondered where he was from; he didn't really have a discernible accent, but there was something about the way he shaped his words that seemed to indicate he wasn't a West Coast native.

In fact, the way he spoke reminded me of Ben, although the timbre of Luke Nicolini's voice was different, slightly deeper. Still, the similarity made me frown slightly.

Everyone clapped, and I belatedly joined in the applause, although I supposed doing so was a little self-congratulatory. Next to me, Ben pressed his hands together, but he only clapped a single time before picking up his wine glass once more. I noticed how he wasn't looking at Luke Nicolini directly, as if he feared that letting his gaze rest on our host would somehow attract his attention. That seemed a little silly to me, but obviously, I wasn't going to comment on his behavior.

"You all give so much to this community," Mr. Nicolini went on, "that I thought it only fitting that I should give a little bit back to you." He paused and appeared to straighten a stack of envelopes that sat on the podium next to the microphone. "And I also figured I'd get this over with so we can all get on with enjoying ourselves." That remark earned him a scatter of laughter, and he smiled. Something about the shift in expression seemed to light up his face, and I was struck again by how handsome he was. "So please," he continued, "as I call your names, come up to the podium."

A nervous thrill went through me. I'd had no idea we would be expected to go up in front of everyone to collect our certificates, or whatever it was Luke Nicolini planned to give out as his little tokens of appreciation. Problem was, I didn't see any way to back out of this. I'd just have to walk up there and pray I didn't trip on my skirt or do something equally mortifying in front of everyone.

At least he seemed to be handing out the envelopes in alphabetical order of the nonprofit involved, so Little Angels Chihuahua Rescue fell pretty much in the middle. When he called out my name, I forced myself to get up from my chair and walk to the podium, although I made sure to keep my gaze fixed somewhere in the middle distance so I wouldn't make eye contact with anyone and lose my nerve.

"Thank you for all your hard work," Luke Nicolini told me as he handed me an envelope. "I hope you can put this to good use."

I murmured a thank-you and managed to smile. There was something about his blue eyes that seemed almost too piercing, as if he was able to look right through me and see all my faults and foibles. Heat rushed to my cheeks, but I was somehow able to turn around and walk back to my table without tripping or otherwise making a fool of myself.

When I got there, I saw that the waiters had already brought our salads. Good. I'd put some food inside me, and then I'd go get another drink. I absolutely hated being on display like that.

"So, what is it?" Ben asked, gaze moving to the envelope I had clutched in my hand. "A nice certificate you can frame?"

I somehow doubted that, just because the envelope was a regular business-sized one, and any certificate inside would have gotten creased from being folded up to fit. Doing my best to ignore my companion's sardonic tone, I said, "I don't know."

Clearly, everyone else at the table had organizations whose titles fell in the second half of the alphabet, since I was the first one to receive an envelope. Trying to ignore their curious gazes, I slid a finger under the flap, breaking the seal, and then peeked inside.

Holy shit.

"Well?" Ben said.

I leaned close to him and murmured, "It's a check for fifty thousand dollars."

"*What?*"

I pulled the envelope open a little further, just enough for him to see its contents. There was something satisfying about seeing the way his eyes widened. It seemed obvious enough to me that he hadn't expected Luke Nicolini to display quite that much largesse.

Still speaking in a low voice, I said, "I had no idea—I just thought this was a recognition kind of thing. I wasn't expecting to be handed a check that would cover most of this year's operating costs."

Ben seemed to have recovered his composure, because his shoulders lifted and he shifted in his seat so he faced forward again. "Luke Nicolini can afford it."

I had no doubt that he could. That wasn't the point. However, the edge to Ben's voice told me I'd better let the matter go. Trying not to frown, I folded the envelope in half so it would fit in my evening bag, then stuffed it inside. Luckily, everyone else at the table had been occupied with watching the other honorees go onstage to get their checks, so I didn't think anyone had noticed our little exchange.

At least now that my moment in the spotlight was over, I could spread my napkin on my lap and pick up my fork and take a bite of salad. It was good, just a simple garden salad with a light vinaigrette, but everything tasted super-fresh, and it gave me something to distract myself from Ben's odd behavior. All right, I supposed I could see why he might still be holding a grudge if he had some kind of history with Luke Nicolini, although I thought it might have been nice if he could have set his dislike of the man aside for just a few minutes so he could be happy for me.

After a brief pause, Ben picked up his fork as well and began to eat. I reflected it was a good thing that our host was still talking, since that meant neither of us had to attempt any kind of conversation. Eventually, though, all the envelopes had been handed out and Mr. Nicolini left the stage to join the rest of the group at his table.

I couldn't quite miss the way Ben's eyes narrowed as they focused on the sandy-haired man and his redhead wife. That is, I guessed they were married, since I thought I'd spied the glint of a large diamond on her left hand, and the man with her was definitely wearing a wedding band.

"Let me guess," I said in an undertone to Ben. "That other guy screwed you over in a business deal, too."

At once, he scowled, and stabbed a cherry tomato with unnecessary violence. "It wasn't a business deal," he said. "But it doesn't matter. I'm over it."

I wanted to remark that it sure as hell didn't look as though he was over anything, but I knew any comments along those lines would only serve to worsen Ben's mood…which wasn't exactly sunny to begin with. Instead, I told him, "Well, I'm fine with slipping out of here as soon as dinner is over. That way, you'll be gone before they even realize you were here."

This reassurance seemed to have the desired effect, since his frown eased itself just a little bit, and the tight lines of his jaw seemed to relax.

"Good idea. I'm sure Luke Nicolini will be so surrounded by people wanting to thank him that we can leave without notice."

His remark seemed to be only the truth, because I could see several individuals come up to him with gratitude clear in their expressions, even though it was fairly obvious that he just wanted to go back to his table so he could sit down and eat his dinner. I probably should have been one of them as well, except I knew Ben would go ballistic if I tried to approach Mr. Nicolini to express my gratitude for the extremely generous donation his foundation had given my nonprofit. No, I'd just have to write a nice thank-you note and mail it as soon as possible; luckily, I had some very cute custom-printed notecards with the Little Angels logo on them—an artist friend had designed the logo for me—and I'd use one of those for my thank-you to Luke Nicolini and the South Coast Foundation.

The rest of dinner passed without incident, and Ben even unbent enough to share some small talk with the other people seated at our table, although I could tell he was itching to get out of there. And because he was antsy, I was, too. The food had been wonderful, and I had to admit that there was something nice about getting out of the house and being around other adults for a change. On the other hand, the boned bodice of the gown

I wore was starting to dig in under my arms, and the clip-on earrings Naomi had loaned we were definitely beginning to bite my earlobes.

As soon as the waiters had cleared the remnants of our tiramisu, I leaned toward Ben and said, "Now is probably a good time to go."

He nodded, relief clear in his expression. We said our goodbyes to everyone at our table, and I picked up my purse with its precious check inside and began to follow Ben toward the exit.

We only were halfway there when Luke Nicolini stepped in front of us, wearing a smile as he asked, "Leaving so soon?"

CHAPTER TWELVE

I GROUND TO A HALT. EVEN THOUGH I DIDN'T dare look over at Ben, I had to assume that the scowl had made a reappearance. "Oh," I said brightly, knowing that we probably looked like a couple of kids trying to sneak off school grounds in between classes, "thank you for everything, Mr. Nicolini, but I've got a litter of two-week-old chihuahua puppies at home that a couple of friends are watching for me, and I really need to get back and check on them."

"Luke," he corrected me, still smiling. "And if you have friends dog-sitting for you, why the need to leave the party so soon?"

"Because they're not exactly dog people," Ben put in, his tone almost defiant, as if he'd decided that he might as well dive headfirst into this confrontation, since there was no way to avoid it. "They're just doing a favor for Jillian."

Without missing a beat, Luke said, "How are you, Ben? You're looking very well."

"Thanks," he replied, sounding so sulky, he might as well have said, *No thanks to you.*

Still sounding way too cheery—although I didn't know quite else what to do—I said, "Yes, I had no idea you and Ben were acquainted. He doesn't talk much about his friends."

That careless remark earned me a glare so sharp, I was half expecting daggers to come flying out of Ben's eyes and stab me in the throat. Oops.

"Somehow, that doesn't surprise me," Luke said. His gaze shifted to Ben. "Why don't you come over to our table for a bit? I know Allan would love a chance to talk to you."

"No, I don't think so," Ben replied. He shoved his hands in the pockets of his trousers. "It looks as if he's busy."

I glanced past Luke Nicolini's shoulder to the table in question, where the sandy-haired man— who I assumed must be this "Allan" person, even if I didn't have any idea what his former relation- ship with Ben had been—was leaning toward the pretty redhead and whispering something in her ear. She laughed and swatted him on the arm, while the brunette who I assumed was Luke's wife sat back in her chair and shook her head in amusement.

"No, we don't want to interrupt anything," I added, figuring I'd better come to Ben's defense, although I had no idea what the dynamic was with these people or why he was so adamantly opposed to spending any time with them. Actually, both of the women looked like they would be fun to know, and I felt a bit regretful that I wouldn't get the chance to meet them.

However, getting Ben out of there was far more important.

"And really," I went on, even as Luke opened his mouth to reply, "I do have some puppies I need to get home to. Thank you for the invitation —and for the generous award. It will be put to good use, I promise."

"Oh, I know it will," Luke said. His smile had faded, but a corner of his mouth quirked just then. "I won't keep you, then. Good luck with the puppies."

He turned and headed back toward his table, and I looped my arm with Ben's and walked quickly to the exit. To my relief, he didn't try to pull his arm from mine, even though I could feel the tension in his muscles right through the sleeve of his tuxedo jacket.

Once we were outside and waiting at the valet stand, however, he disentangled himself from me so he could reach in his breast pocket and pull out the ticket to have his car retrieved. We stood there in silence as I pulled Naomi's pashmina shawl around me and tried to tell myself that it really wasn't that chilly outside.

And even though he could probably tell I was cold—and even though he probably also guessed that I was embarrassed as hell by his behavior—he walked all the way around his Jag, inspecting it from every angle, before he went back over to the valet and handed him a ten-dollar bill.

It was with an overwhelming sense of relief that I fastened my seatbelt. As Ben got in the driver's seat, I blurted out, "I am so sorry. I thought we'd be able to slip out of there without bumping into him."

Looking straight ahead, he said, "It's not your fault."

No, it wasn't, but I'd still been expecting him to blame me, just because he seemed to enjoy finding a scapegoat when he was upset about something. "Still—"

"It's all right," he broke in. "Just—just let it go."

Fine by me. I sat quietly for a few minutes, but then couldn't help venturing, "Are you sure you don't want to talk about it? I mean, I suppose I'm just trying to understand what's going on. Mr. Nicolini seems very nice."

That observation elicited a dry chuckle. "Yes, he's very good at seeming nice. His stock in trade, I suppose. That doesn't mean you should trust him."

Oh, boy. I pulled in a breath and tightened my fingers around the beaded evening bag I held in my lap. Even though Ben had turned on the car's heater, I still felt cold. "I'll return the money."

Finally, he looked over at me. It was dark in the car, but I could still see the surprise in his expression. "I'm not asking you to do that."

"But you just said he wasn't trustworthy. Maybe this money has…strings attached or something. You tell me, since you seem to know him so well."

"I…." The word trailed off into silence, as if he wasn't quite sure what he'd intended to say. When he spoke again, his tone had gentled somewhat. "Once upon a time, I'd would have said there were definitely strings attached. Not now, though. He's on the up and up. You can take the money and use it for your rescue organization without any worries."

I stared at Ben, not sure how he expected me to respond to such a statement. "What, did he used to be in the Mob or something?"

His mouth lifted in a grim smile. "No, of course not."

"Well, that's what you just made it sound like."

"Let's just say he's changed how he does business." Ben tapped his fingers on the leather-wrapped steering wheel and added, "Really, it's nothing you need to worry about. I can't forgive him for some of the things he's done, but I don't want you dragged into it. You earned that money. Don't worry about it."

Don't worry about it? After dropping increasingly mystifying comments about Luke Nicolini, Ben expected me to let it all go?

Apparently, because he said, "None of this has anything to do with you."

Maybe it didn't. Or rather, it didn't have to, because whatever was going on with Ben and Luke, it had all happened long before I came on the scene. And besides, since there really wasn't anything between Ben and me, I supposed you could have said there was no reason for me to get involved.

Only...I wanted there to be something between us, even if all either of us seemed able to do was to throw up roadblocks to make sure it didn't happen.

But I also didn't want to get into an argument in the car—or ever, really. That was probably unavoidable, and yet I preferred to delay that evil day for as long as possible. After being with Tom, I'd had enough arguments to last me a lifetime.

"Okay," I said, and fell silent again. We were both quiet as he finished the rest of the drive back to Angelino Heights and Carroll Avenue.

After he got out of the car and came around to help me climb out of the passenger side, I almost protested when he started to walk me up the front path to the porch. But then I realized that Rufus was inside, and of course Ben needed to get him back.

So I tried to look cheerful as I unlocked the door and let us in, and to sound even more upbeat when I called out, "We're home!"

"In here," Naomi called back.

Ben and I went to the family room, where Naomi and Eloy were watching an episode of *Queer Eye* on Netflix, and the puppies and Frida and Rufus were all on top of each other in a messy doggy pile in front of the hearth, where a fire burned low. It was such a fun, cozy scene that I couldn't help smiling, despite the tense exchange Ben and I had shared in the car on our way back to the house.

"Looks like you all had a good time," I observed, and Naomi smiled and shifted, looking like she was ready to get up. I couldn't help but notice the way she and Eloy had been sitting together on the sofa, even though there was also a recliner in the family room and there was no need for them to sit next to one another.

"Oh, great," she said lightly. "We ordered pizza—gluten-free, of course—and the dogs got bites of cheese and had a great time."

Strictly speaking, it was a little too early for the puppies to be eating any human food, but I decided to let it go. They all seemed fine, if wiped out.

"How was your evening?" she asked.

"It was awesome," I replied. "The party was beautiful, and I got a nice fat check for Little Angels."

Naomi's face lit up. "A-ha! I told you it would be worth it."

"Oh, it was," I assured her.

She pushed herself up from the couch, and Eloy followed suit, although he paused to stop the show and put the remote back down on the coffee table before he stood. "We can dog-sit for you any time," he said, with a knowing glance in Ben's direction, even though my companion only stared back at him stonily and didn't reply.

"Great—I'll let you know," I said hastily. "Although I don't think I have any more charity galas coming up in the near future."

Eloy only smiled a little, and followed Naomi out to the foyer without making any further comments. She called out a good night, and then they were both safely out the door.

I looked down at the pile of dogs on the floor. Frida had opened a sleepy eye to take a peek at us when we first walked in, but otherwise, they all seemed pretty sacked out for the night, Rufus included.

"Maybe we should let them sleep a little while longer," I suggested to Ben. "Do you want a glass of water or something?"

He looked as though he wanted to refuse, but then he appeared to relent. "Sure."

I went into the kitchen and set my purse down on the counter, although I kept the pashmina wrapped around my shoulders, since I tended to keep the thermostat set fairly low and I knew it wouldn't be comfortable otherwise. After I poured some water for both of us and handed one of the glasses to Ben, I said, "The dogs look like they had a fun night."

He sipped from his glass before putting it on the counter. When he turned back to me, his eyes met mine, level and far too direct. "You don't really want to talk about the dogs, do you?"

No, I had way too many other things occupying my thoughts. I just wasn't sure whether any of them were safe to discuss.

"I'm not sure what I want to talk about," I said softly, and drank some of my own water. "Or at least, it seems as if you keep trying to shoot down any topics I bring up."

"Because there's nothing in them that merits further discussion."

"There's no need to be rude," I told him, irritated enough that I really didn't care what I said.

Ben crossed his arms and leaned against the counter. If my comment had bothered him in any way, he showed no sign of it. "I wasn't being rude, only truthful."

"There are ways of telling the truth that are still rude," I shot back. "Just because something is true doesn't mean it can't also be hurtful."

Was that the slightest hint of softening in his expression? I couldn't be sure—I might have been imagining things, or simply looking for a sign that he wasn't quite as big a jerk as he seemed to be in that particular moment.

"I didn't intend to upset you," he said then, and yes, his tone wasn't quite as sharp as it had been just a moment earlier. "There are just some things I would prefer not to talk about."

"Yes, I've noticed that," I said. "A whole lot of things. I mean, I don't even know where you're from, or what you do for a living."

"I live off my investments," he returned. "I wasn't aware you had such a burning interest in how I support myself."

Those must have been some investments. His

remark made me think that my suspicions about him being a trust fund baby weren't completely unfounded, although, judging by the way he'd spoken about Luke Nicolini, he could also have been involved in organized crime of some sort. He certainly hadn't scrupled at breaking into someone's backyard to take the puppies. Yes, it was done in a good cause, but still, there were quite a few people who wouldn't have gone along with my plan simply because they didn't feel comfortable trespassing on someone else's property.

"I don't know about 'burning interests,'" I told him. "I just know that in general, friends talk about these things."

Once again, his eyes met mine. Even though the lighting in the kitchen wasn't the best, I could see glints of gold and amber, green and gray, in his hazel eyes with their frame of dark lashes. Maybe I should have looked away, but something seemed to make me remain as I was, gaze locked with his.

"Is that what we are?" he asked softly. "Friends?"

"I thought we were," I replied, even as I wondered if simply being friends with Ben Blake would be enough for me. Part of me wanted him...while the other part told me he was a raging jerk and that I'd be much smarter to walk away.

And I knew which part was currently winning.

He pushed himself away from the counter and took a step toward me. "What if I'm not interested in being friends?"

Then you should have told me to back off a week ago, I thought then, although I didn't say those words, wasn't sure what I was supposed to say to such a question. If he had absolutely no interest in forming even the most superficial of friendships, then why had he agreed to watch Rufus, and why did he persist in stopping by to chat about the neighborhood or the weather or the dogs or whatever other innocuous topic served to pass a friendly quarter-hour?

A shiver passed over me, and I pulled the pashmina shawl a little tighter around my shoulders. "Then we'll be neighbors and nothing more," I said, trying to keep my tone light, even as something very small and fragile inside me seemed to break.

At once, he shook his head. "No," he said. "That isn't what I meant."

He took another step closer, and then he reached out and grasped my hands, pulling me toward him. Caught off-guard, I stumbled in my heels, and he caught me, his arms going around me as his mouth descended on mine.

As kisses went, it definitely was a little

awkward. Maybe because we were both a little off-balance, or maybe because he really hadn't planned this and so was going on instinct. Whatever the case, it took a moment before our lips lined up and he was able to deepen the kiss, tongue tentatively touching mine.

Oh, yes, that was *much* better. As soon as I tasted him, a shockwave of need went through my body, a flood of desire so strong that I nearly felt dizzy from it. I clung to him as we kissed, felt the strength of his body under the proper tuxedo jacket, breathed in the scent of his skin and the cologne he wore, something warm and sensual without being overpowering. In fact, he'd had to get this close before I could detect it at all.

We remained locked in that embrace for some time, as if, now that he'd initiated the kiss, he didn't quite know how to end it. Finally, though, I lifted my mouth from his, although I remained holding on to his hands so he could know from our continued contact that I was fine with what had just happened.

However, my intended reassurance apparently was a little too subtle, because his face went stony, and he took a step back, pulling his hands from mine.

"That was a mistake," he said, his tone abrupt.

"It didn't feel like a mistake," I replied. Because I thought I was starting to get a better read on him, I tried not to let myself get upset. I had a feeling he'd only made the remark in an effort to safeguard his feelings, just in case I decided to express any regret over what we'd done. "Actually, it felt great."

His expression lightened. "It did?"

"Yes," I said. I slipped my fingers into his, and this time, he didn't try to pull away. "Don't you know I've been thinking about kissing you for the past week?"

"We've only known each other for a week and a half," he pointed out, and I smiled.

"I know."

For a second, his brows drew together, and then the corners of his mouth lifted in a smile to echo my own. "You did a good job of hiding it."

"Well, I didn't want to make a fool of myself." I squeezed his hand and added, "It's not like I was getting any signals from you."

"You wouldn't have," he said. "I didn't want —" Abruptly, he stopped himself there, and I felt my smile slowly fade.

"You didn't want…what? Anything to happen between us?"

"No, that's not what I was going to say." He reached over and touched a strand of my hair, his hand slipping down to caress my bare shoulder before he lifted it away. "I didn't want to make it seem as if I was open to such things if you weren't."

The old Catch-22. I'd been doing much the same thing, after all. Human beings were awfully good at being at cross-purposes with one another.

"Well, I guess it's pretty obvious that we both are," I said. "Open to such things, that is."

"Apparently."

Ben bent down and kissed me again, a little more skillfully than the first time he'd made the attempt. Or at least, it was amazing from the start on this go-'round, rather than the awkward beginning we'd shared during our initial kiss. Once again, I could feel how my body responded to his touch, how parts of me that I'd thought dormant were now awake and sparking with long-repressed desire. God, I wanted him. The dogs were asleep—would it be too awful if I took him upstairs and tore his clothes off? After all, we'd known each other for almost two weeks, so it wasn't as if this would be some sort of one-night stand with a stranger.

However, just as I was about to press myself even more closely against him, to do my best to signal that it was all right if matters advanced a bit further, I heard the click of toenails on the tile floor, followed by a plaintive little whine.

Ben lifted his mouth from mine as if shocked by an electric cattle prod, and looked down to see

Rufus standing a few feet away from us, his head cocked and his dark eyes confused, as if he couldn't quite figure out what Ben and I were doing.

That makes two of us, I thought, although all I did was let out a low chuckle. "It looks like someone is ready to go home," I said.

"Yes," Ben replied. He stepped away from me and pulled at the hem of his tuxedo jacket, as if to straighten it, although it didn't look terribly rumpled to me. "It is getting rather late."

Actually, it really wasn't—the digital clock on the stove told me it was barely ten o'clock—but I didn't protest. I guessed that he needed to put a little distance between us so he could figure out what was going on, and I wasn't about to stop him. After all, I could tell I needed some space of my own. Honestly, I hadn't really expected him to have this sort of effect on me. Yes, I'd known I was attracted to him, but I'd never been the type of person to immediately jump into bed with someone. Something about that second kiss we'd shared, however, had made me ready to run upstairs and remove that tuxedo of his post-haste, and I needed to do my best to figure out what it was about him that got my blood running quite so hot.

"Right," I said. While intellectually I agreed that it was better if he went home, I didn't want to leave the evening on such a flat note, not after those kisses we'd shared. Then I recalled that it was Valentine's the next day. No, I wouldn't make a big deal out of it, but, on the other hand, I thought it might be fun to advance matters between the two of us and see what happened. "Hey," I went on, trying to sound casual, "why don't you come over for dinner tomorrow night? It's Valentine's Day—I'll make something special."

His response was predictably Ben. One eyebrow lifted, and he shot me a skeptical look. "Don't tell me you've fallen into the Valentine's Day trap."

Trap? While I'd admit that I thought it felt like a manufactured reason to make people spend money, I wasn't quite sure I was ready to go all the way and call it a trap. "What's wrong with Valentine's Day?"

"Other than making the day about hearts and flowers when it's supposed to honor someone who was beaten to death and then beheaded?"

Ouch. I honestly had never looked up Saint Valentine's history, so I'd had no idea how he'd died. With a shrug, I said, "Well, if that's the way the poor guy met his maker, then I think it's only fitting that we honor him with some good wine and good food. And no hearts and flowers. I just want you to come over for dinner, that's all."

"'All'?" Ben echoed, and I nodded.

"All," I said firmly. "In fact, I specifically forbid you to bring me flowers. Even the grocery stores jack up the prices on flowers around Valentine's Day. It's a total racket."

He stared at me for a moment, then chuckled. "I knew there was a reason why I liked you, Jillian Torres."

Even though I'd sort of assumed he must have some sort of regard for me, or he wouldn't have let go of his self-control enough to allow us those two kisses, a happy little warmth spread through my body at his words. Ben Blake liked me.

It was definitely a start.

"So, it's a date," I said. "Come over at seven. No flowers."

"Candy?" he asked, his tone arch.

"How about chocolate cake for dessert instead?"

"A much better idea." He came over and kissed me, but only on the cheek that time. Which was fine; I figured it was a down payment on future intimacies. "And now, I will take this dog home."

"Have a good night," I said, still feeling a little glowy from the casual embrace. All right, he'd neatly sidestepped any questions about his past or his history with Luke Nicolini, but I decided to let all that slide for the moment. With any luck, as he became more comfortable with me, he'd feel safe enough to allow a few confidences.

"Tomorrow at seven," he replied, then bent down and patted Rufus on the head, and went out of the kitchen. A moment later, I heard him pause, followed by a faint *click,* and realized he must have stopped back at the family room to retrieve the dog's leash and put it on. Another moment, and then the front door closed behind them.

I looked around the kitchen, realizing it would forever be imprinted on my mind as the spot where Ben had kissed me for the first time. Probably not the most romantic place in the world for such an activity, and yet in a way, I thought it was perfectly appropriate. The kitchen was the heart of my home...and I knew he'd already made a home in my heart.

INTERLUDE

He'd kissed her.

Kissed her.

Had he gone absolutely mad?

That seemed to be the most logical explanation for his completely illogical behavior, and yet Beelzebub didn't feel mad. He felt....

He wasn't sure how he felt. Not like himself, not the demon who'd mocked Asmodeus for his liaisons with human women and thought Lucifer absolutely insane for getting tangled up with some insipid mortal. How could a human female possibly have anything to offer that would make the rulership of Hell or the powers of a demonic lord pale in comparison?

And yet, here he was...fallen prey to the same weakness that had seized both Lucifer and Asmodeus.

It would have been easier if he could have blamed the whole incident on the various weaknesses of this human body to which he'd been confined. At least that scenario was somewhat understandable. But this body only did what he told it to, and so he couldn't rightly blame it for having a mind of its own.

He couldn't blame Jillian, either. If she'd been the one to lean in for the kiss, well, then he could have said this was all her fault. Unfortunately, it wasn't she who'd initiated their contact, but he himself, Beelzebub.

Very well. He supposed he could say she was partially at fault, just for looking so beautiful. However, that particular argument didn't hold up very well, not when he'd previously considered himself utterly immune to female charms.

And the thing was…he'd enjoyed kissing her. This human body had reacted all too well, had told him exactly what it wanted. Even now that he was safely back at home and supposedly well out of reach of Jillian's charms, he found himself aching for her, aching for more.

Which was also insane. Hadn't he previously mocked humanity's need for sex, and laughed at the idiotic faces people made when engaged in such activities?

Only now…now, he very much wanted to do all those things with Jillian. Wanted to taste her mouth, taste all of her. Wanted to see her in all her naked glory, with the magnificent pale mane of her hair spread out across the sheets. Wanted to bury himself in her, feel her surround him with her warmth.

Dear God.

He scrubbed a hand across his face and went into the kitchen so he could pour himself a glass of wine. Also a very human impulse, to have a drink when one's thoughts were so tumultuous, but he didn't know what else to do with himself.

Luckily, he had a bottle of cabernet sauvignon that was already open and sealed with a little vacuum stopper. He removed the stopper and poured himself a glass, then took a large and very disrespectful swallow. The wine wouldn't have quite the same effect on him that it might on someone who was entirely human, but it seemed to help a little, calmed his racing thoughts just a bit and eased some of the tension ratcheting its way down his spine.

Was this Your plan, God? he thought then in some anger. *Did You know all along that I would react this way to Jillian Torres?*

Considering Who he was dealing with, Ben thought this theory completely plausible. But if this actually was God's plan, what should he do about it?

The Beelzebub of even a week ago would have

vowed to have nothing to do with Jillian, to completely freeze her out and see what happened next. At this particular moment, however, he didn't find such an option terribly appealing. He wanted to see her again, wanted to share her company.

Wanted to share her bed.

All right, ignoring her probably wasn't going to work. Or rather, he could attempt such a thing, but he had a feeling he'd only be hurting himself as much as he hurt her.

On the other hand, allowing matters to continue as they now were seemed the surest way to do exactly what God wished. And although Beelzebub knew He generally got His way in most things, it rankled to succumb so easily to His machinations, especially after being removed from Hell in such a capricious fashion. If he'd still been down in Hell, he would never have had to worry about Jillian Torres crossing his path, because he knew she most definitely would not have ended up there.

Damned if he did, and damned if he didn't. A very neat trap he'd fallen into this time.

And he had no idea what to do about it.

CHAPTER THIRTEEN

Since Ben had eaten prime rib without any drama the night before at the gala, I knew I didn't have to worry about avoiding red meat for our dinner. Pot roast seemed a little prosaic for a Valentine's Day meal, so instead I bought a couple of New York steaks, figuring I would cook them in the *sous vide* machine Tom and I had bought ourselves as a Christmas present a few years back. We'd never used it all that much, but I found a little perverse pleasure in the thought of utilizing it to make my new boyfriend a nice dinner.

Okay, calling him my "boyfriend" was probably pushing things just a bit. Still, there was no denying that our relationship had now entered a new phase. Maybe Ben wasn't my boyfriend, but he also wasn't merely my neighbor any longer.

Although I had the urge to go over to Naomi's

house so I could dish about what had happened after she and Eloy left the evening before, I managed to quash the impulse. This wasn't high school, and really, I'd never been one to kiss and tell, anyway. Besides, even if I'd lost all self-control, it wouldn't have mattered, because I remembered that she was attending some kind of Valentine's event over in Santa Monica and wasn't available anyway.

I kind of liked it when circumstances saved me from my worst impulses.

So instead of gossiping, I tidied the house and went to the store to get the items I needed for that night's dinner. I even made the supreme sacrifice of inserting my contact lenses two days in a row, although I wasn't sure why I made the effort. It wasn't as if Ben hadn't seen me in my glasses multiple times. In fact, he'd seen me far more often with them than without. But since I was making a little extra effort with dinner, I figured I might as well make a little extra effort with myself as well.

Not that I planned to wear a dress or anything. Getting dolled up for the gala had been enough to hold me for a long, long time. No, I just put on my best pair of jeans and a knit camisole edged in lace, a pink cardigan, and silver-gray ballet flats instead of my usual sneakers. That was about as dressed up as I ever got, but it wasn't enough to make anyone think I'd spent hours in front of the mirror.

Because the weather was good, I let the puppies out in the backyard for a while, with Frida keeping a careful eye on them. It was sort of astonishing how fast they grew up, and how soon they'd be ready to find new homes…if I was willing to part with them at all. But no, five dogs was too much, even chihuahuas. I'd keep Boudicca and make sure the rest of them went to the absolute best people I could find.

As I went about my preparations—I was making potatoes *au gratin* and pan-roasted vegetables in addition to the steaks—I found myself wondering once again about the strange interaction between Ben and Luke Nicolini the night before. There had been a familiarity about the way they spoke to one another that made me think they had a lengthy history together, that whatever had happened, it hadn't been a one-time business deal that had gone wrong.

And that made me think about doing some research. Maybe Ben wanted his history to be a closed book, but Luke seemed like more of a public figure. It was possible that I could discover a few things about him online, something…*anything*…that might help me to fill in the blanks of Ben's background.

While the steaks were cooking in the *sous vide*

machine—it was basically a big vat of water with a device that heated the liquid to a precise temperature and maintained it for however long you needed, thus guaranteeing meat that was perfectly cooked and melt-in-your-mouth tender—I got my laptop from the office and brought it into the kitchen. After I set it on the table and went back to the family room to double-check that all the dogs were still passed out from cavorting in the yard earlier that afternoon, I brought up Google and did a quick search on Luke Nicolini.

There were several people with that name, but it was obvious enough that he was the only one with any kind of public presence. He had a bio on the South Coast Foundation's website that said he was originally from New York and had attended Columbia University and earned a master's degree in business. His parents died when he was in college, and he was an only child. He apparently was a recent transplant to L.A., having moved here only a little more than a year earlier, and his wife was an editor at *SoCal* magazine.

All very basic, of course, but it gave me something of an idea of who he was and where he'd come from. How Ben—and Allan, the man who'd shared a table with Luke and their respective wives at the gala—fit into that background, I wasn't entirely sure. Supposedly, Luke had a master's in business, but what kind of business? Where had his money come from? Was he a self-made man, or was it his family's money that allowed him to be so generous?

I had absolutely no idea, although I wasn't so naïve as to believe that "business" couldn't encompass some pretty shady doings. Luke Nicolini had seemed very pleasant, handsome and affable and completely at home in his surroundings, but if nothing else, my breakup with Tom had taught me that it wasn't wise to trust surface impressions. On the surface, everything had seemed great with the two of us…until it wasn't.

So maybe Ben and Luke had been involved in some sort of business back in New York, shady or not, and it had all gone sour somehow. Had Ben known that Luke had relocated out here to Los Angeles, or was it just an unfortunate coincidence that they'd ended up in the same city?

Again, I didn't know, and I had a feeling Ben wouldn't be too thrilled if I started giving him the third degree during what was supposed to be a cozy Valentine's Day dinner. But at least I knew a little more than I had a few minutes earlier, which I supposed was a start.

With a sigh, I closed the laptop and took it back to the office. By that point, it was close enough to seven that I knew I needed to set the table, so I went ahead and got everything laid out —I used a tablecloth but not the "good" dishes, which had been a wedding present and had probably seen active duty twice in the entire time Tom and I had been married—and put some soft music on in the background. I also recklessly lit a bunch of candles, since I liked the atmosphere they provided. So what if it looked like I was trying to be romantic? It was Valentine's Day, after all, and it wasn't as though Ben and I were still dancing around each other. We'd kissed. There was no putting that back in the bottle.

At exactly seven, the doorbell rang. My heartbeat sped up a little, although I told myself that it was silly to get too excited. This was just a quiet little dinner at home.

With Ben, I added mentally, and felt a rush of…what? Excitement? Anticipation? Naked lust?

A little bit of all three, from what I could tell.

I went and answered the door. As expected, Ben waited outside on the porch. In one hand, he held a bottle of wine, and in the other was a medium-sized pink box.

"Cake?" I inquired, eyeing the box.

"Of course," he replied. "As requested."

"Perfect."

He came inside, and I took the box from him, then told him to go ahead and put the wine on the dining room table. I'd already had a bottle set aside, just in case, but I'd been inwardly hoping that he would bring something, mostly because I guessed it would probably better than anything I currently had in my own limited wine cabinet.

"I'll be in with the food in a minute," I called to him as I went to the kitchen.

A pause, and then he replied, "Do you need me to help you with anything?"

Well, there was progress. A week earlier when he'd been here for dinner, he hadn't made any such offers. However, the meal wasn't that complicated, and so I called back, "No, I'm fine. Go ahead and open the wine—I'll be there in a few minutes."

I'd had a pan waiting with some butter and shallots, and so I removed the steaks from the plastic bag that had held them while they were cooking, then dropped them in the pan to give them a quick sauté. While they were browning, I slid the vegetables into a bowl and then pulled the potatoes out of the oven and set them on the stovetop to settle down a bit. A quick flip of the steaks, and I took the potatoes out to the dining room and put the casserole dish down on a trivet I'd set out earlier.

Ben sat at the head of the table, extracting the cork from the bottle of wine he'd brought. "You're sure you don't need help with anything?"

"No, I'm good. I just have to go back and grab the steaks and the veggies, and we're set."

He nodded. "I'll go ahead and pour, then."

I smiled at him. "Perfect."

Sure enough, when I returned to the dining room, he'd already poured a measure of wine into both our glasses, letting it air a bit before we got started. I went ahead and put the plate with the steaks on it next to him, and set the bowl of vegetables down in an empty spot next to the potatoes.

"That's everything," I said. "So, now we can relax."

"Good." He reached for his glass and lifted it, and I did the same, wondering what he was going to offer as his toast.

As usual, he didn't disappoint.

"Happy Valentine's Day—I hope it ends with neither of us getting beheaded."

"Or clubbed to death," I added, and his hazel eyes glinted with amusement as we clinked glasses.

"A worthy toast."

We drank and then set our glasses down. The wine was excellent—some kind of Bordeaux, according to the label, although I would be the first to admit that I didn't know jack about French wines. However, it was dark and rich, and would be a great accompaniment to the steaks. And the potatoes as well, gooey with Gruyere cheese and thick with cream. Normally, I wasn't quite so decadent with my side dishes, but I figured eating stuff like this only a couple of times a year wouldn't kill me.

And obviously the food passed muster with Ben, because he took a bite of steak and remarked, "This is excellent. It tastes like something I might have ordered at a restaurant."

"Thanks," I said. "Really, I didn't have to do that much—I used my *sous vide* to cook the steaks, and it's easy."

"'*Sous vide*'?" he repeated, clearly unfamiliar with the phrase.

Well, it was kind of nice to bump into something he didn't know anything about, cluelessness about smart thermostats notwithstanding. I explained how the process worked, and he listened, apparently fascinated. I explained how *sous vide* meant "under vacuum" in French, and how it used a bath of water maintained at a constant temperature to cook your food.

"And it's super forgiving," I added as I cut a piece of my steak, marveling a little at how tender it was, perfectly pink in the middle, even though that was sort of the whole point of cooking *sous vide*. "It's not like when you're broiling a steak and you need to get it out of the oven right away or it'll get too done. I could have left it in for another twenty minutes or so without any problems."

Ben had another bite of the steak, expression approving. "I suppose that would help when you're trying to get several different dishes ready at the same time."

"Exactly."

After that, we were both silent for a few minutes as we ate and interspersed bites with sips of Bordeaux. He looked similarly impressed by the potatoes, and I reflected that there was something to that old saying about getting to a man's heart via his stomach. Of course, he'd already demonstrated his heart's involvement by the way he'd kissed me the day before, but I found something satisfying in watching the way he enjoyed his meal. Maybe that was old-fashioned of me, and yet I wouldn't deny it.

And maybe I was just a little gratified that Ben was so appreciative, because Tom had never been terribly impressed by my culinary endeavors. Oh, he never said anything was bad, but he was spoiled because his mother was a fabulous cook and could whip up all kinds of traditional Mexican foods. Next to her gourmet molé sauce and homemade tamales, my pot roasts and barbecue chicken had probably seemed like pretty tame fare.

"How's Rufus doing?" I asked after we'd slowed down a bit, more because I knew we needed to discuss something that didn't involve Ben's past than because I thought Rufus' existence had materially changed since the day before.

"Very well," Ben replied. He scooped up a forkful of potatoes au gratin, chewed, and swallowed, his expression about as close to blissful as I'd ever seen it. But he became brisker as he went on, "Actually, I've been thinking about it, and I think I might want to keep him permanently...if that's all right with you."

A wash of delight went through me at his request. If it was all right with me? Of course, it was all right...assuming he was truly serious about such a commitment. "That would be wonderful," I said. "I know he's been enjoying himself, and I have to say, I was sort of worried about how he would fare once someone else decided to adopt him."

"Well, you don't need to worry any longer," Ben told me. He swirled the Bordeaux in his glass but didn't drink. "Is there anything I need to do formally?"

I shook my head. "Not really. This isn't the same thing as getting a dog from an animal shelter or a breeder. But I have a little form I sign to show that the dog was a rescue and that you're now taking responsibility for him. And obviously, I'll hand over his vet records. Not that I have much except the paperwork from his last exam and the certification for his shots."

"Still, that's something. It'll show he belongs

with me if anyone contests the arrangement, for some reason."

That probably wouldn't be an issue. Rufus had been in either my or Ben's care for going on two weeks now, and I'd had his photo and description plastered all over every lost dog Facebook group and Nextdoor bulletin board I could think of. If someone really had been looking for him, I was pretty sure they would have tracked him down by that point.

But I only nodded and said, "Yes, might as well cover all the bases. I can give you the paperwork after dinner." I paused before adding, "Thanks, Ben. This is going to mean so much to Rufus."

My obvious gratitude clearly made him uncomfortable, because he looked down at his plate rather than meet my gaze. Fork in hand, he pushed some potatoes around and replied, "It's not a big deal. He's a good dog."

Yes, he was. Of course, I'd always believed that all dogs were good dogs, and the ones who acted out in one way or another just needed some extra love and attention. And honestly, I'd noticed that Rufus had seemed a bit less hyper the past few days, as though he was calming down now that his home environment felt more settled and he had a regular daily schedule. Knowing that his world wouldn't be disrupted once again was a huge relief to me…and I had to believe it would be a huge relief to the dog as well.

"I'll take down the notices tomorrow," I said. "And if anyone does contact me about him—which I sort of doubt is going to happen—then I'll let them know he's already been adopted."

Ben gave an approving nod. "That sounds like a good idea."

Really, for Ben, he was being remarkably mellow. I hadn't caught an ironic brow lift or snarky side-eye the entire evening. It could have been the food, or the wine…or maybe just the understanding that he didn't need to fight the attraction between the two of us any longer.

Whatever the cause of his current affability, I wasn't going to argue with it. He even helped me clear the table when we were done with our meal, and lingered in the kitchen with me as I cut us several pieces from the cake he'd brought, luscious and gooey and positively decadent.

We took the cake into the living room, where he lit a fire in the hearth. I supposed we could have gone into the family room to be with the puppies, but it was probably safer to eat chocolate cake in a place where there weren't any dogs around. Not that either Ben or I would be foolish enough to feed any of our dogs chocolate, but accidents happened sometimes, and I knew I wanted to avoid an emergency trip to the vet because one of us dropped a piece of cake and a dog—or worse, a puppy—swooped in to get the fallen morsel.

It felt good to sit there on the couch, to have him be close to me, so close that his knee brushed against mine as he shifted his weight. Just the faintest of touches, but it was enough to send heat rushing through my body.

Since the light in there was fairly dim, I couldn't see much of his expression, so I didn't know for sure whether he'd noticed the way I'd flushed, or pulled in a quick breath. To cover my reaction, I said, "This is amazing cake. Where'd you get it?"

"A bakery in West Hollywood."

I stared at him, surprised. "You went all the way to West Hollywood to get a cake for tonight?"

His shoulders lifted, and he took another bite of luscious chocolate decadence. "I did some research on who made the best chocolate cake in Los Angeles, and the consensus seemed to be that it was Cloud Cake. So I drove out there to get one."

He spoke as if it was no big deal, but with traffic, that was more than an hour round-trip. True, I didn't think Ben had any huge claims on his time—I still hadn't quite figured out what he did with his days, since he clearly didn't have a job but also didn't appear to have any time-consuming hobbies—and yet the mere fact that he'd given up a chunk of his day for such a trip seemed to indicate he thought our evening together merited such an effort. Once again, a rush of warmth moved through me, and I couldn't help being oddly pleased.

"Well, it's amazing," I said. "Thank you for going the extra mile—or ten—to pick it up."

While he didn't exactly smile, something in his eyes seemed to warm as he looked back at me. "I thought I should make the effort, since you were the one doing most of the work for this dinner. And thank you—the food was all very good. I doubt we could have gotten anything better at a restaurant."

That seemed like high praise, coming from Ben...although I wondered if he was also thinking that it was much less fraught to stay in rather than go out, considering what had happened at the gala the night before. True, L.A. was a big place, and our chances of bumping into Luke Nicolini again were most likely slim to none, but he still had probably wanted to play it safe.

"I don't know about that," I said, which wasn't false modesty, considering how many good restaurants you had in Los Angeles to choose from. "But it's such a mob scene on Valentine's Day, I feel like it's better to stay home rather go out and fight the crowds."

One last bite of chocolate cake, and he set his plate down on the coffee table. "Yes, I'd much rather be alone here with you."

A little thrill went through me at those words. However, I tried to seem cool and calm as I ate the final two morsels of cake on my own plate before putting the plate down on the table next to his. "And a bunch of dogs."

"They seem rather quiet," Ben observed, glancing down the hall in the direction of the family room.

"Oh, I made sure they were all well fed before you came over," I said lightly. "And I bribed Frida with dog biscuits, or she would have been bouncing all around the dinner table, trying to get bits of steak from us."

"That would have been distracting."

However, he didn't look distracted now. No, his eyes were fixed on mine as he leaned forward and pressed his lips to my mouth. He tasted of chocolate and Bordeaux, and in that moment, I thought he was even more lush than the cake we'd just consumed.

Blood rushed through me, heating all my limbs, making me throb with need. His hands tangled in my hair as he held me close, and I pressed myself against him, hoping he would understand what I wanted from him, that I didn't see the need for us to wait any longer.

Apparently, he got the message, because his kisses moved from my mouth and down my neck, and lower still, his breath hot against the sensitive skin of my chest. I gasped, wanting him to push my cardigan aside, to pull down the camisole and bra beneath so his lips could touch my bare breast.

Instead, though, he paused and glanced up at me. I could see the need in his face, so naked that it didn't matter that the room was lit by only a single low-wattage bulb in the table lamp on the other side of the space. Mixed in with that need was a sort of confusion I didn't quite understand, since I thought it should have been obvious to pretty much anyone what I wanted from him.

When he spoke, his voice was rough, almost husky, sounding very unlike him. "Is this—is this what we're supposed to be doing?"

I didn't understand his hesitancy, but I knew I needed to respect it, no matter that my body was fairly pulsing with the strength of my desire for him. "It's what I want to be doing," I said softly. "But if it's not what you want—"

"I want it," he cut in abruptly. "I do."

"Then let's go upstairs," I said. "I don't really want to do this on the couch like a couple of teenagers."

For a second, his expression was almost

puzzled, but then I saw him nod. "Yes, that's probably a good idea."

I twined my fingers in his and pulled him up from the sofa, then led him to the staircase. We ascended the stairs quickly, lust making us hasty. Only a few steps from the top of the stairway to the master bedroom, and then we both fell on the bed, each of us tearing at the other person's clothes, as if we'd both realized that there was no need to hide what we wanted…or what was about to happen.

His body was amazing, smoothly muscled and more taut and firm than I'd expected. Oh, he wore his clothes well, and I'd felt his muscles that one time when I grabbed his arm, but I still hadn't quite thought he'd look like a fitness model under those plaid jackets and bow ties. And no time for me to be self-conscious, to wonder if my own body measured up to his physical perfection, because his lips closed on my bare nipple, sucking, and I gasped aloud, giving in to his touch, to sensations I hadn't experienced for more than a year.

No, that was a lie. We'd only gotten started, and yet I was pretty sure Tom had never made me feel like this.

My hand closed on Ben's shaft, feeling how rock-hard it was under my fingertips. The moan he let out was almost shocked, as if he hadn't been expecting me to do such a thing.

But of course I would. I wanted to touch him, wanted to feel him, wanted to experience him in every way.

It seemed the most natural thing in the world to lean down and take him in my mouth, to savor the faint salt of his flesh, to run my hand up and down as I suckled on him. Another moan, louder this time, and I kept going, wanting to make him come, wanting to show him how much I loved doing this for him.

And he did come not too long after that, filling my mouth with the heavy saltiness of his climax. I swallowed and kissed his belly, felt how his breaths came in short, hard gasps. And then I moved farther upward, so I could kiss him on the mouth.

Finally, he spoke. "That was…." The words trailed off, as if he'd suddenly realized that he didn't have a vocabulary adequate to express what he'd just experienced. "Thank you, Jillian."

I chuckled. "Oh, it's a little early to be thanking me, Ben. We're just getting started."

We kissed again, and my hand moved down to touch him, to feel how he was already starting to harden once more. At the same time, his fingers slipped between my legs, gently probing, and I gasped as little ripples of pleasure began to flood through my body, every inch coming alive as he stroked me.

The orgasm came fast for me, too, as I clamped down on his fingers and rode it out, gasping, breaths coming in quick pants. He kissed me, his body pressed close to mine, and I could feel the heaviness of his cock pressing against my stomach, slipping lower…and then pausing.

"We're supposed to take some kind of precaution, aren't we?" he asked.

That seemed like an odd way to phrase the question, but I wasn't going to worry about semantics. "I'm on the pill," I told him. "As for the rest…it's been more than a year since I was with Tom. And I know I'm safe."

"It has been…a very long time for me," he said, hesitating over the words. Self-conscious about his lack of a sex life? It was nothing to be embarrassed about, but I supposed he just didn't want to admit a lack of experience to a new partner. "So…I suppose I can say I'm safe, too."

"Well, then." I kissed him, then whispered in his ear, "I want you, Ben. I want this."

He didn't reply, but he shifted his position, and suddenly, he was slipping inside me. I was already so wet from his caresses that there was no awkwardness, no positions to be adjusted, only the two of us joining with sudden, shocking intensity, our bodies beginning to move together in their own particular rhythm. I wrapped my legs around him and drove him deeper, wanting to feel as much of him as possible, wanting him to know how perfect this was, how utterly and completely flawless.

My moans soon blended with his, and we clung together, driving toward consummation, to the moment when we both cried out together and held on to each other as we rode the orgasm, letting it flood through us and over us and take us away from the world for a breathless eternity. Eventually, though, it began to ebb, and I lay there and smiled as he kissed me over and over again, his touch almost frenzied, as if he needed to prove to me that this had been as amazing for him as it had been for me.

And then at last we curled up next to one another, arms entwined, and I laid my head against his chest and listened to the strong, steady beat of his heart. There truly was no place else I could ever imagine being.

Best Valentine's Day ever, I thought, and let myself drift off to sleep.

CHAPTER FOURTEEN

I OPENED MY EYES TO SEE BEN SITTING ON the window seat and quietly pulling on his shoes. Disappointment stabbed through me, but I did my best to sound unconcerned as I said, trying to make my words sound like a joke, "Sneaking away under cover of darkness?"

Not that it was really all that dark. The light level in the room told me it was probably around six-thirty in the morning or thereabouts. In fact, when I sent a quick glance toward the clock on my nightstand, I confirmed that it actually was six thirty-eight.

He finished putting on his second shoe, then came over to the bed and bent down so he could kiss me. A nice, lingering kiss, too, not some dismissive peck on the cheek.

"No," he replied. "But I didn't know how long

you were going to be asleep, and I realized I'd left Rufus alone in the house all night long. It's the first time he's ever been left like that, and I wanted to make sure he was all right. He needs his breakfast and to be let out in the backyard."

I should have thought of that. In fact, I rarely slept in this late, so most likely Frida and the puppies were wondering what I was up to, and why I hadn't yet emerged to take care of everyone's morning feedings.

"Right," I said, and pushed back the covers so I could climb out of bed. "I forgot that you didn't bring him with you last night. Of course, you need to get home and take care of him." I hesitated, wondering if I should leave matters where they were and see how things evolved, but I didn't want to be on pins and needles with Ben. I needed to know where we stood...no matter what. I pulled in a breath before saying, "Did you want to come over for dinner tonight? You can bring Rufus."

Ben frowned faintly. "I don't expect you to cook for me every night."

"Good, because I don't plan to," I said with a grin. "We can order takeout or something, if that makes you feel better. But I also don't mind cooking."

"Then yes, I'll come over for dinner," he said, then added, "And we'll get takeout. I'm still not that familiar with the restaurants around here, so you can choose."

I reached over and squeezed his fingers. "We can choose together…but I'll give you my recommendations."

"That sounds like a plan. I'll see you tonight, then."

And he went out after that, making me realize he obviously didn't intend to spend the day with me. Well, that was actually a good thing. We didn't need to be in each other's laps 24/7, after all.

Right, I thought, doing my best to swallow my disappointment.

But even if I was ready for the full Ben Blake immersion experience, I realized that I had other claims on my time. For one thing, I had to get to the bank that morning to deposit the fat check the South Coast Foundation had given me. Also, the puppies had another checkup scheduled at the vet, and then at two o'clock I was meeting with a retired couple who wanted to be added to my list of fosters. I couldn't have spent all day in bed with Ben even if I'd wanted to.

Although at some point, I thought it would be a good idea to clear my calendar, just to see what a day in bed with him would be like….

Naomi came over at noon, bearing with her salads from Oasis, one of our favorite local spots. "So, tell me more about the gala," she said as we seated ourselves at the kitchen table. It was another bright, sunny day, the sun flooding in and making the space even more cheerful than usual.

Or maybe that was just how I was looking at the world that day, thanks to the spectacular lay I'd had the night before.

"It was good," I replied. "I mean, it's kind of hard to beat a free meal at the Biltmore, especially when you get a fifty-thousand-dollar check to go along with your tiramisu."

She blinked at me. "Wow! I mean, I know you said when you came home that you'd gotten a fat check, but I guess I wasn't expecting it to be quite *that* fat."

"Me, neither," I said. "Honestly, I was kind of shocked. I really hadn't been expecting that."

"It was definitely a nice gesture," she agreed. A pause as she dug through her salad and extracted a grape tomato, and then she added, "And…?"

"And what?" I asked, all innocence, although of course I knew exactly what she was asking about.

"What about you and Ben? Did you have a good time? Did he behave himself?"

"Mostly," I said, wondering if I should mention anything about that weird exchange between Ben and Luke Nicolini, or whether I should just let the whole thing go.

However, Naomi must have picked up on some of my vibe, because her brows drew together and she said, "'Mostly'? What happened?"

I shrugged, although I had a feeling she wasn't buying my nonchalant act. "It seems that Ben and Mr. Nicolini know each other somehow. He didn't want to tell me about it, but it seemed obvious to me that there's some sort of bad blood between them."

Her frown deepened. "Did this Luke Nicolini guy seem upset that Ben was at his party?"

"Not as far as I could tell," I replied, doing my best to replay the scene in my head. "If anything, he seemed almost amused that they'd bumped into each other in such a way. I'd say the animosity appeared to be mostly on Ben's part."

"That is kind of weird." She munched on her salad for a moment as she appeared to ponder what I'd just told her. "And Ben wouldn't say what it was about?"

"No. Not that I should be all that surprised, I suppose," I added. "I mean, I've slept with the guy and I still know basically nothing about him."

Naomi dropped her fork into her salad and held up her hands. "Whoa, whoa. Hold up a sec. You *slept* with him? When did this momentous event take place? After the gala?"

"No," I replied, wishing I'd made myself think before I spoke. Not that I was ashamed of sleeping with Ben—far from it—but what had happened between us was special, and not something to be gossiped over like a new pair of shoes or the latest Chris Hemsworth movie. "We—we kissed for the first time when he brought me home from the gala. But we, um—he stayed over last night."

"Wow." She slumped against the back of her chair, looking positively gobsmacked. Since she had her hair tied back in a ponytail and her makeup was somewhat subdued, I guessed that she wasn't filming anything that day. "I'm kind of shocked. Happy for you," she hastened to add, "but shocked."

"It just sort of…happened." All right, maybe that was a tiny little white lie. I'd been hoping it would happen, had sort of orchestrated the evening so it would be easy for us to fall into bed together, but it had only worked because Ben wanted the same thing I did. Or at least, I had to hope he did.

"Was it good?"

"Naomi!"

"Hey," she said with a shrug. "I'm still on my man cleanse, so I need to live vicariously through someone, and right now you're having the most interesting adventures of any of my friends. I mean, a handsome, mysterious man moves in across the street, takes you to a black tie gala, and then makes love to you on Valentine's Day. That's got Hallmark Channel written all over it."

"Do they allow premarital sex on The Hallmark Channel?" I asked, genuinely curious. I wasn't a subscriber, so I had no idea.

"Whatever," she said with a wave of her hand. "Anyway, I can see you're not going to kiss and tell, so we'll leave that aside for now. But were you serious when you said you know nothing about him?"

"Dead serious," I replied, returning to my neglected salad so I could spear a slice of cucumber with my fork. "Naomi, I don't know where he's from, if he has any family. Hell, I don't even know if he has a middle name. I *think* he might be from New York, just because that's where Luke Nicolini is from and it's obvious that whatever happened between them went down before Ben ever moved to L.A., but I don't know that for sure. Like I said, I don't know anything."

"Well, you need to talk to him, girlfriend," Naomi said reasonably. "I mean, it's one thing if you're just casual neighbors. Then yeah, maybe you don't need to know every single detail. But you've slept with the guy." She stopped there, brown eyes narrowing slightly. "I assume it wasn't intended as a one-night stand."

"I don't think so," I replied, although even as I

spoke, doubt assailed me. What if he'd made plans to come over for dinner with no real intention of actually showing up? I told myself that was ridiculous, that Ben wouldn't do something like that, but did I know for sure? However, I tried my best to push those misgivings away. Nothing he'd said or done gave any indication that he intended to dump me now that he'd gotten laid. That was just leftover pain from my breakup with Tom raising its ugly head. Just because my ex-husband was a jerk didn't mean every man on the planet couldn't be trusted. Doing my best to sound confident, I added, "He's coming over tonight—we're going to order takeout because he doesn't want me cooking for him all the time."

"Good man," she observed. "Still, he needs to understand that he can't keep his entire life hidden from the woman he's having a relationship with. Because that's what you have now," she continued, steamrollering over the protests that began to rise to my lips. "I don't care how you want to classify things, but if you're sleeping together and seeing each other regularly, then you're in a relationship. The beginnings of one, but still."

As much as I would have liked to argue with Naomi, I knew she was right. Ben's and my relationship had just begun to blossom, but it still existed, and we both needed to recognize the situation for what it was. However, it was one thing to resolve that Ben needed to be more open with me, and quite another to actually tell him that was what he should do. He could be so…adamant… about things.

"I'll try," I said, knowing how dubious I sounded. "But I can tell he doesn't want to talk about it. And if I push him too hard, I might scare him off."

"In which case, I'm not sure if he was worth having in the first place," Naomi responded, her tone firm. "I mean, it's not right to hide that sort of stuff, if for no other reason than the truth is always way more innocuous than whatever scenarios you might manufacture in your mind. I know if I were in your situation, I'd start inventing all sorts of scenarios—that he's actually married and has a wife and family in another state—"

"Or that he's in the witness protection program," I supplied, and she nodded.

"Exactly. And if he's determined to be a clam, then you'll have to decide if you want to be with someone like that."

I supposed she was right. The current situation couldn't go on indefinitely. While I understood that Ben needed his space, I was now in that space with him…if only barely…and it was wrong to keep me in the dark.

"And in the meantime," she said, "I think I'll do a little digging of my own."

"'Digging'?" I echoed, faintly alarmed. "Naomi, I'm not sure you should get involved."

"Well, not me exactly," she replied. "Just that I meet a lot of people in my work, and a couple of them *might* just happen to be private investigators, so...."

Now I was really wishing I'd kept my mouth shut. "*Please* don't sic a private investigator on Ben. He'd go ballistic if he found out."

For someone who'd just made such an alarming suggestion, her expression was calm. "He's not going to find out."

"How do you know that?"

"Because these people are good." She paused, then said, "Tell you what. If you can get Ben to tell you where he's from and how he had the money to buy that house for cash—"

"He bought it for cash?" I interrupted, somewhat shocked by that revelation. "What makes you say that?"

Naomi sent me a pitying look. "Because I talk to actual people and not just to dogs."

That remark earned her a scowl, but she seemed unfazed. "Low blow, Naomi," I remarked.

"It's the truth." She let out a breath and then pushed her salad away, even though she'd only eaten about half of it. "I was talking to Linda, the realtor who had the listing. She said the property was bought through a trust and that they paid cash. One point nine million dollars. And okay, it was done by wire transfer, not someone walking into her office with a suitcase full of cash, but still. I don't know anyone who can pay cash for a house like that…do you?"

No, I most certainly did not. Oh, sure, my father had paid cash for the land where he'd built a cabin a while back, but that was only about sixty thousand dollars, not nearly two million. Even my ex-husband, who was earning nearly seven figures these days, couldn't afford that kind of cash outlay. On the surface, it did seem, if not suspicious, then at the very least highly irregular. Still, I couldn't quite stop myself from grasping at straws. "You said a trust bought the house, right? So, maybe Ben didn't have anything to do with the actual transaction."

Once again, she gazed at me with something close to pity in her eyes, as if she couldn't possibly believe that I'd be so naïve. "Jillian, people use trusts to obfuscate who owns what and whose money is exchanging hands. Yes, of course there are totally legitimate reasons why you might want to handle those kinds of transactions in such a way, but when you add that to Ben's compulsion to hide absolutely everything about himself from you, you have to admit it doesn't smell very good."

No, it didn't. While his finances were none of my business, so many things here weren't adding up, and those anomalies were only contributing to my overall unease. I made myself eat another bite of salad, even though I'd pretty much lost my appetite by that point. Once I'd washed the food down with a sip of water, I put down my fork and sent her a pleading look. "I don't know what you expect me to do."

Naomi reached across the table and patted me on the hand. "I don't *expect* you to do anything, except to do your best to be smart about this. You need to talk to the guy, Jillian. Like I started to say earlier, if you can get him to cough up a few details—maybe not his entire life story, but enough that you're satisfied, then sure, I won't talk to my private investigator friends. Otherwise…."

The words trailed off, but the threat in them was implicit. Although maybe "threat" was too strong a word. I knew my friend was just trying to look out for me because she didn't want me to get hurt or mixed up in something that could cause trouble for me down the line. And if making sure I was safe meant reaching out to a private investigator to uncover some of the truths Ben was hiding from me, then so be it.

Honestly, right then, I was so conflicted, I didn't know what to do. I wanted to respect Ben's privacy…but at the same time, I also didn't want to be left in the dark. It wasn't fair for him to do that to me.

"Okay," I said at last. "I'll try to talk to him tonight. I can't promise anything, just because I know he's going to dig in his heels. But I'll try."

"I'm not asking you to promise anything," Naomi replied, her tone earnest. She genuinely looked concerned, hands knotted together on the tabletop in front of her, brows drawn together. "And I don't want to be the cause of any trouble between you and Ben. But I also know you can't let things go on like this indefinitely. You need to talk. If he cares at all about you, then he should know it's not a good idea to keep secrets from one another."

This was so eminently obvious that I couldn't really protest. All the same, I couldn't quite fight off the sinking sensation that started somewhere deep in the pit of my stomach.

Ben wasn't going to like this. No, not at all.

INTERLUDE

Was this what being in love with someone felt like?

Beelzebub couldn't say for sure, because obviously, he'd never experienced an emotion like this before. It had been difficult to leave Jillian's house that morning, and yet he'd made himself come home, mostly because he needed some time to gather his thoughts—and, of course, take care of Rufus. He'd fed the dog and taken a shower, and they'd gone out for a walk together after that. During all of these prosaic tasks, however, his thoughts had been consumed by Jillian Torres, by the sound of her voice and the taste of her sweet mouth, by the fresh, clean scent of her hair.

And yes, that hair had looked magnificent spread out on the pillows of her bed.

Just the mere mental image was enough to

make his groin tighten in need. He didn't want to reflect on the irony of being so obsessed by her when he'd spent countless millennia laughing at humans and their—to him, at any rate—insane preoccupation with sex. A mere animal instinct, and certainly nothing that should require so much time and attention.

Well, he knew better now. She had taken up space in his brain, and there didn't seem to be much he could do to get her out.

Not that he really wanted to. No, he found it far more satisfying to replay those scenes in his mind, to recall how lush her body had felt beneath his, how insanely amazing it was to be locked together with her, their two separate selves seeming to become one, if only for a few minutes. The length of time didn't matter so much, because it felt as though he'd lived a few delicious centuries while being caught in her embrace.

The day was fine, and so he'd come to sit in the backyard, to let the sun touch his skin and his hair while he watched Rufus happily sniff around the perimeter of the space, looking for God knows what. Beelzebub supposed he'd been hoping that the fresh air might do something to clear his mind, and yet it didn't seem to matter how much of the cool, slightly damp breeze he breathed in—he still found his thoughts going back to Jillian over and over, as if they were caught in some kind of loop and would never be able to break free.

Yes, this certainly did seem like love. Or infatuation. Did he know her well enough to be in love with her?

Was he even capable of being in love with someone?

A few weeks ago, he would have dismissed such a question as utterly ridiculous. There was no room for love in a demon's heart…or at least, his heart. But it seemed that Jillian had somehow managed to take up space there, despite his earlier belief that he was incapable of such a soft, soppy, silly emotion.

All right, if he was able to admit that he might…just might…harbor some sort of feelings for her, that could only lead to his next question.

What did he plan to do about it?

Most of the time, Beelzebub had an answer for everything. Now, though, he found himself at a loss. Was he capable of doing the same thing that both Lucifer and Asmodeus had done, i.e., attaching himself to one woman for the rest of his existence and living an utterly prosaic life with her?

He couldn't begin to say. On the one hand, if his current preoccupation was any indication, then he certainly didn't seem to fare very well when he was separated from her. On the other, while he hadn't quite decided yet what to do with this earthly existence that God had sentenced him to, Beelzebub hadn't exactly expected to do something so common and humdrum as to pledge himself to one person and settle down with them and a dog—or several, as was currently the case—and live out his life puttering in the garden, or whatever it was that God expected him to do with his mortal days.

This was all so very difficult. Not so long ago, he'd known exactly what was required of him, what his place in the universe was supposed to be. And yet…he wasn't sure whether he would want to return to that life, even if it was offered to him. To be a lieutenant of Hell was no small thing, to be sure, and yet he didn't quite know whether it could ever measure up to the way he'd felt when he held Jillian in his arms.

And as soon as that thought crossed his mind, Beelzebub realized he truly was lost.

CHAPTER FIFTEEN

MAYBE IT WAS SILLY TO BE SO NERVOUS ABOUT having Ben over, but despite my inner remonstrances, I couldn't quite ignore the agitated butterflies flitting around in my stomach as I set the table in preparation for his arrival. Naomi's words had stayed stuck in my mind, for better or worse.

If he cares at all about you, then he should know it's not a good idea to keep secrets from one another.

That sounded so sensible, so true, that I couldn't really dispute her assertion. However, she wasn't the one who would have to confront Ben. No, she'd be safely over at her house—not alone, because I'd seen Eloy's silver Audi coupe pull up a while earlier—doing whatever it was the two of them did together. Some kind of strategy session,

I assumed, since she wasn't filming that day and she hadn't mentioned any kind of event she planned to attend.

Not that it was really any of my business what she and her manager did with their time... although I wasn't sure if Ben was the only one she should be lecturing about keeping secrets. I knew that Eloy hadn't meant for me to see it, but I couldn't help noticing the glance he'd sent Naomi when he thought no one was looking. There had been just a bit too much longing in that look for someone who supposedly wasn't interested in women, although I knew I was too chickenshit to bring it up to him. If any declarations of love were forthcoming, they'd have to come out naturally, and not at my urging.

A knock came at the door, and I hurriedly set down the wine glasses I was holding and went to answer it. Ben stood on the doorstep, a bottle of wine in one hand and an excited Rufus at the end of the leash he held with the other. The dog was practically bouncing, tail wagging like crazy.

"Come on in," I said, then took the bottle of wine from Ben. Our fingers brushed against one another, and a thrill made its way down my back. I couldn't quite forget what those fingers had felt like as he'd stroked me to a climax the night before. Doing my best to push that thought aside, I added, "It looks like Rufus misses the puppies."

"I suppose so," Ben observed. He'd bent down to undo the dog's leash, and Rufus bolted for the family room as soon as he was freed. A moment later, I heard excited little yips coming from that direction, and guessed that the puppies had piled on the moment he entered the room. "It sounds as though they're sufficiently occupied."

"Yes, it does," I agreed. "So, what are you in the mood for? Indian, Chinese, Thai, Mexican? Or we can do pizza, or Italian."

He looked a little bewildered by all the choices I'd just offered him. "I don't know...Italian? We had Chinese not too long ago."

"Sure," I said, pleased despite my nervousness. I'd been secretly hoping he'd choose Italian, just because I'd been jonesing for the lasagna from my favorite local place. "Let me pull up their menu on my phone—it's in the kitchen."

He followed me in, and I scooped up my phone from the counter, unlocked it, and then navigated to the restaurant's Yelp profile so he could take a look at the menu. While he was occupied, I took the wine into the dining room, noting that he'd brought a red blend—and happy for his choice, since it gave us more flexibility in terms of pairings.

"Should I go ahead and call it in?" he asked once I returned to the kitchen. "What would you like?"

"Lasagna—and a garden salad to share?"

"Anything else?"

"Garlic bread," I said promptly. Most of the time, I tried to avoid eating bread, but I wasn't about to skip an opportunity to have some of Francisco's amazing cheesy garlic bread.

A nod, and he pulled his own phone out of his pocket and made the call. I watched him, enjoying just the simple sight of him on the phone, leaned up against the counter, the recessed lights overhead catching little flickers of dark gold and warm umber in his brown hair. He really was insanely good-looking, and I wondered what it was he saw in me when he could have had his pick of any number of beautiful women.

And while I didn't like his secretive behavior, I also had to give him props for not making any snide comments about what I'd ordered. If that had been Tom standing there and placing our order, it would have been almost guaranteed that he would have made a remark about the garlic bread and how I needed to be careful about what I ate. Which wasn't even true, not really, because I did so much running around with the dogs and so much work around the house that my lifestyle wasn't a sedentary one at all. I could afford to indulge every once in a while.

Ben, however, didn't appear to care, or at least, he seemed to realize that I was a grown woman and could make those sorts of decisions for myself.

"All set," he said, once he was done. "The food will be here in about fifteen minutes."

"Great," I responded, although I wasn't sure how "great" it really was. Yes, I wanted to talk to him, but I had a feeling it would be better to delay that discussion until after he'd had a little food and wine inside him and was feeling a bit more mellow.

And since we might as well get started with the wine....

"Let's go to the dining room to wait for the food," I suggested. "It's closer to the front door anyway. And you can open the wine."

"Of course."

We went to the dining room and sat down, and he opened the bottle he'd brought and poured a bit into each of our glasses. The first swallow I took was way too big, but I didn't think he'd noticed. Although he was doing his best to act smooth and casual, I could tell he seemed on edge as well. Probably just post-coital awkwardness, but it didn't make me feel much better about our impending discussion.

"Busy day?" he asked, obviously trying to make conversation.

"Sort of," I said, and then went on to tell him about the puppies' visit to the vet for their checkup, and about the couple I'd met who wanted to become fosters for Little Angels. That meeting had gone really well, and so I knew I was going to add them to our little community of dog lovers. However, I decided not to mention my trip to the bank to deposit the check Luke Nicolini had bestowed on my rescue organization; while there was a good chance that Ben's former associate might come up in our conversation later in the evening, I didn't see the point in instigating a confrontation before it was strictly necessary. I also didn't say anything about Naomi's lunch visit. I doubted it would go over too well if I told Ben that my best friend wanted to sic one of her private investigator acquaintances on him to ferret out the hidden details of his past.

The delivery guy showed up then with the food, and the next few minutes were busy with getting everything set out on the table and trans-ferred to plates and bowls. Ben took the empty takeout containers into the kitchen and then returned and seated himself again at the head of the table. I noticed how he'd neatly taken over the ordering process earlier so he could pay for every-thing but hadn't mentioned it. If what Naomi had told me earlier was true, he was in a much better position to pick up the tab than I.

He lifted his glass. "To not making you cook," he said, and I grinned.

"This time," I amended, and he touched his glass to mine with a smile of his own, albeit one with a tinge of resignation to it. "Although I'll admit that the lasagna at Francisco's beats anything I could make."

Ben had ordered the same thing, I noticed, which in a way was fun, since it made our dinner feel as if it might have been homemade and dished up from a big baking dish that resided somewhere in the kitchen. For a minute or two, we were quiet as we alternated bites of lasagna with bites of salad or garlic bread, or sips of wine. I'd gone ahead and lit the two taper candles that sat on the dining room table but had dispensed with the others, and the overall mood was a bit more prosaic than it had been the evening before.

Or maybe I just wasn't feeling all that romantic because I was steeling myself for a confrontation and really, really would have preferred to avoid it.

You could, you know, I told myself as Ben poured me a bit more wine. *I mean, he doesn't know you talked to Naomi. He doesn't know that you made this grand plan to pry information out of him. You could just…let it go.*

Put that way, leaving things alone sounded awfully tempting. Yes, maybe that was the coward's way out, but would it really kill me to let a few more days pass before I started nagging him to tell me more about himself?

As my father often said, if ain't broke....

I drank some wine and took a bite of garlic bread. Ben spoke then, looking concerned.

"Is something the matter?"

"No," I said hastily. "Why would you ask me that?"

"Because you seem preoccupied."

Well, I was. However, I couldn't admit to such a thing without having him ask what was currently occupying my mind. "Sorry," I said. "I suppose I was just thinking about the puppies."

"'The puppies'?" he repeated, a slight frown creasing his brow. "I thought you said their visit to the vet went well."

"Oh, it did," I said hastily. "No, it's just that I've sort of fallen in love with them, and I'm trying to figure out how angry Frida will be with me if I try to keep all of them instead of just Boudicca."

He blinked. "That's a lot of dogs."

"They're chihuahuas," I pointed out. "It's not like I'm going to have a herd of old English sheepdogs roaming around the place."

"Still."

Maybe he had a point. Yes, chihuahuas didn't take up a lot of space, but five of them would still be a lot of dogs to have underfoot. If I had that many full-time, I'd be a lot harder-pressed to take in fosters on a temporary basis, even for a night or two. But I felt so close to the dogs after hand-feeding them for almost two weeks—not to mention getting thrown in the slammer for taking them away from their abusive owners in the first place—that I didn't know whether I'd be able to give them up when the time came.

"Well, it's just a thought," I told him. "I haven't made up my mind yet. I still have some time before I can even think about posting them as being available for adoption."

"Then don't worry about it," he said as he tipped a little more wine into my glass. "I know you'll choose the right thing to do."

Loaded words. Maybe Ben didn't see them that way, since he could have no idea of what really had been tying me in knots, but I realized I did need to do the right thing. That meant I needed to get my relationship with Ben on a solid footing, one based in truth. I didn't want to continually be guessing what might be hidden in his past, or whether we might run into someone he knew but didn't want to discuss. How was that any way to maintain a healthy relationship?

"About that," I began, and he tilted his head at me, expression puzzled.

"About what?"

"Doing the right thing."

He continued to gaze at me, obviously not comprehending. Or maybe he had a flicker of understanding but didn't want to acknowledge what I was trying to tell him.

I sucked in a breath and glanced at my wine glass, then decided it was better not to take a sip right then. That sort of thing would only make it look as though I needed the wine to give me confidence. And all right, that would only be the truth, but I felt shaky enough as it was and didn't want to give the impression of looking weak.

"I'm—I'm glad about what happened last night," I said. Instead of looking relieved by that statement, he frowned again, as if he'd guessed it was the prelude to something he would prefer not to hear. "But it still bothers me that you won't tell me anything about yourself. I know nothing about you, Ben. You could be married—"

"I'm not married," he cut in, his tone flat. "Anything else you want to know?"

Oh, he was already angry. No, he hadn't raised his voice or anything, but I'd caught the glint in his hazel eyes and knew I was treading on dangerous ground. Unfortunately, it was too late to turn back, so I told myself to toughen up and keep going.

"Everything," I said simply. "I want to know where you came from. I want to know about your family, about where you went to school. I've told you so much about myself, and I still know nothing about you. Nothing at all."

His gaze dropped from mine, and he fussed with the napkin in his lap. "There's nothing to tell."

"There's always *something*," I said, doing my best to keep the mounting frustration out of my voice. "I don't care if you've had the most boring existence on the planet—you still must have a past of some sort. Obviously, or you wouldn't have had the reaction to seeing Luke Nicolini that you did."

"So, you want me to tell you about that?" Now Ben's voice had an edge to it, although his tone was still even enough. He looked up at me, eyes narrowed, all the warmth I'd seen in them earlier gone.

A chill went through me. I had a very good idea that I'd already ruined things between us, but there was no point in backing down now. The dice had been rolled, and it sure looked as though they'd come up snake eyes.

Still, I found myself equivocating, if only the tiniest bit. "You don't have to tell me about Luke if you don't want to," I said quietly. "But I want you to tell me something. Anything. Are your parents still alive?"

"No."

The one syllable came out as though he'd ground it from between his teeth. Still, he'd answered me, hadn't tried to evade the question. "I'm sorry," I said. "That must have been hard."

For some reason, he smiled, although that smile didn't have much humor in it. "Oh, not as hard as you might think. Anything else?"

"Do you have any brothers or sisters?"

"No."

"I'm an only child, too," I told him. "Although you probably guessed that, since I would have mentioned siblings by now."

"I hadn't really thought about it."

He might have been a stranger as he sat there, face hard, eyes not meeting mine. In that moment, it was difficult to remember how he'd held me less than twenty-four hours earlier, had kissed me, had made me feel a sort of ecstasy I'd never experienced before. How I'd fallen asleep in his arms, utterly satisfied, feeling safe and happy and relaxed.

Well, I sure wasn't feeling any of those things at the moment.

"College?" I said desperately.

"I'm an autodidact," he responded, and in that moment, I got the definite notion he was now playing with me in some fashion I couldn't quite comprehend. "What about you?"

"USC," I replied. "That's where I met Tom. I was working in the law library. Otherwise, I don't know whether we would have bumped into each other, since he'd already graduated and was in law school, and I was still a sophomore."

"Must have been fate," Ben said with a slight baring of his teeth that was probably meant to be a smile.

I reached for my wine and took a swallow. Right then, I didn't care what he might think; I needed that drink. "I don't believe in fate."

"How modern of you."

Anger flared, but I pushed it back. Luckily, I'd had years of dealing with that sort of thing; Tom had always done his best to push my buttons, to get me to strike out in anger without thinking, and so I'd learned to tamp down my rage and do my best to think before I spoke. "Look, Ben, the last thing I wanted to do was upset you, but—"

"I'm not upset."

Seriously? He was doing a pretty good imitation, as far as I could tell. However, some men hated to admit to any feelings, and Ben was so closed off, I supposed I shouldn't have been all that surprised to see him react in such a way. "I just—" I paused and sucked in a breath, telling myself to be strong. Nothing ventured, and all that. "I care about you, Ben. I like the two of us together. But I don't like knowing so little about you. After…after last night, I guess I sort of assumed there might be some kind of future for us. Maybe I was wrong. You tell me."

Utter silence after that little speech. He continued to sit there in his chair, gaze fixed on me, although I somehow had the feeling that he was staring at something far beyond this room, something that had absolutely nothing to do with me at all. It was horrible in its way, simply because it made me feel as if I didn't matter to him, that I was only a means of amusing himself and nothing more.

"I don't know," he said at last.

So much for holding back my anger. "You don't know?" I burst out. "Did you know when you fucked me last night?"

The casual obscenity made him blink, but otherwise, he didn't react. Or rather, he didn't say anything, only folded his napkin and set it on the table, then slowly stood.

"I think I'll see myself out," he said.

"So, you're going to run away?" I demanded, figuring I'd already done my worst, and so it didn't really matter what I said. "Why won't you talk to me about this?"

His jaw hardened. "Because there's nothing to say. Have a good evening, Jillian."

After uttering that empty—and cruel—pleasantry, he walked out of the dining room. I heard him call to Rufus, and the clatter of the dog's toenails on the wooden floor. A minute later, the front door shut quietly.

I wished he had slammed it.

The only sound in the dining room was the pounding of my heart against my ribcage. Or maybe it just seemed that way; I knew the roar of angry blood was loud in my ears. For a long moment, I sat there, not sure what I was supposed to do.

Get up, clear the table, go check on the dogs. Pretend none of this had ever happened. That was the logical course, I supposed. After all, I knew from bitter experience that it was easy enough to go on with a broken heart. It would heal eventually. And really, it wasn't as though Ben and I had shared all that much. I'd never told him how much I cared for him, that maybe, just maybe, in a hidden little portion of my soul, I'd allowed myself to admit that I loved him. But he didn't know that. This could have been just about sex.

It wasn't, though.

I should have kept my mouth shut. Irrational anger flashed through me then, anger at Naomi for convincing me that I needed to prod Ben into revealing something of his past. If she hadn't butted in....

Unthinking, I pushed myself to my feet and stomped out of the dining room. Duty forced me to peek into the family room to check the dogs, but although Frida was watchful, her bright dark eyes meeting mine as I looked in, the puppies were asleep, smashed into a little puppy pile in their favorite spot in front of the fireplace, although no fire was burning that night.

Rage pushed me out the back door, down the steps, and along the walkway to the gate that opened into Naomi's backyard. I honestly couldn't even say why I felt the need to have it out with her right then, except that I felt as if I had to expend my rage on something or I would explode.

Her back door was locked. This shouldn't have surprised me, since it was after dark, and even though our street was quiet enough, Angelino Heights wasn't all that far from some fairly rough neighborhoods. I knocked, waited, and knocked again when no one answered the door quickly enough for my taste.

At last, though, Naomi appeared, wine glass in one hand as she stared out at me in surprise. "Jillian? What the hell—"

"Tell him to open up!" I snapped. "Make him talk to you! Great frigging idea, Naomi!"

Comprehension flared in her eyes. "Oh, shit. It didn't go well?"

"No, it did not go well."

"Come in," she said. "No point in you standing out there in the cold. Want some wine?"

Hell yes, I did. I nodded.

There was a bottle sitting on the counter. I couldn't see the label—not that it mattered. What mattered was that she poured me a healthy amount into one of her big blown-glass Mexican goblets and then handed it to me.

"Big drink," she said.

I gulped some down. Afterward, while I didn't feel exactly better, at least I felt as if I could stand there without falling apart.

"Good. Now, come and sit down."

She guided me out of the kitchen and into her family room, which was bigger and airier than mine, with pale gray walls and white linen sofas and cream-washed furniture. An extravagant arrangement of peonies and hydrangeas over-flowed a vase to one side.

Eloy was sitting on one of the couches, a glass of wine in one hand and an expression of some alarm on his face. Several fashion magazines adorned with various sticky notes—research, I assumed—were spread out on the coffee table in front of him. "Girlfriend, what's going on?"

"She had a fight with Ben," Naomi said as she gently pushed me toward the empty sofa so I could sit down.

"Oh."

He looked nonplussed, and I wondered how much Naomi had told him about the situation with Ben and me. Probably not all that much; she knew how to keep a secret, and she'd most likely guessed that I wouldn't be thrilled if she went and blabbed everything to her business partner.

"It's your fault," I said in accusing tones after I'd helped myself to another fortifying swallow of wine. "If you hadn't told me I needed to force him to talk—"

"I didn't say you should *force* him," she said gently. "I just said you should let him know how important it was for him to be open with you."

I waved a hand. "Whatever. Anyway, you're a fine one to talk about honesty and openness."

"Excuse me?" she responded with a blink. "Jillian, I've always been honest with you."

Well, all right, that was true enough. Right then, however, I realized I'd been talking about something else entirely. My gaze shifted to Eloy, and something about his posture stiffened, as if he'd just realized that the wine had gotten hold of my tongue and I was about to say some things that couldn't be taken back.

"Maybe you two should sort this out—" he said as he shuffled the magazines together and looked as though he was about to stand up and flee.

Oh, no way was I going to let him get away with that. If Naomi was all about honesty, then she should start at home, so to speak.

"I don't think it's either of us who have the

honesty problem," I said. "I think it's the men in our lives who have issues."

"I really don't—" Eloy began, but Naomi cut him off.

"Eloy has always been honest with me. Haven't you, Eloy?"

One of the magazines slipped from his grasp and fell to the floor. He ignored it, however, and replied, "Sure, Naomi. Always."

I let out a derisive laugh and drank some more wine, while Naomi started to look as though she was regretting pouring it for me. "Bullshit. If he was so damn honest, then he would have told you he was in love with you."

Then it was Naomi's turn to laugh, only hers was more startled than mocking. "Oh, come on, Jillian. Eloy is gay. How could he be in love with me?"

"Is he?" I asked. "Have you ever met any of his boyfriends?"

"Well, no, but…." She hesitated, as though she'd intended to offer more of a defense and then realized she didn't have one.

"Does he ever talk about a boyfriend?"

Eloy ran a nervous hand through his perfectly coiffed hair and said, "I don't have time for a personal life. Of course, I wouldn't talk about a boyfriend because I don't have one."

"Because you're too busy, or because you've

been secretly in love with Naomi this whole time?"

Expression strained, she said, "Jillian, you're really going too far with this one. Let me walk you home."

But, just as I had in my disastrous conversation with Ben a half hour earlier, I knew I'd gone too far to back out now. I wasn't doing this to hurt either of them, despite how angry I'd been. No, I was just tired of people lying to each other and thinking it was okay.

"Tell her, Eloy," I said.

He was quiet for a moment. Then, still in silence, he put down the magazines he was holding and faced her. In that moment, he was barely recognizable—all the affectation was gone, and his even, handsome features were strained, worried.

"I do love you, Naomi," he said quietly. "I've loved you for a long time."

"But…." The word trailed off, and she stared at him in utter confusion. "You let everyone think you were gay. Including me."

"A guy can like girly things and not be gay," he told her, still in that quiet, measured tone which didn't even sound like him. "Besides, would you have let me get close to you like I have if you'd thought I was straight, someone who might try to make a move on you?"

It was her turn then to be silent. She crossed her arms, glass of wine still held in one hand. "If we're all being honest here…then no. I wouldn't have let you get close."

He pushed a hand through his hair again, utterly messing it up this time. In a way, though, that looked much better. He seemed more approachable when he wasn't so perfect. "There you have it," he said simply.

She glanced over at me. "You knew and didn't say anything?"

"No, I didn't know," I told her. "Lately…I started to guess. I could have been wrong. But I just thought it would be better if you two were honest with each other."

"I don't—I don't know what to do," she said, and the helplessness in her voice wrung me. It was so unlike the confident, fix-anything Naomi Klein that I—and the rest of the world—knew.

"It's okay," I said, and patted her on the arm. "I'll leave you two to figure it out."

And I set down my glass of wine and walked out of the room.

INTERLUDE

It would have been easier if he hadn't loved her. Then, he could have simply been angry and nothing else. Now, though, all his anger was bound up with his feelings for her, and he didn't know what he was supposed to do about that.

Didn't she understand that there was no way in Hell—pardon the pun—that he could ever tell her the truth about himself? About what he was, where he'd come from? He was supposed to be living a simple mortal life, and confessing to the woman who'd somehow managed to insinuate her way into his heart that he was a former demon with no family, no origins, no past other than countless millennia spent toiling in the under-world, was simply not in the equation.

And it was even more awkward that she had

to be living right across the street from him. Avoiding her was going to be exceedingly difficult.

He'd taken Rufus home and spent the night brooding while he played Bach far too loud on the stereo system in the living room. The precise, elegant music didn't soothe him in the way it normally did, however, and he finally went to bed, although sleep eluded him for the most part. Therefore, he was in an even fouler mood than he'd expected when he got up the next morning and peeked past the curtains to see if there was any activity at her house. None that he could tell, although he noticed that the silver car which had been parked in front of her neighbor's home the night before was still there. Odd, since he couldn't recall Naomi having overnight visitors before this.

Well, it was none of his concern.

He ventured out to walk Rufus and was relieved when he still saw no sign of Jillian Torres. However, he'd barely gone inside his house and shut the door when she finally emerged from her own home, Frida at the end of a leash, trotting along with her head held high. Jillian's chin was also lifted, although he couldn't see much of her expression, since her eyes were shielded by a pair of large dark sunglasses...prescription, he assumed.

Not that it mattered. He would have to remind himself that nothing she did mattered from now on. They'd connected briefly, but it was obvious enough to him that he'd been fooling himself when he'd thought he might be able to participate in a normal human relationship. Such a thing simply wouldn't work…at least, not for him.

He wondered if there was any way to convince God to give him a different house. Frankly, the idea of spending the next several decades doing his best to avoid Jillian Torres was appalling. Bad enough to stay away from her, but what if she eventually found someone else? Could he really stomach the sight of her with some human who most certainly wouldn't deserve her? From what he'd seen of humanity so far, Beelzebub had no reason to think the next specimen she attracted would be any better than the philandering dolt who'd been her first husband. If there were still a Hell, then Tom Torres would most definitely be headed there. As it was, about the most Beelzebub could hope for was that his current fiancée would make his life as miserable as he'd made Jillian's.

Problem was, he couldn't exactly pull out his cell phone, call his Creator, and make a request for a change of residence. God contacted you, not the other way around.

The second night was even worse than the first. Beelzebub lay in bed, wakeful, staring at the ceiling and wondering if he would ever be able to sleep again. This human body required it, and although when he'd first been sent into this mortal exile, he'd hated the thought of giving up so many hours of each day to oblivion, now he wished he could lose himself in such blessed forgetfulness. However, sleep was now a will o' the wisp, something he found himself chasing but unable to catch. He fancied he could still smell the soft perfume of Jillian's hair, and his body craved the sensation of her curled up against him, even though they'd only spent one night together.

A night that seemed destined to haunt him for the rest of the days. Right then, Beelzebub was glad he was now mortal, because at least he would eventually die and be released from his torment.

When he went to shave that morning, a bleary-eyed, scruffy self stared back at him from the mirror. He put down the razor, realizing he didn't give a damn whether the lower half of his face was covered in scruff or not. Honestly, he didn't give a damn about much of anything at all.

Although he hadn't yet picked up the human habit of drinking coffee, he realized he needed some kind of stimulant. Tea seemed far too insipid to him, and so, once he'd walked Rufus— managing to avoid Jillian altogether this time, for which he was grateful—he got in his car and drove down the hill to a coffee house he'd passed several times but had never set foot in before that moment.

Almost at once, he realized he'd made a mistake. The place was crowded and noisy, and the sight of a young woman with hair almost as fair as Jillian's made him realize that it didn't matter where he went, as it seemed he would be haunted by her absence no matter where he was.

He took the café au lait he'd ordered back to his car and sat there for a long moment, trying to decide what he should do. The mere thought of entering his empty house seemed anathema to him, although he knew he would have to return at some point to feed Rufus his lunch. Still, that particular task was some hours in the future. Maybe he should simply drive around aimlessly in an attempt to gather his thoughts, but doing so didn't seem like a very good use of his time. Besides, Los Angeles traffic was so abominable that he guessed such an endeavor would only put him more on edge.

As he sat in the parking lot and sipped his coffee, he realized he wished he had someone he could talk to about his situation, if only to have them reassure him that he'd done the right thing by walking out on Jillian. But he knew no one in L.A., and besides, spilling his heart to a human would be a pointless effort. It wasn't as if a mortal could begin to understand what he was going through.

A thought occurred to him, one so ridiculous, he almost dismissed it out of hand.

Except....

He knew he was being a little disingenuous when he tried to tell himself that he didn't know anyone in Los Angeles. He knew two people, both of whom were former demons and therefore uniquely suited to understanding his current situation.

However, he knew he would never talk to Lucifer. The former lord of Hell would only pretend to be sympathetic, but would probably be laughing internally at his former subordinate.

But Asmodeus...he was the closest thing to a friend Beelzebub had ever had. Maybe he, too, would find his former associate's current situation amusing. On the other hand, he might be able to offer some advice.

Advice to go groveling back to her, Beelzebub thought then with a curl of his lip. *After all, Asmodeus's entire reason for being had been to bed human women. He certainly isn't going to tell you that you were right to leave.*

Maybe not. But advice didn't have to be taken, and Asmodeus was probably the best—and only—sounding board Beelzebub currently had.

Thus resolved, he finished the rest of his

coffee, then got out of the car so he could put the empty cup in one of the trash receptacles at the border of the parking lot. That task done, he climbed back into the Jag and recited the address for Asmodeus's Century City office into his phone's navigation system.

Although it was nearly ten and the morning rush hour mostly over, it still took him almost an hour to get to Century City. Scowling, Beelzebub took the ticket from the machine at the building's gate-guarded subterranean parking, then navigated his way to a parking space relatively close to the elevator. When he reached the lobby, he scanned the directory, saw that Asmodeus's office was located on the fifteenth floor, and took another elevator to reach his location.

The place was elegant in a cool, sparse way. An extremely pretty Asian woman sat at the reception desk—no surprise there. Asmodeus might have found the love of his life, but that didn't mean he wasn't going to hire someone decorative as the public face of his business.

"Can I help you?" she asked pleasantly when he approached.

"Is Allan D'Alessandro in?" Beelzebub responded, using his former compatriot's human alias.

"Who's asking, please?"

"Benjamin Blake. We used to work together."

"At Hart Hathaway?" she said.

That was the agency where Asmodeus had first worked in human form before striking out on his own. "No," Beelzebub said. "Before that."

The receptionist didn't seem too put out by his response. "Oh. Well, let me see if he's available." She touched her headset and said, "Allan? I have a man out here who'd like to speak to you—a Benjamin Blake. I—" A pause, and then she said, "Of course. I'll bring him right over." Another touch of her index finger to the headset, and she looked up at Beelzebub and smiled. "Right this way, Mr. Blake."

She got up from the desk, and led him out of the reception area and down a short hallway to an office that apparently took up most of the space on that side of the building. It was enclosed in glass, and so Beelzebub could clearly see Asmodeus get up from his desk and come to the door. What the purpose of that door was exactly, he didn't know, since the office was a fishbowl, but he supposed that if it was closed, then at least it would keep any sound from escaping.

"Ben!" Asmodeus said with a big smile. He clapped his former associate on the shoulder, and Ben did his best not to wince at the familiarity. "Great to see you. Thanks, Miko," he added, obviously addressing the receptionist. She nodded and went back to the front desk, while Asmodeus guided Beelzebub into his office and closed the door. "Coffee?" he asked, inclining his head toward a stainless-steel monstrosity of an espresso machine that sat on a table off to one side.

"No, thank you," Beelzebub replied.

"Water?"

"No."

Asmodeus paused there and tilted his head to one side as he regarded his visitor. Beelzebub had to admit that his former partner-in-crime was looking very well, tanned and relaxed, an expensive watch gleaming on his left wrist. Quite the contrast to how he knew he himself had looked that morning.

An observation confirmed by Asmodeus, who said amiably, "You look like shit, Beelzebub. What's going on? I was hoping for the best for you, especially after I saw you with that gorgeous blonde at Lucifer's little party the other night."

"Jillian and I aren't together," he said shortly, making Asmodeus's eyes narrow in sudden comprehension.

"Ah," he responded. "No wonder you look like hell. What happened?"

"I—" Now that the time had come to explain his predicament, Beelzebub wasn't sure whether he had the courage to tell the truth. Coming here had been a huge mistake.

"She dumped you?"

"No," he said at once, a little nettled that Asmodeus would immediately jump to the conclusion that Jillian had been the one to end things. "I walked out. She was asking for things I couldn't give her."

Asmodeus ambled over to his desk—a large L-shaped hunk of glass and metal—and leaned against it, hands stuck in his trouser pockets. "Such as?"

"She wanted to know more about me—about where I'd come from, my family, those sorts of things."

"Sounds like a pretty rational request to me."

"Well, on the *surface*," Beelzebub replied, trying not to grind his teeth. "But of course, I couldn't tell her the truth."

"Why not?"

He blinked. "Why not? Are you joking?"

Asmodeus lifted an eyebrow. "No, I'm not joking."

Clearly, living a mortal lifestyle had made Asmodeus completely lose touch with reality. "I should think it would be patently obvious why I couldn't tell her who I really was."

"I don't think it's as obvious as you believe it is," Asmodeus said. "After all, Christa knew exactly who Lucifer was and loved him anyway, and it was only when Belinda discovered that I was a demon that she realized she actually could be with me. So, I guess I don't understand what the big problem is with you telling Jillian the truth as well."

"The circumstances are completely different," Beelzebub gritted. Obviously, his instincts had been correct. Asmodeus was being absolutely no help at all.

A shrug. "I don't think they're as different as you think they are." Asmodeus removed his hands from his trouser pockets and straightened, then came over to where Beelzebub stood. "Considering your former stance on relations with human women, I'm going to go out on a limb here and guess that this Jillian is a pretty special person."

"She is," Beelzebub allowed. Or at least, he'd believed she was. Now he wasn't quite as sure. If she was truly as extraordinary as he'd thought, wouldn't she have understood that some secrets needed to be kept, no matter what?

"Well, then," Asmodeus said. "If she's that special, then why won't you give her the benefit of the doubt and tell her the truth? After all, it's not as if you're a demon anymore. You're not going around possessing people and causing havoc."

"More's the pity," Beelzebub growled, and Asmodeus chuckled and patted him on the shoulder again.

"You say that, but I don't think you mean it.

Not really. Anyway, being a demon is in your past. It's not who you are now."

The words slipped out before he could stop them. "I don't know who I am now."

His former compatriot sent him a look of almost pity...but definitely one of understanding. Voice gentle, he said, "Then I think it's time you found out."

For a long moment, Beelzebub didn't respond. Then, slowly, he nodded.

As humans said, the past was prologue. Now he needed to decide how to write the rest of his life's story...

...and he knew he needed Jillian to be a part of that story.

"Thank you, Asmodeus," he said. Those were the only words he could give voice to, but his fellow demon seemed to understand. A corner of his mouth lifted.

"That's what friends are for, Beelzebub."

CHAPTER SIXTEEN

I pushed my glasses up my nose and did my best to focus on my laptop's screen. The day before, I'd taken in two rescues—and thank God for that, because getting them to the vet to be checked out and then off to my newest foster family had taken enough mental energy that I could almost forget the way Ben had broken my heart—and now I needed to get the two rescues up on the Little Angels website. Wrestling with Wordpress was not usually my idea of a fun time, but it gave me something to do. I couldn't spend all my time crying on Naomi's shoulder…not that her shoulder was terribly available, since my temper tantrum of two days earlier seemed to have succeeded in driving her and Eloy right into each other's arms.

"What about your 'man cleanse'?" I'd asked

her only that morning, when she'd come over to share a cup of coffee while he was off getting a haircut.

Her expression went dreamy, which led me to believe she'd gotten spectacularly laid. And her next words only seemed to prove my suspicions. "Oh, I've been cleansed, all right," she remarked, and took a sip of coffee.

"Spare me the gory details," I said, and she chuckled.

"Not to worry," she replied. "I know that you don't want to know. But…things are looking good."

"For some of us," I muttered, and her smile disappeared as if it had never been there in the first place.

"I'm sorry. That was insensitive."

I waved a hand. "No, it's okay. I never want to be one of those awful people who can't be happy for someone else just because their own life is in the shitter."

Naomi's expression grew stern, and she set down her mug of coffee. "Your life is not in the shitter. What happened between you and Ben sucks, but it's not the end of everything. Maybe that was the universe getting him out of the way so something really spectacular could happen for you."

Good words, and ones I probably should have

been trying to take to heart. But after she headed back to her house and I sat down to update the Little Angels website, I thought that I didn't want the universe to send me something spectacular. I just wanted Ben back in my life.

"No, damn it, I don't want that photo resized," I muttered, clicking on the image in question so it wouldn't show up like a teeny thumbnail on the web page for the dog whose information I was entering. No tag, so we'd named her Tinkerbell, a tiny little apple-headed girl probably not even a year old. I had a feeling she'd get snapped up pretty quickly; her big brown eyes just begged you to pick her up and love her, and she was the popular brown and black combo, a really lovely pup. Thankfully, Terry and Michael had been able to foster her right away, or she might have stolen my heart as well, and I had enough puppies underfoot as it was.

The doorbell rang then, and I looked up from my laptop in annoyance. I had a "no solicitors" sign next to my front door, but the written warning still wasn't always enough to ward off the kids selling candy for school fundraisers or any particularly overzealous Mormons and Seventh Day Adventists. Maybe if I ignored it, whoever was at the door would go away.

No such luck, because the doorbell rang again. I let out a hiss of annoyance from between my teeth, clicked "save draft," and then shut my MacBook and got up to answer the door.

To my shock, Ben was standing on the front porch. He held a bouquet of hydrangeas tinted pale green and soft pink, and his expression was impossible to read. "May I come in?" he asked.

Part of me wanted to say, "No," and then slam the door. However, I told myself that wouldn't be a very mature response. Besides, I really wanted to know what he was doing on my doorstep after pulling a disappearing act for the past two days.

"Sure," I said, trying to sound unconcerned. I stepped aside and let him enter the foyer. "Let me put those in some water. You can go sit in the living room."

He nodded, and I took the flowers from him and went into the kitchen. To my surprise, I realized that my hands were shaking as I set the flowers down on the counter and rummaged through the cupboards for a suitable vase. I located a pretty carnival glass one that I'd found at a garage sale years back, and filled it with water before dropping the flowers into it. With them taken care of, I carried the impromptu arrangement back to the living room and set it down on the mantel.

Ben hadn't actually sat down, but was sort of hovering in front of the sofa, as if trying to make up his mind whether he should take a seat or not. "I need to talk to you," he said.

"All right, we're talking," I replied. "After two days, but I suppose better late than never."

His expression slipped a little then, and I could see the contrition in his eyes. "I needed to sort through a few things."

"And now you're done sorting?"

He hesitated before giving a very small lift of his shoulders. "I hope so." His gaze strayed to the couch as he added, "Maybe you should sit down."

"No, I'm good," I responded. I didn't want to give him the impression that I intended this conversation to go on any longer than it absolutely had to. "What did you want to tell me?"

Another of those long pauses. I noticed how his eyes wouldn't quite meet mine, how he glanced out through the big picture window, although I didn't quite know what in the world he was looking at. There wasn't anything out there except a lone SUV driving slowly past. Looky-loos, probably; we got a lot of those on our historic street.

"You're sure you don't want to sit down?"

"I'm fine," I told him, an edge creeping into my voice. Jesus, did he think I was on the verge of collapse simply due to his sudden reappearance?

"All right." He jammed his hands into the pockets of his trousers, a subtle herringbone tweed that I didn't think I'd seen before. "There were reasons why I didn't want to talk about my past."

"Such as?"

He didn't answer right away. In fact, there was such naked apprehension on his face that I began to feel sorry for him...even as a small tendril of doubt started to creep in. What if he really had been hiding some kind of terrible truth from me?

When the silence got too awful, I said, "What...are you a serial killer or something?"

"No," he replied, although he didn't crack a smile or give any indication that the truth he intended to reveal was any better. "I'm a demon."

I blinked at him. As he continued to stare at me, obviously waiting for some kind of response, I managed to say, "You're joking, right?"

"No joke." He straightened then, and suddenly his jaw seemed firmer and his eyes glinted with a sort of cold pride. "I am Beelzebub, Lucifer's lieutenant, chief among the princes of Hell."

His words had a ring of sincerity to them, but did that mean anything? If he was suffering from some sort of delusion—which of course he had to be, if he was making pronouncements like that—then he would believe what he was saying, wouldn't he?

"You don't look like a demon," I said, since I

really didn't know how else to respond to such a statement.

A bitter sort of smile touched his lips. "This is what I look like as a human. Actually, I am human...now. Or at least, this body is."

All right, now I had absolutely no idea what he was talking about. "A minute ago, you said you were a demon."

"I was a demon ever since I and the rest of my cohorts were banished from Heaven and sent to rule Hell," he said. "Unfortunately, a few weeks ago, God decided that Hell was an outmoded concept and decided to lay all of us off."

My head was swimming, and I didn't think I could blame it on an empty stomach and too much coffee. I sort of wobbled my way over to the couch and sank down on it, realizing that it probably wasn't a good idea to remain standing.

Ben's expression was almost smug. "I tried to tell you that you should sit down."

"Well, I'm sitting now," I returned. "So, you're a former demon who's out of a job, and now you're living in a restored Victorian house and driving a vintage Jag and adopting rescue animals."

"In a nutshell." He came over and sat down next to me, and took my hand. His fingers felt human enough, and far warmer than my own.

I probably should have yanked my hand away.

However, I was shaky enough right then that I didn't want to get into a tussle with him. And besides, as confused and as shaken—and yes, still angry—as I was, I couldn't deny that it felt good for him to be touching me. I liked the strength in those fingers, liked how they felt wrapped around mine.

"You know I can't possibly believe any of this, right?"

He hesitated. When he spoke, he sounded calm, almost resigned. "I know it all sounds crazy. If I were in your position, I probably wouldn't believe me, either. But...." The words drifted away into silence, and I saw his chest move as he pulled in a breath. He looked so very human...sounded human. For God's sake, I'd slept with the guy. I'd seen him, touched him, tasted him. How in the world could he be a demon?

"But?" I prompted.

"But I very much doubt a human could do this."

He lifted his hand from mine and spread his fingers. From his outstretched palm, a gout of angry-looking orange flame burst forth, shooting across the room. I let out a screech of fright and started to push myself off the sofa so I could run and get the fire extinguisher...only to pause as the fire abruptly disappeared. As far as I could tell, it hadn't caused any harm, even though it should have left scorch marks on the wall opposite us.

I stared at him, breaths coming from me in quick, terrified pants. "That's impossible."

"Not for a demon. Former demon," he amended. "But I was left with some of my powers. Not all of them, though," he added as he gazed down at his hands, as if even he wasn't sure what he was capable of any longer. A flick of his fingers, and the heavy curtains that framed the window blew wildly for a second, even though it was a cold day and everything was shut tight.

"This is…." I'd been about to say "crazy," but I thought we'd gone far beyond that and so out into left field that I couldn't even begin to guess where we stood.

"It's a lot to take in," he agreed. He shifted on the couch so he could face me directly, and I was so shell-shocked that I remained where I was, gazing straight into the shifting, cloudy depths of his hazel eyes. "You see now why I didn't want to say anything to you about my past. There's nothing normal about me, Jillian. I don't have a family, or friends."

That scene in the Crystal Ballroom at the Biltmore leapt into my mind. "How do you know Luke Nicolini? Is he another demon?"

"Not exactly," Ben replied with a resigned smile. "He's the Devil. *Was* the Devil," he amended. "He found love and was released from his rulership of Hell. His associate, Allan D'Alessandro, is actually Asmodeus. The two of us worked together on many occasions."

Even though it was only a little past ten in the morning, I found myself thinking that I needed a stiff drink. "Well, I guess it's better than being in the Mob," I joked feebly, and Ben reached over and took my hand again.

"Possibly. This is the truth, Jillian. This is what I was hiding from you."

For some reason, I found myself compelled to ask, "And the house?"

"The house...the car...the 'trust fund'... they're all part of my retirement package, so to speak." His fingers tightened on mine. "I understand if this is too much for you. But even if this doesn't change anything between us—even if you want nothing more to do with me—I wanted to tell you the truth. You deserved that much."

I stared at him, throat tight.

The truth.

Some part of me still didn't want to believe what he was saying, wanted to believe that flash of impossible flame and the wind from nowhere had only been a couple of parlor tricks. Except...I knew they couldn't be. I'd been standing right next to him the whole time. I'd held the hand he'd used only a few seconds before he produced the flame. There were no gizmos attached to his fingers, no tube connected to a tank of propane or kerosene or anything else that could have created such a flame, no controls for a fan he'd hidden somewhere to produce the wind effect. The sleeves of his crisp white shirt were rolled up, proving that he truly didn't have anything up his sleeve, so to speak.

No, he'd produced that flame from thin air and made the curtains billow in an unseen breeze because he wasn't exactly human, no matter what he looked like.

And no wonder he'd tried to walk away from me. If I'd been hiding a secret like that, I wouldn't exactly have been shouting it from the rooftops, either.

But he'd come back. He'd come back to this house and told me the truth because he believed I deserved it. That was a lot more consideration than I'd ever gotten from Tom, who'd tried to sell me his lies right until the very end, when he finally realized there was no way to hide what he'd done.

This demon...former demon...was a hell of a lot more honorable than many people I'd known.

"Thank you," I said quietly. "Thank you for that, Beelzebub."

The corners of his mouth lifted ever so slightly. "I prefer Ben these days."

"Ben," I repeated, and paused, not sure what else to say. A moment later, though, a question bubbled up in my mind and found its way to my lips. "What about the other demons?"

"'Other demons'?" he echoed.

"You said God closed Hell and you demons were all laid off. Did everyone else get a 'retirement package'?"

A thoughtful look passed over Ben's face. "I hadn't really thought about it, but I suppose they must have. But, other than Lucifer and Asmodeus, I don't know where they were sent or whether they were given exactly the same deal." A pause, and he added softly, "I can only hope that they ended up somewhere even half as good as here."

Our eyes were still locked. I didn't want to look away. In that moment, I wanted to take all of him in—the sensual lips, the dark stubble on his cheeks and chin, the way his left eyebrow arched ever so slightly more than the right. Did it matter where he'd come from? He was here now...and he'd somehow managed to make me understand that there was still a lot of love left in my heart.

I didn't know which one of us moved first, but in the next second, our lips were locked together. Warm, welcome heat flooded my body, and I let him press me down into the cushions, his weight on top of me, holding me in place as we tasted one another again, my legs wrapping around him and pulling him close, even though we were fully clothed and nothing was going to happen.

Well, not at that exact second, anyway.

We came up for air at some point, his gaze fixed on me, intent. "Does this mean you forgive me?" he asked.

"I'm not sure there's anything I need to forgive you for," I told him. "I know now that you had your reasons for keeping things from me. It's okay."

"You're sure?"

I nodded, then pushed my glasses back in place. During that embrace, they'd gotten knocked a little askew—no big surprise, I suppose. "I guess there's something to be said for contact lenses," I said with a shaky laugh.

He surprised me by saying, "I like your glasses."

"You do?" Yet another statement I knew I would never have heard from my ex.

"Yes. They're part of you. Or rather, you're beautiful with them, and without. But when you wear them is entirely up to you."

I leaned against his shoulder and drew in a big, contented breath. "Man, I love you."

His body stiffened beneath my cheek. "You what?"

"I love you," I repeated, then straightened so I

could look him in the face. "Does it bother you that I said that?"

"No," he said firmly. "I liked hearing it. I suppose...I suppose I never thought anyone would say such a thing to me."

If he'd been a demon toiling away in Hell, I could see why he thought those three little words would never be directed at him. But he was here on Earth now, and I knew he was eminently lovable...even when he was being a jerk. "Well, then, I'll have to make sure I say it to you a lot. I love you, Ben Blake."

"And I love you, Jillian Torres," he replied, and smiled at me.

I didn't know whether it was the good vibes circulating through the house, or whether the dogs had finally figured out they weren't alone. Either way, they all came running into the family room then, cheerful little bundles of energy with Frida bringing up the rear. She looked around, as if checking to see whether Ben had brought Rufus with him.

He seemed to understand, because he said, "No, he's not here. But I'll bring him with me the next time I come over."

Then there wasn't time to talk for a little bit, because we had to get down on the rug with the puppies and pet them and tell them how good they were being. I watched Ben run his hand over Boudicca—nearly obscuring her in the process, since she and the other pups were still so small—and wondered if I'd ever been quite this happy. Maybe right after he and I had made love, but this was different…this was more a contentment, a realization that both of us were exactly where we needed to be.

After a while, once the puppies had gotten their fill of petting and decided to pass out on the rug, he looked over at me. "How are we going to do this?" he asked.

"I don't know," I said frankly. "But I think the fact that you're almost always coming over here has to mean something."

His expression was thoughtful as he glanced down at the pups, then back in my direction. "I think you're right. That will be a lot of dogs, though, if Rufus comes with me."

"It's okay," I said. "I always wanted a big family."

For a second, Ben just stared at me. Then he laughed and came over and took my hands, and pulled me up so I was standing in front of him. "A big family, it is. All of us in this house."

"Yes," I said, then went up on my tiptoes so I could kiss him again. "All of us together. And you're okay with that?"

He brushed a strand of hair away from my

face, fingers gentle, caressing. "I never thought my life would be like this. And yet...."

"And yet?" I prompted.

Another smile, one so beatific that I remembered he also had been an angel in a forgotten time before he became a demon. "And yet, it turns out it's the one thing I wanted."

And he took me in his arms and held me, and the puppies woke up and began butting against us, and we laughed again, knowing that this was exactly who we were and where we were meant to be...and nothing else mattered.

The End

ALSO BY CHRISTINE POPE

THE WITCHES OF WHEELER PARK

(Paranormal romance)

Storm Born

Thunder Road

Winds of Change

PROJECT DEMON HUNTERS

(Paranormal Romance)

Unquiet Souls

Unbound Spirits

Unholy Ground

Unseen Voices

Unmarked Graves

Unbroken Vows

THE DEVIL YOU KNOW

(Paranormal Romance)

Sympathy for the Devil

Charmed, I'm Sure

A Wing and a Prayer

THE WITCHES OF CANYON ROAD*

(Paranormal Romance)

Hidden Gifts

Darker Paths

Mysterious Ways

A Canyon Road Christmas

Demon Born

An Ill Wind

Higher Ground

Haunted Hearts

THE WITCHES OF CLEOPATRA HILL*

(Paranormal Romance)

Darkangel

Darknight

Darkmoon

Sympathetic Magic

Protector

Spellbound

A Cleopatra Hill Christmas

Impractical Magic

Strange Magic

The Arrangement

Defender

Bad Blood

Deep Magic

Darktide

THE DJINN WARS*

(Paranormal Romance)

Chosen

Taken

Fallen

Broken

Forsaken

Forbidden

Awoken

Illuminated

Stolen

Forgotten

Driven

Unspoken

THE WATCHERS TRILOGY*

(Paranormal Romance)

Falling Dark

Dead of Night

Rising Dawn

THE SEDONA FILES*

(Paranormal Romance)

Bad Vibrations

Desert Hearts

Angel Fire

Star Crossed

Falling Angels

Enemy Mine

TALES OF THE LATTER KINGDOMS*

(Fantasy Romance)

All Fall Down

Dragon Rose

Binding Spell

Ashes of Roses

One Thousand Nights

Threads of Gold

The Wolf of Harrow Hall

Moon Dance

The Song of the Thrush

THE GAIAN CONSORTIUM SERIES*

(Science Fiction Romance)

Beast (free prequel novella)

Blood Will Tell

Breath of Life

The Gaia Gambit

The Mandala Maneuver

The Titan Trap

The Zhore Deception

The Refugee Ruse

STANDALONE TITLES

Hearts on Fire

Taking Dictation

Night Music

Golden Heart

* Indicates a completed series

ABOUT THE AUTHOR

USA Today bestselling author Christine Pope has been writing stories ever since she commandeered her family's Smith-Corona typewriter back in grade school. Her work includes paranormal romance, fantasy romance, and science fiction/space opera romance. She makes her home in Arizona's beautiful Verde Valley.

Don't miss out on any of Christine's new releases —sign up for her newsletter today!

Christine Pope on the Web:
www.christinepope.com

www.ingramcontent.com/pod-product-compliance
Lightning Source LLC
Chambersburg PA
CBHW021127260626
47169CB00005B/1490